EDGE OF TIME

DAVID DARLING

Novels by David Darling

The Noah Hunter Series
The Tipping Point
Grave Choices
Course of Action
Hunter's Gambit (forthcoming)

Novella
Grim Measures

Standalone
Serve in the Shadows: Recruitment

Science Fiction
Edge of Time
Edge of Eternity (forthcoming)

Thank you to Ryan Steck, who saw the vision and set my feet on the path to polishing this novel. Also, to Gareth Worthington and Jonas Saul for your time and thoughts in making the story shine.

I want to thank the University of British Columbia staff for my countless questions about the TRIUMF building and grounds. No janitorial staff was harmed in the making of this novel!

I also wish to thank my early beta readers that caught the inconsistencies, errors, or sections that needed clarification. It's greatly appreciated.

"On 28 June 2009, the world-famous physicist Stephen Hawking threw a party at the University of Cambridge, complete with balloons, hors d'oeuvres, and iced champagne. Everyone was invited, but no one showed up. Hawking had expected as much because he only sent out invitations after his party had concluded. It was, he said, 'a welcome reception for future time travelers,' a tongue-in-cheek experiment to reinforce his 1992 conjecture that travels into the past is effectively impossible."

- Scientific American Publication, Lee Billings, 09/02/2014

Prolog

Golden energy flickered across a dark landscape like a nebula exploding in a distant galaxy or a universe-sized Tesla experiment gone wrong. Lightning clusters twisted in endless loops before vanishing. Ripples of green light shimmered like a cosmic aurora borealis stretching into infinity. However, the most fantastic views of the universe didn't occupy his attention—he remained focused on the other two men.

He stood in a triangle formation, facing two others. He wore jeans and a white T-shirt, while the man on his left wore a black suit and tie. The man on his right also wore a matching jacket and tie, which was blue. He had a week's stubble, while the other two looked fresh from the shower, hair combed to the side, still damp.

"This is awkward," the man in the black suit joked.

He nodded at the same time as the man in the blue suit.

A casual conversation would be appropriate if they were standing on a street corner or in a park. Instead of such a mundane venue, they met in an area without time.

The quantum realm.

The man in the dark navy suit gestured to his companions. "I have no memory of this event. It must be new."

"Agreed." He ran a hand through the scruff on his face and glanced over his shoulder. All light was swirling in a circular pattern like water going down a drain. Space and time were being bent along with reality. "I've done everything possible, but it wasn't enough."

Despite the different clothing, the men in the suits had his mannerisms. Their right hands rose, and all three rubbed their chins with their thumb and index finger. The men in suits were identical and could have been his brothers, but they weren't. They were much closer than siblings could ever hope to be.

Moments passed, and he was lost in thought, as were the others. But a minute could have been an eternity in a realm where time can't be measured. While reality was being destroyed, he questioned his sanity. Were the others real? What if my mind snapped? *I have to check.* When he stepped toward the other two, vibrations on the sub-molecular level reverberated across the universe. Sheets of lightning flickered behind his eyelids as his teeth ground together, and he scrambled to his original position. Once they resumed the spacing, the vibrations halted. The sensation of being torn in two wasn't one he wanted to repeat.

There was only one possible answer, and the others came to the same conclusion.

Dark Suit Man slipped a hand inside his jacket pocket, and Blue Suit Man copied the move. "The answer was right here all along."

The lingering headache was painful, but he could still function. He turned his back on the others and faced the anomaly in the distance. "We won't remember this, will we?"

"Doubtful. However, we *must* remember. Somehow. Three is too much. Two as well? Not sure." Blue Suit Man moved to the side but not closer to the others. "I will go first."

"I'll go second." Black Suit Man cupped an object in his right hand.

"Three is too much." He stood back and repeated those four words, hands in his jeans.

Blue Suit Man looked at the others and winked. Like a fastpitch at the World Series, he wound up and whipped his arm forward with a grunt of exertion. An object flew from his palm and rapidly grew as it hurtled across the quantum realm toward the pinpoint of light. Another golf ball-sized stone thrown by Black Suit Man immediately followed with the same results.

All three turned to avoid the brilliant flash of light, but it was too late.

There was no time to scream before he was erased from the universe and his atoms scattered throughout time and space.

*****

Three is too much.

The thought was echoed by a fourth man dressed in a Hawaiian shirt and cargo shorts hidden in a fold of time. His eyes squinted against the power of a collapsing universe, and a golden nimbus surrounded him for a moment. The shield parted the energy, and he was safe.

He rubbed his chin with a thumb and index finger, an old habit. "It will come down to just one, but *which* one?"

Faster than a firing neuron, he disappeared from the quantum realm.

Space and time collapsed too fast for the human mind to comprehend as all matter in the solar system fed the anomaly, but no one was around to witness the occasion, as all life on the planet ended instantly.

Chapter 1

Boston, Massachusetts
2 November 1783

Clement stared at the two ceramic mugs on the farmhouse kitchen table, and his eyes watered. For twenty-five years, he had made tea each morning for them both, and it was the third time this week he rested two mugs on the table instead of one. Each time he did, a little piece of him died.

"I'm losing it. Sorry, dear."

The desire for tea fled, and with difficulty, he controlled the urge to hurl the cup across the room. Instead, he gently placed it on the open wooden shelf. Trembling fingers turn it to hide the chip. After Clement slipped on his jacket to ward off a sudden chill, he grabbed the wicker basket, and with a final look around the kitchen, he stepped outside the cabin.

Bare fields stretched before him, covered with a light blanket of frost. Most of the leaves had fallen with the autumn weather, allowing him to see deep into the farm's woods. Within four weeks, winter would have Massachusetts firmly in its grasp—it was in the air and long overdue.

When the rooster crowed from the barn, Clement blazed a trail across the whitened lawn to collect the morning eggs. The frozen weeds crunched underfoot, and his breath plumed as he followed the worn path under the frost. He would let the chickens out to roam once it warmed up in the afternoon. It was part of the morning chores and life on a farm; frankly, it was welcome right now.

"Come on, girls. Only four eggs? You can do better."

Clement returned the basket to the kitchen and filled the water pitcher from the well. Soon he was sweeping the kitchen and living area, but it only took a few minutes. He needed to keep busy, and as usual, he turned to the pile of logs. Cords of wood were stacked six feet tall, the same height as Clement, running the length of the thirty-foot cabin. There was enough seasoned wood to last many years, not just one winter, no matter how brutal. But there could always be more, and it would keep him warm.

A calloused hand gripped the worn shaft of the heavy chopping ax. The pile of rounds to be split had taken a week to accumulate, and his back and arms still ached. A wrist flick buried the ax head into the two-foot log, and Clement placed the column on the chopping block with one hand. Biceps, the size of most men's thighs, easily lifted the weight. With a twist, the blade came free, followed by a continuous arc of momentum. As the ax passed the apex, a second hand rose to grip below the first and guided the edge through the log with a well-aimed blow. It sounded like a gunshot as the dry elm cracked, and two halves fell. With further efforts, the halves became quarters and were tossed to the side. After a few minutes, the physical work warmed him, and he removed the light brown coat. The pile of split wood steadily grew to either side of the chopping block as he found his rhythm.

Clement's mind wandered as usual when he performed repetitious work. It started when his eye caught the apple tree on the far side of the field.

A coughing sickness caught hold of his wife the year before, and by early spring, she didn't have the strength to carry on. She had loved the spring blossoms—her favorite spot—and they had countless meals in its shade.

He tore his eyes away, picked up the splits, and stacked them in a new row along the cabin. When his kids were young, this was one of their chores. However, both sons had died in the war against the British several years ago, and his heart still ached. He couldn't do the mundane task without them coming to mind. The farmer shook his head and ran a hand through his short brown hair.

By the time he turned forty-five last summer, Clement had more heartache than many carried. Besides his family, there were many years with failed crops or weather which would not cooperate. A blight had destroyed eight acres of corn four years ago, and there was barely enough money to last that winter. Belts were tightened, and they had made do.

Life without his wife devastated Clement, and he had no idea how he kept placing one foot in front of another. Gods will? More likely, I'm too suborn to die. However, he continued to do so daily. He vowed not to place a second mug on the table the next morning.

Being physically exhausted daily left no time to grieve or wallow in misery. When falling into bed, sleep came swiftly. Clement's feet hung over the end, but he never complained. The mahogany bedroom set was an expensive gift from his wife's parents, and she loved it.

In the middle of another backswing, Clement froze. The hair on the nape of his neck stood on end, and he had the feeling of being watched. On the other side of his main field, the low rumble of thunder echoed off the tree line.

He spun around as a bright blue and orange ball of fire, wreathed in black smoke, streaked through the crisp morning sky. The roll of thunder intensified, reverberating in Clement's chest, and stole his breath. He swore when the fireball clipped the tallest pine, vaporizing a twenty-foot section like a match stick, "Mary, Mother of Jesus."

The fireball hurtled over the eight-acre field and roared into the leafless woods in the blink of an eye. An invisible shockwave rippled outward, and there was no time to run or think. Clement's heavy-set frame lifted like a pile of dried leaves, and he crashed through a pile of tinder and rolled to a painful stop on the porch. The cabin creaked and groaned in protest. The window beside the front door rattled in the frame before shattering into a thousand pieces. Clement scrunched his eyes and covered his head as shards of glass rained over him.

Slow to regain his feet, Clement shook his head as the high-pitched ringing in his ears faded. Across the field, swirls of dust and leaves rose twenty feet in the air before settling in concentric rings. The urge to hide inside the cabin was real, and he even stepped back, grasping the handle with a shaking hand.

Contrary to what happened, silence reigned, and the sky remained clear as he waited for death. Was the world ending? *Not going to lie, Lord. I'm okay if that happens.* Wildlife and even the light breeze stilled. Clement hoped the horses in the far pasture hadn't bolted. His eight hens and rooster, still inside the barn, were now silent, the usual clucking noise absent. The vapor trail across the sky slowly dissipated.

The silence was unnatural and did little to appease the sudden dry throat and queasy stomach. After looking down at the glass shards, Clement was surprised to find he wasn't cut or injured beyond a few bruises.

"That doesn't happen every day."

His whisper seemed unusually loud. Clement had seen meteor showers across the night sky, but nothing like this. Past the apple tree, the rock should have landed a hundred yards farther into the woods. There had been little rain this fall, and the threat of a forest fire was real. *The way this year has been, having my lands burn wouldn't surprise me.* He shouldered the ax and strode across the field.

After two-hundred yards, his steps slowed. Clement removed a small branch before the gravestone, threw it off to the side, and shifted a handful of leaves to clean the area. He knew it to be a fruitless gesture with the season, and more would fall, but he didn't mind. It had been almost eight months since his wife passed, but it seemed like yesterday to him. The world had lost a bright light, and everything dimmed in comparison. They had spent many nights staring at the stars, and she would have leaped at a chance to see a meteor up close. Clement kissed his fingertips and laid them on the crude, hand-carved headstone under the apple tree.

"I miss you every day, Jeanne. You wouldn't believe what I just saw."

Clement swallowed the lump in his throat and entered the woods. He followed an animal trail up the hill north through the trees. After a few minutes, the scent of burned wood let him know he was getting close, and the fear of fire returned.

The meteor had collided with a stout oak and won. Eight feet above the ground, the thick tree was sheered through, and tendrils of smoke still rose from the stump. The remainder had fallen to one side and was hung up in a neighboring pine. A swath of broken branches decorated the forest floor leading to a large limestone slab.

The rock, like the oak, was two feet thick, and the meteor had passed through the corner without effort. A hole lay on the other side, burrowed into the ground. Debris had blown clear in a wide circle from the impact revealing the bare forest ground. Steam rose from the earth, and a sharp scent of sulfur tickled his nose. A ticking noise echoed off the trees like a wet kettle on a hot wood stove.

Maybe this isn't such a good idea.

Damp palms gripped the ax handle, turning his knuckles white, and his knuckles cracked. He tried to ignore the nervous flutter in his stomach and rushed forward. Once he stood beside the crater, Clement waved away the smoke and peered down, his eyes wide.

Almost two feet in diameter, a jagged black rock lay at the bottom of the narrow shaft bored into the hillside. Sparks of lightning flickered under the surface before vanishing. His jaw muscles unclenched, and the tightness in his shoulders disappeared.

"You don't look dangerous." Clement peered at the eight-foot-wide path the meteor had cut through the forest canopy and shook his head. "Not now, anyway."

He leaned the ax against the limestone rock and searched along the swath of destruction. It didn't take long to find a straight branch.

Clement held it firmly like a spear and moved to the hole's edge. Before prodding the meteor, a dull thud sounded behind him. His heart leaped in his chest, and he spun around with the stick held high, ready to use if needed.

There was nothing to see, and he was alone. There wasn't a chance a squirrel or any wildlife was within a mile—they were too smart, unlike him.

Clement turned back to the hole. His foot knocked a pebble from the edge, and it fell into the depression. Before it could strike the meteorite, the little stone hung in midair. It neither rose nor fell but hovered in place, defying gravity.

"What in God's name is happening?"

Clement's jaw dropped as his heart rate doubled. He was too old to believe in magic, but before his eyes was a trick he could not explain. He took a firm hold, extended the branch, and poked the small rock. Every time the end of the stick got close to the meteor, it went in a different direction.

As a child, he played with lodestones. When aligned, the magnets would attract, but you could push one away without touching it when you flipped one over. When the end of the stick got near the stone, it reacted in the same manner. *Is it a giant magnet?*

Clement had done rather well for the last few years, growing and selling tobacco since the corn had failed, but he could always use more money for labor around the property. With such a rarity, someone in Boston would buy it. A lot of the city folk had more money than sense. With that decision made, he threw away the branch and picked up the ax. It was too expensive to leave behind.

As he returned to the cabin, Clement thought about the meteor's strange properties and what it could mean. Cautious, he kept one eye skyward in case more were about to fall. He leaned the ax against the chopping block and headed to the barn.

It was a simple structure with a large double door, horse stalls, and a pen for the chickens inside. The loft stored enough hay for the horses to get through the winter, and there was still room in the back for farm equipment. Outside, a large overhang ran along the side, protecting his tools and equipment from the rain or snow. He loaded a shovel and a length of rope into the wheelbarrow.

Clement crossed the field and followed his footprints in the dew past the apple tree. The morning sun had burned off the frost, and his leather boots kept the damp chill from his feet. He could only bring the barrow so far into the woods. Roots and uneven ground made it difficult, and he had to abandon it. He carried on with the coil of rope over one shoulder and shovel in hand.

Short of the impact site, Clement froze when a noise filtered through the woods. A flicker of movement ahead sent his heart racing once again. He wasn't a woodsman but could move silently enough to hunt, and he used those skills to remain hidden. Clement gingerly felt with his toe for sticks, and walked along the outside edge of his heels with bent knees, and rocked forward. Slow and steady. But most importantly, quietly. Using larger trees as cover, he made it to the base of the sheared-off oak and peered around the trunk.

A large man stood at the crater with his back to Clement. The figure leaned over to place something down against the big rock. *Is that a short-barreled musket?*

Clement peered around the trees, concerned for his safety, searching for others, but the man appeared alone. The stranger picked up a long branch before facing the hollow once more. It was the same limb Clement had used to poke the meteorite.

A nervous sweat beaded Clement's forehead, and his hands grew clammy. A chill ran down his spine, and the shovel slipped in his grip. The blade arced into the tree trunk with a *thunk.* Panicked, he ducked behind the oak. The man beside the meteorite didn't see him, but he got a good look at *his* profile.

Clement's stomach churned, and he swallowed a few times while a second chill rippled through his body. He clutched the shovel tight against his chest so his hands wouldn't shake.

He looked down at his white cotton shirt and tan work pants. The rugged dark leather boots were still wet from crossing the field. His light coat still lay across the woodpile beside the cabin. It took a minute, but slow deep breaths calmed his nerves, and the tremor in his hands vanished. There should be no reason to be calm, but he was.

Once again, Clement leaned around the tree to observe. As the stranger poked the meteor, he studied the man's clothing. The stranger also wore a white shirt and tan work pants. Clement's wife had repaired his left boot, and the red stitching down one side was unique. Even the man's boots appeared the same, down to the red thread.

Clement shaved every few days looking into a small polished-steel mirror that rested on a shelf outside the outhouse. He caught the man's profile by the impact crater again.

Clement knew that face *very* well.

It was his own.

Chapter 2

Captain O'Sullivan was a lean man in his early thirties with a thick red beard, sharp cheekbones, and dark eyes. His nose had been broken several years ago and never healed straight. He absently straightened his dark brown uniform and then patted the side of his mare's neck. Molly was a great horse with an even temperament. She had seen him through many years of service, and they had grown quite fond of each other.

After John Hancock became the first governor of Massachusetts in 1780, resigning from his position as senior major general of the militia, O'Sullivan worked with the man, and they were uncomfortable years. Handcock's effectiveness as a leader of six thousand troops remained in question by many, and the militia leadership sighed in relief when he retired. One of Hancock's first acts as governor was to hire his former militia to patrol the roads in and around the Boston area. Brigands, highwaymen, and Indians were still known to lay an ambush, and the constant patrols helped keep the peace.

O'Sullivan led his troops along the southeastern road for an early morning patrol. They adopted various marching formations: staggered lines, single file, and parade riding while covering their arcs of responsibilities. The horses steamed from their excursions in the crisp autumn air, and their breath billowed in plumes.

Fallen leaves littered the road and quieted the clomp from the horses' hooves on the hard-packed soil. The bare trees allowed them to see deeper into the woods and helped alleviate the paranoia of an ambush—they wouldn't be surprised or taken unawares. It didn't stop him from constantly scanning ahead.

After the patrol passed a dairy farm, they stopped at a narrow creek to water the horses and rest. The six-man detachment dismounted and alternated, leading their horses to drink. The stream continued to flow steadily with clear and cold water, but it'll be frozen solid and covered with snow next month.

"Don't let them drink much. The water's too cold for that." Brandan took a deep breath of the fresh air and enjoyed the view over the valley below. A hawk circled on the rising thermals, and two squirrels chattered. After a few days in the city, he was glad to get out into the country. The city of Boston was crazy as they filled in the swampland and marshes to give them more room to expand. They brought in more gravel by the wagon load daily than he had ever seen.

When an ear-splitting thunder parted the heavens that was felt as much as heard, O'Sullivan jumped in his saddle. Three of the younger horses reared, eyes rolling in fear. A trooper missed the reins of his horse when the front hooves left the ground and lost his footing in the creek. The young man stepped into the knee-deep water as his mount, mad with terror, raced down the road.

"Sir, over there!" His second in command, sergeant Harding, pointed above the tree line. A miniature sun hurtled across the sky, trailing fire burning in its wake, and Brandan turned to blink away the afterimage. The brilliant yellow and orange ball continued to dance across his vision. Brandan looked back to see it crash a few miles distant into the woods. He felt the impact in his chest, and had he not been in charge, the Irishman would have fled. Once they gained control and quieted their mounts, everyone turned to their captain and awaited orders.

A brief look over the trees confirmed his suspicions. "I believe that's the Wallace farm. Let's go." Despite the calm assurance of his orders, the men glanced at one another with worry. Brandan had patrolled this length of road for the last fifteen months and knew everyone in the area. "Mount up. Simon, double with someone until we find your horse."

After stepping out of the creek, Simon took a few seconds to dump the water out of his boots. "Yes, Captain."

The horses had nervous energy to burn, so Brandan let them set their own pace. The patrol passed a hog farm on the north, then turned and rode along the laneway to the Wallace farm within fifteen minutes. Captain O'Sullivan gave the order to dismount while he looked in dismay. He had stopped here on the last rotation and watered the horses while catching up with the farmer. The property had changed over the previous three weeks, and not for the better.

The cabin was a simple dwelling with an open main floor and a loft above. The building used to be well-maintained along with the rest of the property. Clement worked extremely hard and wouldn't let his cabin or property go to seed long as he still drew breath.

I hope Clement isn't dead. He's a good man.

The scene that greeted the patrol was one of neglect and abandonment. A corner of the cabin roof had rotted, exposing the interior to the elements. The fields were ready for winter, except for a large swath of tobacco not harvested and left to rot. The yellowed and withered two-foot-tall plants stretched from the cabin to the field's far edge in a direct line.

As the horses passed the barn, Brandan shook his head. Weeds had grown along the tracks, and some topped four feet tall. One of the double doors had rotted and had fallen outside the barn, acting like a drawbridge. The second door was propped open with an old stump, and thick weeds grew through the boards—not three weeks of neglect but years.

Trooper Ferguson dropped his reins. The horses had calmed and would not wander while the others stayed in place. At the cabin's front door, he knocked lightly before stepping inside.

It didn't take him long to emerge. "Sir, from the dust everywhere, no one has been here in a long time. I would easily say three years, Captain, maybe more."

With the report, O'Sullivan shook his head. Whatever was going on here was beyond a simple Irishman. He had no answers, but he knew where he could find some.

"Leave the horses here under guard. The rest follow me."

His second in command, Peter, found a volunteer, and the remainder followed, keeping the tobacco column on their left. Captain O'Sullivan led the troops across the field and halted beside the apple tree. He shook his head again and couldn't find any explanation or words of comfort for his men. At this time of year, the tree should be barren of leaves and ready to face the cold, harsh winter that Massachusetts would soon throw at it. To their dismay, green leaves covered the tree, and the bright red apples made the branches bend low, heavy with the ripe fruit.

A young private, barely old enough to shave, picked an apple and was dumbfounded. "Sir? What's going on?"

Brandan didn't have an answer. "Let's keep going. Keep your eyes open."

After following a game trail and going uphill, they stumbled across an impressive limestone slab. The stone was partially buried and covered with moss. However, a portion near the top was missing. Brandan ran his hand along the edge, and the cut felt smooth as wet glass. What drew his attention was the large hole in the forest floor. It certainly wasn't natural and resembled a collapsed bear den. Like any forest floor, several fallen logs and branches covered the area.

"Simon, get down in there and look around."

"Yes, sir."

Once in the hole, he pulled out handfuls of leaves, dirt, and branches before reporting. "Nothing in here, sir."

O'Sullivan knew, without a doubt, this would have been where the meteorite had landed. His judgment of distances had always been accurate, and after years of patrolling, he was certain of the location. He stood next to the hole, and the thrill of locating the impact area made him grin. But there were too many questions remaining. Where was the meteor? What happened to the cabin and Mr. Wallace? The brief moment of being an explorer had disappeared and left him uncertain.

More questions came to mind as he studied the area and his men. Then he made a decision. "Head on back to the horses and grab some apples. Carry as much as you can. There's no point in wasting them. I'll join you shortly."

As the men followed the orders, he sat on the large rock and shook his head. He failed to come up with any answers. Nothing made sense. What am I going to report to the major? O'Sullivan would be laughed out of the militia.

I was just here three weeks ago. How's this possible?

The captain waited, but no one arrived to explain what happened, and the answers didn't come to him. He pulled a watch from a small pocket on the front of his uniform and checked the time. The timepiece was a gift from his father when he joined the Masonic Lodge at the age of twenty-one. The square and compass design were finely engraved on the domed cover and a constant reminder of the brotherhood.

Time to go back. There are reports to write.

The chain's link broke as he was about to stand, and the watch fell to the forest floor. A gap had widened with the soft metal and would need to be repaired.

With a sigh, he knelt, but before he touched the timepiece, the captain paused with his fingers mere inches away. He blinked several times while trying to make sense of the situation. The minute and hour hands spun backward before they paused, then flew forward at a more incredible speed before halting altogether.

His hand had a slight tremor as he quickly picked it up. Brandan was pleased to discover the second hand had resumed its usual pace, even if the time was incorrect. When a foot shifted a layer of dried oak leaves, a shiny black rock, the size of two fists, lay exposed.

More curious than fearful, he moved the pocket watch closer. The hands moved erratically once again.

With a deep exhale, he closed the watch with a sharp click, and his thumb caressed the engraving. His thoughts whirled in various directions. The implications were outside his imagination. Nothing in his life had prepared him for this moment.

Conflicted, he studied the design of the pocketwatch cover and came to a decision. The Irishman recalled an oath to make the liberal arts and sciences his future study. Turning this stone over to the governor did not sit well, but he had a straightforward solution that would fit and ensure that he followed the chain of command.

A brother from an outlying district regularly visited his lodge in Boston, and he also happened to be the commander-in-chief of the continental army. Although Brandan heard rumors that the continental army would soon disband, he knew that brother George Washington would be the man to trust with this discovery.

Captain O'Sullivan slipped the watch into his pocket and picked up the black rock brushing away the dirt. The stone weighed almost four pounds and was just over eight inches long and four inches in diameter. It wasn't smooth but rugged and had many small flat areas, like facets, that caught the morning sun.

Brandon tucked the rock under his uniform jacket with a quick look around to ensure he wasn't observed and returned to the horses.

He did not know what he had in his possession.

Time would soon tell.

Chapter 3

Fort Knox, Kentucky

Present Day

 Police Chief Christopher Lockhart waited for the gate to open before his dark blue Crown Vic, then slowly pulled forward until the rubber blocks stopped the front tires. He glanced in the rearview mirror and confirmed the gate had closed behind him. It corralled the vehicle within a twenty-by-twenty-foot processing area.

At sixty-three, the chief was ready to retire with almost forty years of service with the Mint Police. He'd worn the same dark square-framed glasses for most of his life, whether in style or not. Despite his age, he still had a full head of dark brown hair. However, a few grays had started to show on his mustache.

The X-ray sensors activated and started a rotational sweep around the government-issued car, resembling the control arm from a touchless car wash. The officer in the shack looked down at the digital display. Once he confirmed the scale readings and the all-clear from the X-ray scan, he reached for the clipboard.

"All good, chief. Sign out here, please."

Constable Walter Hansen's wife delivered a baby girl two weeks ago, and the sleepless nights took a toll. The dark circles under his eyes and stunned expression made him resemble a zombie. The officer left his shack and handed a clipboard and a pen through the driver's window. The United States Bullion Depository logo, vehicle plate, and information columns were on top and center of the form. He signed beside his name, and the chief filled out the time of sixteen-hundred hours in the departure column, then handed everything back.

"Thanks, Walt. Have a good weekend, and try to get some sleep." Chris couldn't help but grin at the young man. He had been there with many sleepless nights for all three of his children. "It does get better, just not for a while."

"You as well, chief. I'll do my best."

Once inside the shack, Hansen punched a five-digit code on the LED panel, then pressed the large green button. The rubber blockers in front of the tires moved to the side. At the same time, the tire spikes lowered to the ground. The gate slid inside the tracks to the right, which allowed the chief to drive away.

Fort Knox is the most secure bullion depository in the United States, and the security extends to those who wish to gain entrance and those who want to leave.

Fort Knox could also double as a secure storage facility in times of crisis. During World War Two, the Magna Carta, the

Constitution, and the Declaration of Independence were protected and returned in 1944. After the war, the Holy Crown of Hungary was also stored at Fort Knox and returned safely in 1978. The utmost caution and security to safeguard the contents were taken. The Mint Police is one of the oldest police forces in the state. There haven't been any successful robberies or attempts since it opened in 1935, which made all who served quite proud.

The actual gold is stored underground with incredibly thick walls made of granite, all behind a blast door that weighs nineteen tons. After 9/11, Fort Knox's security was upgraded, with all the world's best security systems implemented within and without. They guarded over nine million tons of gold, each bar weighing just over twenty-seven pounds. There was a reason no visitors were allowed, but maintaining tight security was always the prime response.

With a quick wave, the chief placed the vehicle in gear and drove slowly from the employee parking area to head home. His mind had already turned to a list of items his wife wanted from the grocery store. After driving past the gates, he turned on a local news station for a weather report. Dark clouds were rolling in fast, with high winds from the west pushing a storm front. They hadn't called for rain earlier; now, he wasn't sure they were correct.

Thirty feet from the gate, an unexpected bump in the road caused his car to jump. As the tires turned, the wheel spun in his hands, and he fought for control. Then the rear tire hit the same obstruction. Chris stopped the car, unbuckled his seatbelt, and parked the vehicle. His right hand automatically rested on the butt of his Glock 19.

The chief's first instinct was to look for signs of trouble and danger, but there was nothing in the area except open fields. The distant military buildings were almost a mile away. At Fort Knox, the military police kept civilians from this part of the base with checkpoints and patrols. With one hand on his pistol grip, he opened the car door. After he gazed at the road behind the vehicle, the police chief gasped. For the first time in his life, he stood frozen in shock.

Thirty-nine years ago, a young man applied to the Mint Police Department after a five-year stint in the Navy. After training, Constable Christopher Lockhart was given his first posting at Fort Knox. During his orientation tour, they ended underground, and his guide showed him the main vault door.

All new officers were taken inside to reveal what they guarded to help quell any rumors and satisfy their natural curiosity. They would see it soon enough, anyway. The vault was ninety-feet wide and one-hundred-fifty feet long, with shelving units lining the outside walls and four rows through the middle. Gold bars were stacked several rows deep and six bars in height. There were many nooks and locked rooms off the main vault, with more shelving units and even more gold bars.

While he stood in awe, his guide passed Chris one gold bar.

"Not only are we police officers, but we guard our nation's treasure."

When he hefted the bar in his hands, the weight surprised him. It was an instant that he never forgot, and it had made a deep impression on the young police officer. That experience and moment as a rookie are etched in his mind forever.

At first, the disbelief at what he saw froze him in place, and it took six seconds before the police chief could fully draw his weapon. He fired his pistol outside the training range for the first time in over three decades. He emptied a full magazine of 9mm rounds into the ditch. This moment was the second event he would never forget in his career. The impossible had happened.

A few seconds later, a klaxon alarm sounded as the bullion repository went into full shutdown and alert. The remote audio gunfire locator system can detect gunshots fired up to a mile and begins the escalation process for threat assessment levels. The military base would also receive the alarm, and the full shutdown would happen within ninety seconds. The twelve rounds fired were enough to flag the emergency system to start security procedures.

All this went through the chief's mind as he stared at the gold bar on the road. The dulled shine didn't cast a reflection, but it was no doubt real—the serial number was visible with the Fort Knox stamp engraved on the bar's end.

Within minutes, the police had established a full security perimeter around the dark blue Crown Vic. The quick-reaction assault team from the repository encircled the area with their rifles as they scanned the terrain in all directions.

In response, military police sealed the base, allowing no one to leave or enter. Chief Lockhart immediately sent officers to check the vault and test all security systems. The civilian repository employees were relocated within the building while the strongroom was sealed. Rules and procedures established several decades earlier were finally implemented.

A flurry of reports came in. The security and backup systems registered no alarms triggered, and all the camera feeds showed nothing. An immediate full inventory had begun, and with all employees turned to that task, it would still take over thirteen hours. After they verified the count, the second part of the assessment would begin. Each bar would be examined, weighed, and tested to ensure purity.

That could not explain the twenty-seven-and-a-half-pound bar of solid gold on the road. After an investigative team finished photographing the area, the gold bar would be taken by the Treasury Department and analyzed.

The police chief's phone rang. "Go ahead."

"Initial sweep of the interior showed nothing disturbed, and we are conducting an audit of that area of the vault where that serial number matches." Sergeant Henderson sounded exasperated. Chris waited for him to announce that this was an elaborate new test. "Only one other abnormality. The secondary vault door was ajar, and the presidential chest was open and empty."

Since its establishment, only one sitting President had ever visited Fort Knox. Franklin Roosevelt officiated at the grand opening. The metal-reinforced locked chest carried in by the secret service before the ceremony was not made public. The agents had placed the box in the secondary storage vault and had left detailed instructions.

Engraved on the top of the chest was: *To be only opened by the President of the United States - FDR.*

Over the last seventy-nine years, rumors and wild speculations have occurred by all the Mint Police and Fort Knox employees as they guessed what President Roosevelt had placed in storage.

"Empty?" Chris was even more dumbfounded at that news than when he found the gold bar.

"Yes, Chief. Empty."

"I'm on my way."

"Roger that."

He called his deputy chief over and explained what was happening when his phone rang for the second time.

An unknown number flashed up on the screen. A feeling of apprehension grew. "Hello?"

"Chief Lockhart?" The woman's voice was crisp and abrupt—no nonsense.

"Speaking."

"Hold for the Secretary of the Treasury."

Jesus Christ.

The situation escalated quickly. Chris didn't know what he would say to the secretary with no information available.

After a minute of silence, there was a *click*, then a voice spoke abruptly. "Full report. Go."

"Yes, sir." The top Mint Police officer said everything he knew about the situation with zero speculation. It was not his job to guess but to report factual information.

During the long pause, the secretary clicked a pen over and over.

Abruptly he spoke. "Treasury agents will be on scene shortly. Turn all information over to them, as they will handle the investigation. I have to brief the President."

The secretary disconnected the call, and Chris Lockhart stared at the display on his phone while everyone waited for further direction.

What else could go wrong?

Chapter 4

FBI supervisory Special Agent Brad Holman stepped off the jet onto the private runway at Washington Dulles International Airport. He squinted at the early morning sun as it rose in a clear sky over the hangar. Washington's cooler weather contrasted sharply with Phoenix, Arizona, where he had boarded less than four hours prior.

He wore a dark navy suit, blue pin-striped shirt, and matching tie. Brad was an imposing figure standing six feet tall and nearly two-hundred pounds. Most of his weight was on his shoulders and chest, giving him the tapered look of a quarterback.

The bulge in the jacket was from a shoulder-holstered Glock 22. When he was on official business, it traveled with him. At times, Brad would also carry a secondary backup pistol. However, that depended on the severity of the case and his comfort level when not at work.

He had received a phone call from the special agent-in-charge (SAC) in the middle of the night. Brad had twenty minutes to grab his "go-bag" and be at the airport. He parked the agency's vehicle at the steps of a Gulfstream jet and left the keys in the ignition. Moments after boarding, the plane departed on a priority runway.

Brad Holman was considered a rising star within the bureau, with the highest percentage of solved cases recorded in the last twenty years. Brad's ability to process seemingly random information and connect the dots led to an impressive arrest record. The chance that gave him the most recognition and likely his current situation was only a few years ago.

Coordinating with other agencies, Holman led the arrest of William Ulbricht, the Silk Road's creator. An underground deep-web site designed to trade drugs, money laundering, computer hacking, and even fake identification had collapsed like a house of cards. Ulbricht would still be free if not for Special Agent Holman's ability to read into his LinkedIn profile and connect the varied information.

Soon after that case was closed, a thirty-six-year-old Special Agent Holman applied for the position and was quickly promoted to a supervisory role at the bureau, with a team of twelve special agents working under him. His ability and success have continued at the Phoenix field office.

Brad wondered what was important enough to pull him across the country with first-class treatment during the four-hour flight. He rubbed his left eye to calm a twitch before running a hand across his unshaven face. As he reclined in the leather seat, his jaw dropped.

Brad had finally noticed that he wore white gym socks instead of black.

Seriously?

In his rush to leave, he didn't notice until it was too late. He groaned and tried to pull the pant legs lower to hide his ankles. Brad wasn't sure what was vital enough to pull him across the country, but he knew how important first impressions were. Wearing white socks with a dark suit wouldn't be forgotten. Ever. He grabbed his bag to change them when the seatbelt sign came on, and the flight attendant informed him they were about to land. Four minutes later, it was too late to worry about a fashion slip-up as he stood outside the jet.

He was jarred from his thoughts when he heard a voice. "Special Agent Holman. This way, please."

An older man waved to him from thirty feet across the tarmac. He wore a light gray suit and blue tie and stood beside a limousine parked off the jet taxi area. Brad carried his travel bag in his left hand, and his dress shoes clicked on the tarmac. He tried to adjust his pant leg with the last gust of wind, but he wasn't sure if he was successful.

That limousine is familiar.

It was heavily armored, and the oversized wheels were not factory standard. A glance at the hood showed where the flag posts would slide and lock into place. It was not a regular feature on any Cadillac. Over the years, he had worked with enough secret service agents to know the vehicle was named "The Beast" or "Cadillac One" by reputation.

The presidential limousine.

His disbelief grew stronger as he identified the man who waved him over. The man's picture hung on the Phoenix field office wall. It was Director Adams of the FBI. The twitching in his left eye resumed when his boss held the rear door for him and gestured for Brad to enter first. It took a second for his eyes to adjust to the limousine's interior, but when they did, a feeling of dread grew in his stomach, and a chill ran up his spine. The President of the United States sat with his legs crossed at the ankles and waited for Brad to settle in.

"Scooch over." The director gestured for Brad to slide over, which placed him directly opposite the President.

Brad placed his bag on the floor before his seat, trying to block their view of his socks. The worst-case scenario had arrived, and it seemed surreal. He could not believe what was happening, let alone the director using the word *scooch.*

"Special Agent Holman, thank you for coming at such short notice." The President shook his hand and smiled.

President Kelly Bower was in his second term, and the warmth he broadcasted on television with his Hollywood smile was just as genuine in person. It made the American people love him, but it was nothing compared to sitting directly across from him.

"My honor, Mr. President."

The limousine pulled away from the jet and toward the gate. Brad glanced at Adams but was getting no answers from the director.

"I've looked at your file, and I am *very* impressed. Not too many things impress me much anymore."

"Thank you, Mr. President. What can I do to help?"

Bower tapped one of two large manila folders beside him. His smile dropped, and the lines on his brow deepened.

Director Adams cleared his throat. "We don't normally do things this way, but—"

"This is not a usual circumstance," President Bower interrupted.

The President removed several pictures and a report from the large envelope and handed them to Brad.

"Yesterday late afternoon, we had a breach at Fort Knox. The Mint police chief ran over a gold bar lying on the road. Right now, there is no indication of anyone breaking in. No one knows how it happened, and everyone is stumped."

The pictures showed the gold lying on the road like an ordinary rock. It was a *very* costly rock. The reports confirmed that the security systems were not activated and were functional. The next page proved the bar was solid gold with the RF spectrum analysis.

Brad handed the papers back. "This smells like an inside job, Mr. President."

"That's what I thought as well." The director smiled at his assumption. "They checked everyone and the system as well. There isn't a way for someone to smuggle out twenty-seven pounds of gold. All the systems have been triple-checked."

"Here is another report from the treasury investigation." The President handed over another set of pages. While Brad reviewed them, he continued. "The Treasury Department confirmed the gold bar found outside was *from* the vault. No other gold is missing. They found prints on the bar that matched prints in a specific area of the main vault. I've called in favors, but there's no match worldwide."

The limousine increased speed, and a quick look out the windows showed they were on the highway. The usual motorcade of the secret service was absent, but they had no traffic problems.

The director added, "There is one item you *must* find and return. That's why you are here. The theft and thief are secondary and expendable."

He placed the paperwork back in the first folder, and President Bower took the thicker second folder and handed them to Holman.

"If you could look this over and get back to me as soon as possible."

Director Adams spoke up. "We'll be at the headquarters in a few minutes. A secure situation room has been set aside for you."

The situation rooms were for meetings of the utmost importance and shielded from electronic intrusion. It ensured the occupants were safe from being overheard. Inside, the FBI discussed critical information that could jeopardize national security. Special Agent Brad Holman never had the clearance or cause to enter a situation room, but he knew they included a hardwired telephone connected to the White House.

Brad's eyes widened at the severity of the situation, and the thrill of the challenge coursed through his body with an adrenaline spike, his headache forgotten.

The President reached inside his jacket and produced two folded sheets of paper. "Before you read and accept or decline, I have a few things to mention. First, we do not know how critical this item is. It *could be* the most important thing on the planet. Secondly, this is real and not a joke. Period."

The hair on his arms stood on end as the President echoed his recent thoughts. Bower handed over the two pieces of paper and leaned back to watch Brad's reaction. The President appeared concerned and worried.

Holman couldn't believe what he held. The first page was a surety of a presidential pardon. If any federal crimes were committed at the President's behest, he had a free pass citing national security. At the bottom was the presidential signature, witnessed by Director Adams.

The second page was a letter stating the bearer acted directly on behalf of the President of the United States and to obey and assist FBI Special Agent Bradley Holman to their fullest extent. If there are any issues or problems, contact the President directly at the number listed below.

"You are one of the finest investigators in any intelligence field. Anything this country can do to help in any way, ask. *All* federal resources are yours if needed."

The realization hit him like a bolt of lightning. Brad knew he could do almost anything with these two pieces of paper. He had a literal get-out-of-jail-free card in his hands. Lost in thought over the implications, Brad discovered the limousine had stopped before the FBI headquarters building on Pennsylvania Avenue.

He slid both folders and letters into his bag. For the first time as an adult, Brad didn't have a definite plan to tackle the problem.

"I will let you know as soon as possible, Mr. President."

The driver opened the door, and Brad stepped onto the sidewalk.

"Go upstairs to the third floor, and I'll be up once you have settled in."

He knew a dismissal when he heard one. "Yes, Director."

Curious, Brad entered the FBI headquarters lobby. His mind whirled around the impossible break-in and theft, and he could barely concentrate on his surroundings.

The stolen object had to be one of the most valuable items in the country. It could be nuclear codes or proof of aliens, and he grinned.

It could be anything.

He'd never backed down from a challenge.

He wouldn't start now.

Chapter 5

As Brad walked through the front door, two security guards waved him over and had him sign in. The director must have briefed security ahead of time. They had expected his arrival and had written his name in the logbook. He wasn't surprised when they handed him a silver security passkey with his current stock work picture. He clipped it on his breast pocket and placed his old ID in the bag.

Over the last ten years, Brad had visited FBI headquarters in Washington several times and knew the routine, or he thought he did. He placed his items in the gray plastic bucket at the metal detectors and X-ray conveyor belt, but the large guard behind the desk shook his head.

"Sir, you can go to the fast gate with your clearance level. Your authorization will grant you access."

Brad placed his new ID pass on the sensor. The LED light turned green, and the gate swung open. Only a handful of people had that clearance. When Brad ran his fingers along the smooth edge of the silver card, the importance of the task ahead sunk in. Doors wouldn't be a barrier to his investigation—should he accept the case, that is.

The elevator door stood open for him, and within a minute, Brad arrived on the third floor.

When the doors opened, a young woman dressed in a light green dress and matching jacket waited for him. Her short-spiked hair was bright blond, with a purple streak over her right ear. Her thin face brooked no-nonsense as her eyes narrowed, scanning him head to toe.

"Special Agent Holman, I'm Stephanie. Come with me, please."

She didn't wait for a reply but turned and briskly walked down the hall. Brad followed and tried to match her pace but fell several feet behind. She could put a speed walker to shame. Her chiseled calves must have seen thousands of steps at the gym daily.

Her heels clicked rapidly on the polished stone floor, and then she abruptly stopped at a large double door. "My office is right across the hall. Anything you need, just let me know."

Again, Stephanie didn't wait for a reply but opened her office door and disappeared. He was alone, with a faint hint of lavender. A series of locker cabinets beside the door was for electronic storage before anyone entered. The situation didn't call for that measure, so he left his cell phone in his pocket.

The new badge opened the security door, and the smell of fresh coffee on the side cart and water and muffins drew him over. One wall had a large whiteboard, and the large conference table dominated the twenty-foot-long room. It could easily seat two-dozen people. He sat closest to the coffee and quickly settled in.

He removed the paperwork from his bag and dug around until he found the small bottle of aspirin. Now he could deal with the persistent headache.

After he tucked the surity and presidential order of request into his jacket pocket, Brad spread the items from the second folder and found an old journal. It made up the package's bulk.

The journal was slightly larger than a typical paperback novel and appeared old. The smell reminded Brad of an antique bookstore, and the hand-stitched binding confirmed his guess. The bound red leather had faded over time, yet it was well preserved.

Brad sipped his coffee before he dived in. The spine cracked when he opened it, and the earthy smell made his nose wrinkle. He turned to the first page with great care and began to read.

5 June 1789

With the utmost discretion, studies have begun on the small rock sent from the Heavens, which had been entrusted to my care. It had displayed properties that baffled some very learned men.

We will continue our endeavors.

Brad scanned the first page again without believing what he had just read. He held the writings of the first president of the United States. Someone could have faked the journal's apparent age down to the faded ink. But when he considered the source *and* the warning that it was not a joke, he knew the book had to be authentic.

If I can't trust the president, who can I trust?

Brad's awe increased as he gently turned the pages, and the moment seemed surreal. The journal had been passed down from president to president over the last two-hundred and thirty-plus years. Some entries were a full page long, while others were just one line or a quick notation.

Occasionally, he found loose papers inserted between the pages. They were reports from various scientists over the centuries with recorded facts observed and suggestions about the object's nature.

As he turned the sheets, Brad paused to read an entry different from the others.

18/09/35

Due to an overexuberance during testing, the meteorite has been broken in twain. One result is that the effects have lessened per individual piece, but they resumed their original properties when conjoined.

Brad tilted his chair back and set aside his cold coffee while digesting the new information. From the previous entries, the fact that a small piece of a meteor could alter or distort a time would be the most revolutionary discovery since… well, in forever, would be his best guess. He couldn't help but shake his head at the implications while running a hand through his short hair.

A green light flashed once above the door, and a subtle *beep* sounded as Director Adams stepped into the room. Brad began to rise, but he was waved back to his chair. Adams grabbed a bottle of water before he sat beside him at the conference table.

"How are you handling this?"

Brad paused to collect his thoughts, although he didn't have much precedent to form an opinion. "This is incredibly remarkable, sir. Something like this could change—"

"Pretty much everything we know about the world, science, and potentially history itself." Director Adams leaned forward and tapped the journal. "Less than twelve hours ago, the president briefed me. We have just joined a club that only a few living presidents know. Also, I am assuming the thief knows as well."

Being in such an elite group didn't sit too well with Brad. "Sir, I have only had a brief time to read everything. The main target for the Fort Knox break-in would have been the meteorite piece. As to why the thief left the gold bar, I have no idea. It doesn't make sense."

After giving a brief nod in agreement, the director voiced his idea. "There's only one explanation that comes to mind. Anyone that can break into the heart of the world's most secure building does not need the gold. They probably found it too heavy and ditched it."

"If they can get into Fort Knox undetected, anything else in the world shouldn't pose a problem." Brad was comforted by the fact that the director shared his opinions.

"Well?" Director Adams pointed to the spread-out paperwork and gave him a half-smile. "Are you in?"

Brad dragged a finger across the leather cover of the journal, then cleared his throat. "Yes, sir. One hundred percent."

"I'll inform the president. Any resources that the government has available are now at your disposal. However, the fewer people that know about this, the better. But if you need to bring in a few people, they must be trustworthy."

"Yes, Director. I understand."

"Keep me updated. Stephanie now works for you. She is competent and will help you move mountains when required."

"I'll get right to work, Director. Thank you for the opportunity."

Director Adams stood and then paused near the door. "You are known for getting results. Continue to do so. A lot rides on this."

Brad read for thirty minutes before the ideas coalesced into a game plan. He walked across the hall with both folders and knocked on Stephanie's door. He paused a moment before stepping inside her office.

She sat behind a large desk with three computer monitors that guarded her like a wall. When she saw Brad, the flurry of typing paused with her fingers poised above the keyboard.

"Yes, sir?"

"I have taken the case, and the director mentioned you would be able to help me."

"I'm looking forward to working for you, sir. What would you like done?"

Brad could tell that her focused energy would indeed be remarkable. "First, I need the Cheyenne military installation on full alert. Secondly, I must be at Fort Knox as soon as possible to meet with the Mint Police chief for a tour inside. Then, I will be flying out to El Paso County, Colorado, immediately afterward." After placing the folders on her desk, Brad added, "I also need these sent back to the director."

To give her credit, Stephanie didn't even blink at the requests. She just reached for her phone. "Your car will be downstairs in one minute."

"Thank you."

Brad had no idea how hard it would be to stop the impossible so it wouldn't happen again, but he had an idea that would at least give him a chance.

Everything depends on the accuracy of an old journal entry.

How bad could it get?

He tried not to grimace when he entered the elevator.

Chapter 6

Brad ran his hand over the soft leather seat and custom stitching. The sleek and modern jet was a considerable improvement when the FBI assigned him a vehicle and a gas card.

I could get used to this type of travel rather quickly.

He rifled through his small carry-on luggage while balancing a sandwich on his lap. He would need to buy a few items to get through this assignment. His go-bag carried the essentials but not enough for a long-term period. However, one thing made the top of his list of immediate things to do—black socks.

Too wired to rest, Brad reviewed his notes and studied various notations. There were more guesses and question marks on the pages than facts, something he hoped to remedy soon. The process was underway, and the method had worked for him thus far—no point in changing what wasn't broken.

A subtle chime sounded, and the jet descended into the Louisville, Kentucky airport. He barely felt the wheels on touchdown before the Gulfstream smoothly taxied to the northern section of the airport's private reception area.

The clamshell stairs deployed, and Brad descended the nine steps to find a young agent waiting for him. He wore a dark suit and tie and gestured to a black Tahoe with government plates parked nearby.

"Cole Downey, from Louisville field office."

"Nice to meet you. How long to Fort Knox?"

"About thirty minutes, sir."

"Let's go."

Cole moved to open the rear door, but Brad raised a palm out to stop him. "I'm good."

If Cole was nervous, it didn't show as the Tahoe ate up the miles and navigated the traffic. Twenty-five minutes later, they arrived at the main entrance of the base.

A large tank on top of the welcome sign reminded Brad that Fort Knox was a military base. It covered over one hundred and seventy square miles, with the gold depository on a thousand acres.

He showed his identification at the security building behind the entrance. The soldier told Brad to wait in his vehicle, and the military police would escort him to the depository visitor parking area.

With the incident still fresh, extra precautions were in place.

Shortly, a white police cruiser arrived, and the driver waved for Cole to follow. Fifteen minutes later, they pulled into the parking lot, where a man leaned against a Crown Vic. He wore the standard blue uniform of a police officer, black boots, and tactical pants, with shoulder badges for the Mint Police.

There were only a few other cars parked in this private lot.

"I'm not sure how long I'll be. If you need anything, give me a call," Brad said.

Cole turned off the vehicle and nodded.

Brad walked over to introduce himself.

"Special Agent Brad Holman, FBI."

"Mint Police Chief, Chris Lockhart. Nice to meet you." After a quick, firm handshake, the chief asked, "Armed? If you could leave the weapon with your driver, it would speed things up."

Not willing to argue the point, Brad moved over to Cole's window and pulled his Glock from the shoulder harness. After he pressed the release, the magazine dropped into his palm. He canted the weapon to the left and pulled the slide. A round ejected, and Brad snagged it in midair with a neat catch.

"Hold on to this."

"Yes, sir." Cole fed the loose round into the magazine and placed it in a cup holder.

When Brad rejoined the chief, they turned south and headed toward the mint.

"Not too sure what's going on," the chief said. "However, I just talked to the secretary for the second time this week. I'm to roll out the red carpet for you with full access."

"It's appreciated." Brad couldn't brief him on the chest contents, but any information he could impart—he would.

"The public used to have access to the Mint, but that has long since changed. The employee parking is on the other side of the security pen."

The chief went over the events, including finding the gold bar. Having just read the report, Brad was happy to hear no inconsistencies with the chief's testimony. After they followed the road's bend, Brad saw the employee parking.

Thirty feet before the gates, the chief stopped and gestured at the ground. "This is where I found the gold bar. Ran over it, actually."

Brad couldn't see anything special about this exact location. The small ditch on the side had gravel and weeds along the bottom, but it wasn't deep enough to offer concealment. The open grass fields surrounding the depository led to the base of the massive walls. The first impression reminded him of a castle. Each corner of the building had machine gun turrets, and with their combined fields of arc, there wasn't a blind spot.

The chief walked toward the front entryway. "We have various detection devices out on the grass. Pressure plates for mines, listening devices, thermal imagery detection, you name it, it's out there."

As both men continued, a question popped into Brad's head. "How do you cut the lawn? What about wildlife?"

"We turn off the devices in a specific area while the lawn is maintained. A team is out front, visually monitoring the area when that happens. As to wildlife, the sensors are *now* adjusted not to go off under a certain weight. We may have had a few issues with rabbits versus the mines when we first installed the system."

Brad tried not to wince over the mental image and followed the chief into the depository. Everyone entering went through screening and the Millimeter Wave ATI X-ray scanner.

The Mint Police were on full alert and watched everyone with equal scrutiny. Brad signed for an identification badge after being searched by hand, then by an electronic wand. A somewhat intimidating officer told him not to take off the ID badge.

They descended a broad set of stairs and passed through another checkpoint before Brad arrived at the vault's exterior. The open circular vault door was over twelve feet tall, and the reports showed it weighed over nineteen tons.

There shouldn't be a way to get through that massive door.

Heavy shelving units created rows up the interior length inside the main vault. Various alcoves lined the exterior walls, and as far as Brad could see, there was nothing but gold. His eyes fixated on the bars, and he had trouble blinking as he stared at the vault. The smell reminded him of an old library, stale and musty.

Before he spoke, the police chief let him take it all in momentarily. "Each bar is approximately worth five-hundred-thousand dollars and weighs twenty-seven and a half pounds."

The sheer wealth scrambled his senses, and the dollar amount seemed hard to grasp. *There were thousands of bars. Tens of thousands!* "Can you please show me the gold bar you found?"

The chief led Brad down the rows and over to a side alcove. The small ten-foot square room had a metallic gray desk and shelving against the wall. "We just got it back from the treasury agents."

A digital scale and four glass jars filled with a clear liquid capped with blue rubber stoppers sat in the middle of the desk. A digital gauge occupied most of the space.

Behind the desk, an older man wore a white lab coat. He appeared in his late sixties, with bifocals perched on his nose. He combed over several straggled wisps of white hair across his head.

The older man pulled on a pair of white gloves and opened the bottom desk drawer after a quick nod to the chief. The gold bar looked like the others in the main vault, even the stamp and lettering on the top and end cap.

"Put these on." The chief handed him a pair of gloves before the technician handed over the gold bar.

Surprised at its heft, Brad turned it around to view it from all angles. "Is stamping on it consistent with the other bars?"

The man behind the desk nodded. "Yes, sir."

I am holding over five years of my salary.

"Is there anything different about this versus the others?"

He shook his head. "Identical. Just the fingerprints they lifted."

Brad thanked him and left the gloves on the desk. He turned toward the chief. "Can you show me the secondary storage vault? I would like to see the chest."

"No problem, follow me. Thanks, Hank."

The man behind the desk nodded and again secured the gold bar before resuming his work.

The police chief led the FBI agent to the far end of the vault to a steel door, where he scanned his ID on the sensor and punched in a five-digit security code on the keypad. A green LED light above the door blinked, and they heard it unlock. Heavy-duty shelving lined the walls of the smaller room, with several shelves stacked with more gold. In the middle were skids filled with plastic boxes. They were bound in blue plastic sheets and secured with nylon strapping. A two-foot-long iron-bound chest sat on an open shelf on the far wall.

"What's on the skids?"

"A cache supply of morphine sulfate. In 1955 the government bought a large supply of morphine and opium in preparation for the cold war. Thirty years ago, the government didn't know what to do with all that opium, so they refined it, and now we guard drugs no one can use."

Brad shook his head while his hand rested on millions of dollars worth of drugs. The government safeguarded the most massive cache of narcotics he had ever seen.

Inside the iron chest was a small wooden support structure, and once Brad closed the lid, he saw an engraving across the top.

He ran a finger over the FDR initials and asked the chief, "How do you think the burglar did it?"

"I have given this a lot of thought." The chief pointed to the stacks of gold and the pallets, then gestured to the sensors surrounding the interior door. "I could guess someone hacked our system and disabled all the electronics. It would have to be an inside job." He sounded unsure of the answer. Brad knew many of those systems were standalone and not connected externally. "In a nutshell, no one could have done this without inside help."

Brad scanned the room a final time and made up his mind. "That's all, Chief. Thank you for your time."

Surprised at the short inspection tour, the chief shook his hand and led him out. They were both scanned and patted down before leaving the building.

As they walked toward the parking lot, the chief asked, "I didn't have much time before you arrived, but I did find out you are an outstanding investigator. Do *you* have any ideas on how someone could have done this?"

They stopped a few feet before the Tahoe, and Brad rubbed his forehead. The headache had returned. "My best guess is that the gold you ran over was never in the depository. It well may have been a decoy allowing someone to get what they were after."

"That is one *very* expensive decoy."

"I would double-check the entire inventory. You may have one extra bar of gold. Right now, that's my best guess. However, I'm only speculating, so don't hold me to that."

Chief Lockhart nodded slowly. "That makes more sense than someone breaking in."

"Thank you for the tour. If possible, I'll let you know if I find anything."

After a firm handshake, Brad climbed into the Tahoe and loaded his Glock 22 before sliding it into the shoulder holster. He was ready for the next step but had a few things to accomplish to ensure success.

He didn't like leaving things to chance.

Chapter 7

The mall was busy as people shopped or went to dinner after work, so Cole had to park far from the doors. Brad didn't mind the walk, and it allowed him to stretch his legs and get a little fresh air.

Brad gestured to the food court once they were inside. "Go ahead and grab something to eat. I'll pick up some things and join you shortly if you can save me a seat. Keep your receipts."

"Sounds good." Cole agreed. "I always forget that part, thanks."

With a nod, Brad merged into the crowd. Malls over the world were the same no matter where he went. It took him eight minutes to find Round One Arcade and Bowling. A small group of kids hung out in front of the store. Most were glued to their phones, while some stared at the crowds that filtered past. The bench seemed to be their home turf. He would have gone to the parking lot outside the movie theater if this venue had proved a bust. One of them always paid off.

Their pants hung low in an attempt at style, and their baseball hats were backward or sideways. The amount of jewelry made it look like Mr. T was returning to fashion. Occasionally, one kid would join the group and discreetly sit closer to the older one in the middle of the bench before wandering back into the mall.

Brad took out a small pad of paper, scribbled a quick note, and then tore the page out, folding it in half.

Hopefully, I look more like a businessman than a cop, but this should work.

Beside the arcade, Brad leaned against the wall next to the entrance. The folded paper stuck out between his fingers in plain sight with his arms crossed. He waited while playing out various scenarios of his visit to the military base.

During the drive back to Louisville Airport, Brad had toyed with telling Chief Lockhart the truth—the chest contained a rock fragment from a meteor that may be contrary to the laws of space and time. Brad didn't fully believe it, let alone share that information with someone else.

I will know more if this plan works. Everything will ride on what happens next.

Agent Holman emailed and arranged with Stephanie for the operation's next phase. There was one thing that she couldn't help him with, but Cole could.

"Before we hit the airport, I need to go downtown and pick up a few things and dinner. I didn't have a chance to pack for a long assignment."

"Yes, sir. I know a good place. Jefferson Mall is nearby."

Brad had agreed and found himself playing a familiar scene again. It didn't take long for one of the younger kids to wander and pretend to look in the store. The teenager brushed against Brad and took the note. The maneuver was unnoticed and would have made a clandestine officer proud.

When the kid returned to the bench, the paper suddenly appeared in the hands of the ringleader. His hooded gaze and expression didn't change, and when he caught Brad's eye, he flashed four fingers.

Brad didn't blink at the amount but gave him a quick nod.

Reassured, he made his way to JCPenney. A few minutes later, he strolled through the mall with extra black socks, underwear, and aspirin in a plastic bag.

A skinny twelve-year-old appeared beside him within three minutes of leaving the large retail store. He carried a small white paper bag and walked shoulder to shoulder with Brad.

After removing four folded bills from his pocket, Brad exchanged them for the bag. The kid peeled off and merged into the crowd while Brad dropped it in the bag with his purchases.

Before returning to the airport, he joined Cole for a quick dinner at the food court.

*****

When the strong hands lifted the ring in the floorboards, a three-foot hatch swung open on hinges and revealed the dark cellar below. After the flick of a lighter, the man hung a lantern on an old nail hammered into a rafter beam. The dancing flame illuminated the old wooden stairs and cedar-framed room. The smell of damp earth flooded his nostrils as he descended a few steps, and cobwebs broke across his face. An old and familiar sensation, the dark held no fears for him. He slid a black leather bag off the kitchen floor, and the planked steps creaked ominously, but they supported his weight.

The flame from the thick beeswax candle barely illuminated the cellar, and deep shadows lingered in the corners and behind the steps. The ceiling was just under six feet tall, and the man hunched while moving to the opposite corner.

"I was here not too long ago. It looks like the spiders have been busy." His baritone whisper filled the area, and there wasn't a response. Not that he expected one.

The man brushed the cobwebs off his face and dropped the sack in the dirt at his feet. He removed a thick hand towel wrapped around a small rock from the bag. The dark stone was almost four inches long, three inches wide, and three inches thick. It resembled an irregular-shaped black gem with many facets. The surface reflected the candlelight, which seemed to amplify depending on the angle. The end of the small rock was flat and smooth as if sheared with a laser.

A similar stone fragment glinted in a thick gold ring on the man's left hand. With the small rock in the palm of his left hand, he covered it with his right and remained still with his head bowed. He barely breathed while concentrating.

The light dimmed as the air shimmered above the small table, like a heat distortion above a wood stove. Without warning, a concussive air blast knocked the man backward on his behind.

Plumes of dust billowed off the dirt floor and obscured the cellar with a cloud of particles. The lantern squeaked as it rocked back and forth on the nail, and the shadows leaped and danced.

The dust made his eyes water, but the man grinned.

On the table sat a much larger stone, twenty-four inches long, that resembled the small fragment. A subtle flicker of lightning leaped from one end of the stone to another under the surface. A split second later, a second pulse made the rock glow from within before it grew dark.

The man brushed the dust off his pants and placed the small fragment into a divot on the right side. It fit and matched perfectly.

A deep vibration grew in intensity and was felt throughout the small cellar as he rested his fingertips gently on the stone. A flare of light matched the sparkle in the ring.

The air above the stone distorted as the shimmer arrived again, and the vibration increased enough to make the rafters pulsate. With an audible click, the fragment merged with the large rock, and the two were whole once again.

The calloused fingers ran over the remaining depression before the light flared bright enough that he turned his head to the side.

When he turned around, the stone was gone.

"Almost done."

The dust lingered like a morning mist on the pond, and he coughed into his sleeve as he climbed the stairs. After the lantern was removed, the hatch slammed closed behind him. Once he blew out the flame and placed the lantern on a hook in the kitchen, the man did the impossible. He disappeared.

Chapter 8

"Everything will be fine. Don't worry or move."

The young field agent nodded, but her eyes betrayed her confidence. Having a loaded rifle aimed at your head tended to unnerve most people. Brad Holman stretched his arms to his sides, parallel to the ground, palms up. He didn't make any sudden gestures, and he didn't show any expression, despite the nerves that turned his stomach in knots.

The HK416 was held at the ready with the FBI agent in the soldier's crosshairs. The young military police officer stood twenty feet away, dressed in a green camouflage uniform and Kevlar helmet with black body armor. The MP armband was on full display. Despite the raised weapon, he had a calm and solemn look, which Brad did not want to test. Being shot on the first full day of the investigation wasn't how he wanted to start the case.

After landing at Colorado Springs Airport, Brad was met by another junior field agent, Tanya Bradford. He soon sat in the backseat of another black Chevy Tahoe, and they didn't waste any time. She knew the roads and the best route.

As a junior agent, Brad couldn't count the number of times he was tasked as a driver. He drove politicians to senior bureau officials around at all hours of the day or night. The reversal of being seated in the back felt strange.

At thirty minutes to midnight, the traffic was almost non-existent en route to the Cheyenne Mountain complex. During the flight, Brad had read and marveled at the engineering accomplishment.

The complex under the mountain was the center of the United States Space Command and NORAD from 1957 for over fifty years. They monitored the airspace above and around North America for a possible attack. Since 2008 the complex has been turned over to the Air Force as a military base. In a catastrophe, the mountain facility was also a backup command station for the United States government.

The complex was protected against nuclear blasts, electromagnetic pulses, biological or chemical attacks, and earthquakes. The main chamber was over a thousand feet underground, with fifteen three-story buildings inside. Each building rests on springs to prevent any movement from an earthquake.

The long tunnel connecting the outside world to the complex has two blast doors weighing twenty-five tons. Once sealed, the development was self-contained with a power supply and water reservoirs. The Cheyenne Mountain complex is an impregnable fortress that rivals Fort Knox's gold depository for security.

Brad wasn't surprised at the reception they received at the front gates—they had driven past three flashing yellow signs and a soldier stationed at the base of the road. Brad had told Tanya to ignore the soldier, go around him, and continue driving to the security gate.

Calmly, Brad told Tanya to turn the vehicle off, place the keys on the dash, and not move or obey their orders—she nervously complied.

When he stepped out of the Tahoe, it caused the soldiers to go into a flurry of shouted commands. Brad just stood there, arms outstretched, and waited. One MP raised his HK and kept him in his sights. The area was well-lit, with floodlights around the security shack and the tall fencing lining the road.

A second soldier stood by the control arm and yelled, "Get back in your vehicle and leave the area! No admittance."

No kidding, Brad thought.

"Can I show you my ID now?" Brad didn't want to move without warning in case they were trigger-happy.

At a nod from the soldier by the gate, Brad announced, "FBI Special Agent Bradley Holman. I instigated the lockdown." With slow movements, Brad reached inside his jacket pocket and showed the guards his badge and ID.

"Sir, regardless of who you are, you're being asked to leave this area."

"Get your duty officer. I need to speak to them. I'll wait here." Brad ignored the soldier who kept him in his sight, opened the

Tahoe's back, and climbed inside. He tried not to slam the door, but his nervous energy got the best of him. Tanya jumped at the loud noise but quickly recovered.

With a sigh, Brad slumped in the seat and waited.

"Are you okay?" Tanya was nervous as she watched the drama unfold.

"All good. Relax, it was just a show. At least, I hope so."

The junior field agent didn't understand the situation, and she kept making eye contact in the rear-view mirror. Shortly, a green military jeep appeared, and a tall man in a combat green uniform got out and talked to the two men at the gate arm.

The officer gave the order to stand down before he stood next to the Tahoe. The man was six feet tall, receding hairline and broad shoulders. Double bars for his rank were on the collar of his uniform, and the nametag read Captain Sheridan. Brad removed a letter from his jacket pocket and exited the vehicle.

"How can I help you, Agent Holman?"

Instead of answering, Brad handed him the folded paper to read. When the officer finished, a look of surprise washed over his features.

As he finished, Brad produced another letter from his jacket and waited until the soldier finished.

"Do you understand, Captain?"

Sheridan scanned both pages before returning them, "Yes, sir."

Brad opened the rear hatch of the Chevy and removed a small white plastic grocery bag. After a quick look inside, he passed it to the officer. "I'll wait here."

The captain's long strides brought him back to the jeep, and after a three-point turn, he drove quickly into the Cheyenne Mountain complex.

Brad closed his eyes in the vehicle and tried to catch a quick nap. After thirty minutes, Brad could tell by the deep breathing from the front seat that Tanya had also taken advantage of the break.

Brad lowered his window when the same jeep returned and parked beside the Tahoe. Passing the same white bag to Brad between the vehicles with the captain's long reach wasn't difficult. He issued a few verbal orders to the officer before raising his window.

"We're good. Back to the airport."

The captain turned his jeep around and drove into the complex while Tanya started the Chevy and used the full area to complete a U-turn. The soldiers retreated to give her room and gave him a deadpan look. They were not impressed, but it didn't matter. He had a job to do.

"Everything okay, sir?"

Brad could see she was curious and kept glancing in the rearview mirror. "I believe so. The next half an hour will tell. Don't stop for anything and drive straight to the jet."

Brad called the pilot. "Ready for take-off in thirty minutes, as soon as I arrive. We are en route."

After he sent a confirmation email to Stephanie, Brad scrolled through the pictures he had taken of the journal. The president hadn't mentioned whether he could have a copy of the writings. Better to ask for forgiveness than permission.

Scrolling through his phone, Brad paused at the picture he had taken of one journal entry. Everything had hinged on this one log, and it had paid off.

Certain fail-safes were installed at the mountain complex for a nuclear catastrophe to ensure the government and the human species would survive. The seed catalog had enough samples stored in deep freeze to provide many things, from flowers to crops, to rebuild civilization.

Brad hoped the plan would pay off, believing he had everything covered. *The cheese is in the trap—time to catch the mouse.*

Chapter 9

President Bower leaned forward on the Resolute desk and slowly scanned The Oval Office. He knew most of the security electronics in place by the secret service were there to monitor him, from the sensor pads within the floor to the thermal imagery scanners. While in The Oval Office, the president acted as if he were always being recorded. He didn't last this long in politics by being careless and erring on caution.

Bower looked out the window at the South Lawn with the presidential journal in his hands. Reporters and staff were gathered for a briefing, but more pressing matters weighed on his mind. He stood in the historical headquarters and governing center of the country. One of the most secure places in the world, yet someone had access. He didn't know how anyone besides the president could access and read the journal.

Then again, I didn't know how anyone could break into Fort Knox. He opened the journal to the first blank page with his favorite pen and wrote.

31 October 2019

I have just sent an agent to the Cheyenne Mountain Air Force base to confirm that half of the meteorite is safe and secure. The other half was taken from Fort Knox with no clues. The impossible was achieved; it will not happen again.

Once the ink dried, the president opened the bottom right drawer of the Resolute desk and pressed on the inside trim's decorative carving. A panel inside the foot-well revealed a hidden drawer with a subtle click. The journal fit with several inches to spare, and once he pushed the board back into place, it was locked away—another secret this office held—one of many passed down from JFK.

He would keep the journal for a week, then return it to the FBI director for safekeeping. Having read Special Agent Holman's note, he followed the detailed instructions, despite not understanding them fully.

*****

The man focused on the thick gold ring with his arm held at chest height. Like a paused movie on the television, everything froze.

The constant background roar from the electrical hum of lights, cars in the distance, birds chirping, insects, and even the light breeze suddenly stopped.

Perfect silence.

Without any noise, he could hear the blood as it rushed through his veins. His heartbeat pounded in his ears like a drum.

Once he lowered his arm, the man began the long walk on the paved road. It could have taken a thousand years, or it could have taken a second. When time has no meaning, it can't be measured.

Everything was overlaid in a red tinge, from the soldiers to the vehicles, even the ground. He didn't panic when everything turned color. The tall man was used to the effects of the time-stop.

The soldiers were immobile, and he briskly strode around. One woman stood with her foot an inch above the ground, her step incomplete. Another man stood beside the road and flicked a cigarette into the ditch. The butt defied gravity and hung in mid-air, inches from his fingertips. All of them were completely unaware of the man that passed through. They resembled lifelike statues.

The road into the mountain was littered with four-foot-high concrete barriers that would slow a vehicle as it entered the tunnel system. It ensured no one could drive through directly, forcing them to swerve and slow on the slalom course. The man ignored the road, and his hiking boots closed the distance along the pedestrian pathway. Fifteen hundred yards later, a solid door filled the tunnel.

The blast door stood fifteen feet tall and twenty feet wide, and the markings on the polished concrete floor stopped at the barrier.

The thick twenty-five-ton door could withstand a nuclear blast without windows or a viewing port, but it was easily circumvented, not for most people, just him.

With his back to the wall in the large chamber, the man once again held his ring out at chest height, and his tanned brow furrowed.

Inch by inch, a bubble of *change* expanded around him. A neutral shade of gray replaced the red tinge that colored the world as the dome increased. Reality shifted and encompassed the cavern and the security door.

It started with flickers of movement along the road. The massive blast door suddenly swung open, a golf cart drove *backward* into the mountain, and a group of soldiers ran rearward inside. Two military police officers appeared from the interior and stood guard at the entrance. Their hands rested on the grip of their holstered pistols.

Once he passed through the seven-foot-thick door, the man with the gold ring quickly stepped inside. The gray haze moved with him.

The tunnel opened into an expansive room with security screening and conveyor belts connected to X-ray machines. Against the eastern wall was a second blast door, the same dimensions as the first. The security door was unlocked and opened several feet.

Once inside, the man paused, and the gray overlay vanished, only to be replaced by a bright white light that covered everything like a flash.

When the white light illuminated the area, people and objects moved forward normally. A high-pitched noise sounded from the ground underfoot. It increased in tone steadily until it vibrated beyond the human ear's range. The perfect silence returned when the man resumed his journey into the mountain complex. The red tinge once again covered everything.

The seed storage area lay off a side tunnel carved deep into the mountain, with a separate power supply to operate the deep freezers in the event of a collapse. They would last a hundred years, past the downfall of man.

The #501044 bin storage resembled a sizeable deep chest freezer sold at a retail outlet. Two stainless-steel latches were lifted, and the top swung back on hinges. Only one item was inside the ceramic container: a rock the size of his fist.

What the hell?

Right away, he knew this wasn't the stone he needed. A handwritten note was taped to the underside.

```
To my talented thief,
    I believe you are after what I now have in my
possession. I will be at the John Hancock Tower at noon on
Sunday. I am looking forward to our meeting.
    Special Agent Brad Holman, FBI.
```

He crumpled the note and whipped the rock into the bottom of the freezer. As he gripped the sides of the unit, the sense of frustration slowly turned to amusement.

"Well done, Agent Holman. However, you'll lose this game. I have all the time in the world, and I always win."

He left the rock and chuckled at the meeting place. He used to know that location all too well.

Chapter 10

At 200 Clarendon Street, the John Hancock Tower was a massive sixty-two-story skyscraper completed in 1976 and is the tallest building in downtown Boston. Its mirrored windowpanes reflected the sky and could be seen against the horizon for miles. The building was named after the John Hancock Insurance company, and the locals referred to it only as The Hancock.

The observation deck showed stunning views of Boston, and it used to be open to the general public. However, after 9/11, it remained closed. While it could be rented out for private functions, the building owners wanted to fill the space with more offices.

It took Stephanie several phone calls to make the arrangements, but Brad was pleased. They had prepared for everything short of having a satellite tasked to monitor in real time.

The observation deck had been rearranged. Much like an interrogation room, one glass table and two chairs to either side were the only items on the northern platform. Chairs and tables were stacked together on the far side. The management had the rooftop arranged as ordered.

Brad looked over the city and marveled at the views as he stood at the railing. He had an unobstructed view of the Boston harbor and could even see ships near Long Island in Massachusetts Bay. The east wind gusted, and he absently patted his hair back in place and buttoned his suit jacket. A bank of dark clouds would arrive within the hour, and Brad could tell by the telltale wisps that trailed off the ends that it would rain.

"Nice view, isn't it?"

Brad's heart leaped in his chest as he spun around. A man sat at the table ten feet behind him. He appeared to be between thirty and forty years old, deeply tanned with short brown hair. The blue T-shirt and jeans did nothing to hide his muscular physique; his arms and chest stretched the material.

Holman had agents surrounding the building at each possible entry point and spotters in the neighboring condo building. Teams were also deployed on each floor, covering the stairs and elevators. He had heard nothing from his earpiece.

"It is."

Looking around the observation deck, the FBI agent sat in a chair directly across from him. "Glad to meet you finally. I'm Brad Holman."

Brad held his hand across the table, letting it hang for a few seconds. The man across from him didn't offer his hand or give his name in return. The thief just sat there with an amused smile and kept his hands below the tabletop.

"I'm guessing you found my note."

Brad wasn't sure he could handle him physically, but with the quick reaction support in the hallway, he just had to hold him for a moment.

The man gave a slight nod. "I'm not at liberty to go into details, but I need that small rock."

Brad was good at reading people, gauging guilt and lies from their facial expressions and body positioning. He couldn't get a reading off the thief. The man seemed *very* relaxed and not worried or guilty in the slightest, one hundred percent confident and sure of himself.

That worried Brad. He should have been the one in the position of confidence, but he felt outplayed. The thief shouldn't have entered the building without alerting the teams. Then again, he shouldn't have been able to penetrate Fort Knox or the mountain complex.

Yet, here he sat.

Brad smiled and raised two empty palms in the air. "It seems I have forgotten to bring it with me. Maybe you could answer a few questions."

"If you did not bring it with you, I'm afraid my time here is over."

Brad picked up a slight accent but couldn't identify it.

Agent Holman leaned forward, and the muscles in his legs tensed. Ready for action. "I'm sorry, but I can't allow you to leave. There are many questions that you *will* answer."

Brad pressed the panic button inside his jacket sleeve and activated his earpiece. "Target is on the roof with me. Move in!"

The man grinned, spun out of his chair, and darted to the rooftop door. Brad ran around the table and sprinted in his wake, but he tripped when his legs collided with a plastic chair. He skidded a few feet on his chest as his hands tried to break his fall on the decking.

Brad scrambled to his feet, but the man had reached the door and walked through. He glanced at the chair before running to the door. Four seconds after it closed, the door flew open and slammed into the wall. Two agents in tactical gear rushed forward with rifles at the ready. The muzzles swept the area as they looked for the target.

"He just left. Start searching and lock down the building!"

The two men ran back through the double doors without responding while shouting orders in their communications set. Brad's earpiece lay on the ground after it jarred loose.

In disbelief, Brad stared at the chair on the ground. He had carefully set up the observation deck in his favor, with *two* seats at the table. Over seventy feet away, the remaining chairs and tables were stacked along the west railing. The two chairs still were positioned at the table, but now there was a third in the mix.

The chair allowed the thief to get away with seconds to spare.

Once he fitted the earpiece, he heard the tactical coordinator relay commands. The perimeter doors were sealed, and no one would enter or leave. Other teams cleared the building floor by floor, and with over sixty levels, he knew this would take a while. There would be too many places for someone to hide.

Only three or four seconds had passed when the thief walked through the door, and the tactical team rushed out. There wasn't any concealment in the hallway for a child, let alone a full-grown adult.

Brad kicked the rogue chair in frustration. He had more questions than answers.

~

The FBI crime scene investigators finished processing the scene under Holman's watchful eye. It was reasonably straightforward, considering they only had four possible processing locations: the door handles, interior and exterior, the table, and the chair tipped over on the ground.

Brad was sure the suspect never touched the table, just the armrests on the chair.

They found two sets of prints on the observation deck door, one matching Special Agent Holman and one other person. The table was clean, but marks on the tipped-over chair matched the door handle.

Special Agent Holman uploaded the information to the FBI database, and the search began in earnest. He booked the bureaus' forensic artist, and hopefully, he would have the drawings to distribute by morning.

Chapter 11

Doctor Virginia Kincaid rushed into the staff lunchroom, waving a set of papers above her head. "Good news!"

The white lab coat flapped like a dove's wings behind her. Her blond hair was pulled into a ponytail, and the end flicked over each shoulder as she ran. Doctor Kincaid was one of the leading researchers in subatomic physics working out of TRIUMF in Vancouver and headed the cyclotron quantum mechanical project.

Virginia's team had successfully created a miniature black hole in the cyclotron, the approximate size of an atom. It had evaporated almost instantly, but the last run produced a double event horizon. *It lasted nearly a full second!* The rarity was unexplained, but the documented results were timely as their subsidy was to be continued at the University of British Columbia. Already the accomplishment had been shared and marveled at worldwide in the appropriate circles.

"We got it! The funding has been approved!"

The staff and technicians cheered, and the excitement was contagious. Virginia grinned, pushed her oval glasses back on her nose, and added, "It looks like we will actually be paid too."

The last three weeks were almost considered volunteer work at the lab. The funding grant from their initial endeavors had all but vanished.

"I want to recreate the run we had for the double. I have booked the cyclotron already, and we have a full week to prepare."

Buoyed by the announcement, everyone went back to work in the lab. Pleased with the funding Virginia had a bounce in her step when she headed to her office. A definite chance to prove Hawking's radiation theory and investigate and hopefully study small black holes and quantum fluctuations had been a long-time dream. Should Hawking's radiation prove viable, a limitless energy source should be possible once it is harnessed correctly.

*****

As he slumped in the desk chair, Brad rubbed his eyes before taking another sip of coffee. Despite being on assignment for the president, there wasn't escaping the paperwork the FBI demanded. Reports had to be generated, and a paper trail for the use of the two tactical squads and the forensic team. Even with the late hour, agents were busy at the Boston field office, catching up on their endless reports or meetings. However, it was similar enough to the Arizona field office that he felt at home.

With a subtle *ping* from an incoming text message, Brad checked his phone.

\>> How much longer are we to remain in the air?

Brad glanced at the time and figured the immediate danger had passed. *Do you still have the package?*

\>> Affirmative.

I'll meet you at Norwood Memorial in thirty minutes. Land once I have given you the all-clear.

\>> Roger.

Brad slipped into his suit jacket and took the elevator to the underground parking. Despite the offer for a driver, Brad preferred to be independent and had signed out for a vehicle. He did not want to endanger anyone if he could avoid it. The thief's actions revealed holes in their security, which could jeopardize safety.

He passed a yellow taxi on the southbound parkway, but there was barely any traffic at the late hour, and he made good time. With a quick flash of his credentials to the airport security, Brad drove through the gates and parked at the private landing area near the north hangar. Short of bringing in a team to confirm the location was clear, he was confident no one was watching.

All clear to land, area secure. Taxi to me.

\>> Landing. I'll be there in a few minutes.

Before he left Colorado, Holman had little choice for a secure storage place for the meteorite fragment. If the thief could break into Fort Knox and the Cheyenne complex, there was little else he could do to offer more protection.

Keeping the Gulfstream jet airborne was the most secure place that came to mind. The answer seemed obvious with the latest modification of the refueling nozzle mounted on the nose of the G550 series.

Within a few minutes, Brad heard the jet's engines reverse as it came around the corner of the hangar and taxied toward him. There wasn't any ground crew in this area, especially at this hour. The landing wasn't scheduled and was off the books. It was about as safe as Brad could make it.

Soon as the jet came to a full stop, the stairs lowered, and agent Tanya Bradford walked over to Brad.

"Here you go, sir." She handed over the meteor fragment. "To let you know, there were a few issues when I approached the cockpit area. Instruments started to act up, so I stayed in the rear lounge."

"Good call. I appreciate your help."

"Sir, can you tell me what this is all about?"

"To be honest, I'm not too sure myself. I also need answers, and this is my only bargaining chip."

Chapter 12

The twisting pattern of black and gray swirled like paint in a blender about the man without touching or coming close. Designs and shapes without meaning formed and then dissolved. He could have witnessed the display for years or seconds. Where he stood, time was a concept that only existed in his thoughts.

He concentrated and raised the gold ring to chest height. The ring didn't need to move, but centuries of habit prevailed. The inset gem flashed with an inner light before everything paused. When a white light bathed everything in its brilliance, he was ready.

As he moved forward through time, the man passed the benchmark of his prior attempts. The previous threshold left him stranded and frustrated him countless times. It was like hitting an invisible wall that he could not navigate through. Adding the one fragment to the stone had extended his abilities, even if only marginally, into new territory.

His destination was a void—a total absence of light and dark. Nothing at all.

The man could almost pinpoint the location with the extra piece of the puzzle. So *very* close, but it may as well be across the universe. Approaching the void, he attempted to slip into a different pattern resembling a wave harmonic, but the invisible wall halted his progress again.

He would need the remaining fragment to push the threshold back farther. The answers were just out of reach for now.

Everything depended on this.

*****

Instead of returning to Washington to catch up on paperwork, Brad stayed in the Boston field office. All he needed was an empty cubical, and he could log in to the system to complete more work. He couldn't keep the jet in the air indefinitely, and if the stone were kept on his person, he would have tighter control.

Brad slowly turned the meteorite fragment around and examined it from every angle back at the desk. According to the journal, the stone was severed in two to see what lay inside. Traditional X-ray machines failed to function correctly, and all studies said the same thing. It was a rock. Approximately four inches long, three and a half inches at its widest point, and three inches in depth, the stone fit very comfortably in the palm of one hand. One end was flattened as if cut with a laser.

Tapping it on the desktop produced nothing except a few scratches on another government-issued desk. The black material had a gem-like quality and caught the fluorescent lighting, making it sparkle. The scientific testing had shown time passed differently close to the fragment.

"This should be easy to prove."

On vacation several years ago to the Bahamas, he had taken a resort SCUBA course and had picked up the sport. He had replaced his old Timex with a new Seiko known as an 'Arnie.' It was named after a certain governor and action-movie star that made it famous. Once he removed the watch, Brad wrapped the rugged black band around the rock to see the results. The dive watch had a digital and analog display with a date calendar. The digital display would still work if the mechanical aspects were to fail.

The hair on his arms and neck stood straight as he stared at the second hand. The dial spun forward, and at other times it would circle counter-clockwise before it paused. It didn't stay still for long; for seconds, it resumed its stately pace before going crazy again.

The digital display mirrored the same abnormality.

"To read about it is one thing. I feel like I'm being punked." Brad had a quick look around the office. No one recorded or laughed at his expression.

He placed the watch to the side and let out a whistle under his breath. *The journal entries were correct.*

Brad logged in to the computer and held the stone to the bottom right corner of the screen. He wondered if the time display would react the same way, but nothing happened.

Out of ideas, he made sure no one was watching and gave it a good sniff. It smelled like a rock, which didn't surprise him.

In the desk drawer, Brad routed around until he found a stainless-steel letter opener. He had a pocket knife, but this would work better. With the rock in his left hand, he scratched the point across its surface, but the opener didn't leave a mark.

On a second attempt, Brad was caught off guard when the letter opener's point slipped and dug deep into the palm of his left hand.

The sharp sting of pain in his left hand vanished once the blood quickly pooled in his palm and coated the lower half of the meteorite fragment. He dropped the letter opener in reflex as his hand spasmed.

"Holy shit!" The blade floated in mid-air. It should have fallen but hung eighteen inches above the tiled floor instead.

The instant silence was the strangest experience, with the usual background noise of the office stopping. No one talked on the phone. The clicking of keyboards and even the sound of the air coming through the vents were absent.

When he spun around, everyone in the office had frozen in mid-movement.

Don't panic. There must be an explanation for this.

After dropping the stone fragment on the desk, the roar of life rushes back. The letter opener rang as it hit the ground before it settled. Agents continued to talk, and the electrical hum from the lights resumed.

Fearful of his sanity, Brad picked up the meteor fragment and headed to the small kitchen to wash his hand at the sink. He tried to calm the sudden rapid beat of his heart and take slow deep breaths.

When he washed the blood away, he was even more shocked to discover that the wound was gone.

"What the hell?"

The one-inch jagged scar looked like it had healed years ago. Brad turned the stone over to learn that his blood was no longer on the underside. A few dried flakes fell to the floor.

Brad had an analytical mind and could process information with intuitive leaps. He could solve problems and questions well ahead of his peers at the bureau. This ability had given him an unprecedented number of solved cases with the FBI. However, all roads pointed down a path outside the normal parameters. No answers came to mind that didn't question his sanity.

"Scary, isn't it."

As he spun around, Brad saw the thief leaning against the kitchen counter. He had an amused smirk, and his arms crossed his chest. Brad noted the clothing hadn't changed, a blue cotton T-shirt and jeans. Now that Brad stood beside him, he could tell they were approximately the same height, six feet tall.

"How did you get in here?"

Ignoring the question, the man stepped away from the counter and held out his hand. "You can figure that out on your own. Right now, I need that rock."

It is standard for agents to lock up their weapons in their desks or armory while doing paperwork when in the office. Brad's hand twitched to his empty shoulder holster before quickly pulling out a pocket knife. With a quick flick of his thumb, a four-inch blade appeared.

"If it makes you feel any better, you can try to stop me with that."

Brad's opponent appeared amused.

"I will."

The man took a deep breath and moved another step forward as Brad moved back. Brad adjusted his grip on the knife and stabbed himself in his left palm. Once again, the world stopped. This time, there was an exception.

The thief's eyes opened wide in surprise at the sudden turn of events, and he held both hands out wide. Brad couldn't recall what had happened, but it felt like a tornado had picked him up. He wasn't moving, but everything else about him did. Waves of light swirled, and a loud, resonating, humming noise filled his being. He couldn't tell which direction was up or down, and Brad's eyes rolled back as his knees buckled. His mind couldn't handle the onslaught of sensations and shut down.

Before Brad lost consciousness, strong arms picked him up as he was thrown over a shoulder.

Chapter 13

The pounding headache grew every second, and cracked lips cried out for moisture as a dry tongue scraped across like sandpaper. Opening his eyes was a mistake, and Brad pulled the pillow over his head to block out the light. He nearly sneezed as the scent of wood smoke made his nose twitch. With eyes closed, Brad patted his pants pockets as he searched for the white bottle of pills.

Where the hell are they?

Tentatively, he pulled the pillow away and scanned the room. It was a small open-floored cabin about a thirty-foot square. The kitchen had a rough wooden table and chairs next to a lit built-in stone fireplace. A thin wisp rose from a burned log on an iron grate and floated around a blackened metal pot hanging from a hook. Split wood lay stacked against the side, ready to use. Cupboards lined the far wall above a long counter.

Brad finally realized he lay on a coarse woolen blanket on a double bed. On a wooden chair beside the bed sat his knife, wallet, and bottle of pills next to a tin cup filled with water. The chair matched the other three around the kitchen table.

The only other feature in the cabin was a steep set of stairs, more a ladder, that allowed access to the loft. The lone window beside the door had a crack in the glass. Outside, the sun was overhead, and the shadows were short—close to noon.

"What the fuck is going on?"

He winced at the sound of his voice, and the grip crushing his skull tightened another notch. There wasn't a response. Brad didn't expect one.

Am I dreaming?

Brad rubbed his temples before fumbling for the pill bottle and water as his legs swung off the bed. If he was dreaming, it didn't explain the situation. He wore his dress shoes, suit pants, shirt, and tie. The empty shoulder holster hung off the back of the chair, and his tie had been loosened. Presumably, his jacket and gun were still at his desk in Boston. His watch and cell phone were missing as well.

Brad tossed two pills in his mouth, then hesitated with the cup. What if it were poisoned? If someone wanted him dead, it would have been done while he was helpless. The water was refreshing with a slight mineral taste, and he drank it all.

Brad placed his things into his pockets before exploring the cabin. The ceiling was lower than average, just a few inches above his head. He had enough height to walk without banging his head, but it certainly left no room to jump.

From the lower step of the ladder, he had a quick peek into the loft. Two small beds were against the far wall underneath the sloped roof. There wouldn't be room to walk around in the attic. Anyone there would have to crouch.

The kitchen was simple, with wooden cooking utensils, ceramic plates, and mugs on a shelf, but there was no sign of a cell or landline phone. Brad hefted a thick knife from a cutlery drawer and briefly considered keeping it as a weapon but placed it aside. The cedar chest at the foot of the bed held blankets, linen clothing, and towels.

"Where am I? Hello?"

Brad stood at the front door and looked out the small window, but the fractured glass only gave him the impression of a field. He heard birds but not any vehicles. Brad guessed he was far from the city. The door handle was a simple iron latch that rattled when he pressed on the thumb plate. He was relieved to note there wasn't a deadbolt or lock.

The hinges creaked, and Brad knew he was correct about the distance from the city. Open fields stretched before him, and a small barn stood fifty yards to his right. Midway between the barn and cabin, next to a bucket and rope on the grass, was a three-foot pile of rocks forming a pyramid with an opening at the top. A well?

The fresh, clean air felt good and helped clear his head.

On the far side of the fields, a dense forest surrounded the property. Brad's woodcraft was weak, but he recognized pine trees and the odd birch. Towering above the forest like masts on a ship were massive oaks.

"I was kidnapped and taken to the country. Lovely." Only a few clouds dotted the blue sky. Brad stood underneath the overhang on the porch.

Brad spotted a blue T-shirt against the forest backdrop on a second sweep of the field. The man who stole the fragment, and captured him, knelt under a tree. The man's head snapped over when the cabin door slammed. His captor stood and brushed his jeans. With firm strides, he walked across the field toward the cabin.

Brad spotted an ax embedded in a tree stump twenty feet away. Besides the pocket knife, he didn't see any other weapons available, and he waited while the man approached. There wasn't any point in panicking now. If he wanted Brad dead, it would have already happened.

Brad wanted to hear him out, and then he could subdue him if necessary, then go for help and call reinforcements.

"We have to talk about a few things. Grab a seat."

The pile of logs made for an excellent impromptu office area, and when he sat on a large stump, Brad felt a little nervous but also anxious to get some answers. His gaze flicked to the ax handle. He could reach it first if required.

The man took a deep breath and ran his hands through his short hair. He wasn't sure how to begin and seemed hesitant. "I have a few problems, and I'm unsure if you are one of them or a potential solution."

Brad leaned forward and placed his hands on his knees. The pills swept away the fatigue and headache. He had interviewed countless people, but this situation was different. "Fill me in on the background and what the problems are. Then I will tell *you* about the problems you'll have."

The man crossed his arms and stared at the trees. His eyes were out of focus as he collected his thoughts. He didn't seem to be concerned about the ramifications of his actions.

"How about you start with your name and where we are?" Brad switched on the interrogator mode in his brain. *He* was in charge, and he would get answers.

"I'm Clement Wallace, and you're at my farm." With a gesture behind him, he waved in the general direction of everything in sight. "We are currently southwest of Boston."

Brad knew that area well but had already doubted Clement's statement. He should have heard the traffic or spotted a plane as it landed at Logan International. "Kidnapping a federal agent is a felony, let alone your other endeavors. You'll be going to jail for a long time. Start explaining."

Clement paced while he continued. "You may already be aware of some abnormalities with no explanations. I have an explanation, but please keep an open mind." After he cleared his throat, he stared at Brad. "I believe it starts with the world ending and everything we know ceasing to exist."

Chapter 14

Clement sat back down on the tree stump and stared at the ground. "Everything that I am going to tell you is at the limits of my understanding, but I'll try." He adjusted himself for comfort. "A scientific experiment in the future created a miniature black hole that produced an irregularity. Instead of disappearing, it feeds on itself. Normally it would take billions of years for a small black hole to grow large enough to absorb matter to pose any threat. However, this seems to happen within an instant, and it destroys the world. It's imminent."

Brad's jaw dropped while he tried to digest the information. He had interrogated hundreds and asked thousands of people questions to probe the truth and detect lies. Clement believed that statement and knew it as fact, or he was skilled enough that Brad couldn't tell. People that believed their own lies were the most dangerous.

"What about the meteorite piece? How does that play into this?" Brad eyed the ax, mentally preparing to dart for the wooden handle.

"I have an idea, but it seems the rock was sent to try and stop everything. It's the key." Clement shrugged.

Brad's mind whirled. All the puzzle pieces alluded to something he couldn't explain. He hoped Clement *could* explain before he arrested him. Most noticeable were the strange effects that he witnessed. Letter openers do not just hang in midair. "Where are we… exactly?"

"We are at my farm. I have owned this property since I was twenty-three years old. That isn't the question you should be asking. Try, *when* are we?"

Brad rubbed the scar on the palm of his left hand, and he thought about it. There was no point in being rational. Best to play along with the man's delusions. "I give up. When are we?"

"The fall of seventeen-eighty-two. I had just found the meteorite in the woods over there." Clement pointed across the fields where Brad had first spotted him. "We're in an instance, a time-variant if you will, that I can return to at will. This moment is on a loop. A moment saved outside of the normal timestream."

"How is any of that possible?" Brad frowned and gestured to the surrounding land. He remembered the letter opener and how it hung in mid-air without any explanation, which gave him pause. He would love to hear any logical reason and how it connected to the theft.

How could Clement break into Fort Knox and the mountain complex? I need real answers!

Clement continued. "Where we are now sitting, I watched a meteor fall into the woods, and when I found it, I discovered how to use it for time travel."

Brad also had figured that Clement knew of the presidential journal. Specific facts that led to the hidden pieces of stone were only written in the journal, not on social media.

Despite the circumstances, Brad believed Clement had a severe mental disorder. He wasn't about to join him on the funny farm. "You never answered my question. *How* is it possible?"

"I have thought about that particular question for a long time."

"How long?" Brad felt compelled to ask.

"Near as I can figure, several centuries."

Until now, Brad had tried to keep an open mind, but this last statement was hard to swallow.

Impossible.

"Okay…."

With a wry smile, Clement stood and gestured to Brad. "Come with me."

Brad stepped toward the ax, but Clement had already turned away. He didn't feel threatened by the delusional man. For now, he would play along.

Clement led Brad to the kitchen inside the cabin and grabbed a lantern off a wall hook. He pulled a lighter from his pocket, and the small glass door swung open. Once the candle was lit, Clement gestured for Brad to step back. He had been standing on a hatch built into the plank floor.

Clement pulled an iron ring and lifted the cellar door, revealing a steep wooden staircase. The lantern was hung on a nail below. "Watch your head, low ceiling."

As his right hand drifted toward his pocket knife, Brad tensed and mentally prepared for an assault. Being lured into a basement wasn't his idea of playing it safe. However, he didn't get any bad vibes from Clement, but there wasn't any way he was going down first.

The cellar was about fifteen square feet smaller than the cabin's floor plan. The floor was compacted with hard earth and had a damp smell. The ceiling was six feet tall, and Clement and Brad hunched to avoid banging their heads on a low beam. The only object below was a simple wooden table less than a foot in height, placed in the cellar's far corner.

At the table, Clement knelt and brought up his right hand. Brad noticed the gold ring on his middle finger, and the gem glinted in the candlelight.

Unable to look away, the light flickered and danced across the gemstone faster and faster. An airwave of concussive force pushed them back like a flashbang. The lantern rocked on the nail, and Brad blinked and rubbed the dust out of his eyes.

He had seen stage magicians perform and knew the tricks were all sleight-of-hand or accomplished with props. However, he was in a dirt-floor cellar with wooden beams above, not a studio. There wasn't any room for fabrications or a stagehand to help perform an illusion. On the table in front of Clement rested a large stone. The small fragment Brad had tried to protect also sat on the table. One second, the table was empty. The next, it wasn't.

Brad tried to speak, but he didn't know what to say.

Clement rested his hand on the rock. It was real. "When I added the first fragment to the larger stone, it amplified the abilities by just a fraction. Enabling me to get closer to where the experiment occurred. I'm trying to figure out what went wrong and hopefully prevent it."

Picking up the fragment, Clement turned to Brad. "I figured that adding this to the original would enable me to push closer through the barrier."

A mental fog wrapped Brad in its embrace when the large stone appeared on the table. Reality seemed to unravel around the edges. Nothing in his training or his past had prepared him for this.

"However, you have stumbled across how to bond with the stone. I can't connect this last piece to the larger one, but *you* can."

Clement stretched out his arm, and Brad automatically put out his hand and caught it when it dropped into his palm.

"Come over here." Clement gently guided Brad by the shoulder and stood before the meteorite. "Take the stone and place it against the larger one in that divot. It will only fit one way."

Brad numbly followed the instructions and fit the pieces together. A small, repeated *click* could be heard in the small room. The clicks sounded faster and faster, turning into a high-pitched whistling tone that quickly exceeded their hearing range. With a gesture from Clement, the stone disappeared.

Brad waved his hand through the air above the table. It was gone. "How did you do that?"

Clement firmly grabbed Brad by the shoulder. "Let's go see how much of a difference this makes."

Suddenly the two men disappeared. The lantern swung back and forth in the empty cellar while the shadows danced alone.

Chapter 15

Ginny grabbed her backpack and briskly walked out of her dorm room. She hurried across the quad for her next lecture on the dynamics of particles and rigid bodies in her physical mechanics course. Absorbing the information like a sponge, Ginny had fully immersed herself in her classes at the University of Regina in the province of Saskatchewan. Her full scholarship was earned through hard work and an innate sense of mathematics, which was almost instinctual.

"Kincaid! Let's go."

Ginny spotted her friend Amy waiting at the end of the path. After a few weeks of classes, they became close once they discovered shared interests. Both young women were five-foot-ten with long blond hair tied back in a ponytail. Ginny had freckles dusted across her nose, and Amy wore frameless glasses. Otherwise, they could have passed for sisters.

"Coming!" With a little laugh, Ginny ran ahead to join her. She moved around two men as they sat on a bench but didn't pay them any attention. Rest areas all over the quad were used by faculty and students.

Looking at her watch, Amy asked, "Do you think we have time for a coffee? Professor Bestman never starts on time."

"I could use a tea. Let's hurry, and we can still make it."

Shoulder to shoulder, the young women chatted as they hurried to a nearby café before class.

*****

Brad crossed his legs while sitting on the bench and watched the two students walk briskly away. Despite the evidence, he still couldn't help but feel he had slipped off the deep end. As Brad was hurled through time and space, the full range of emotions coursed through his body—denial to confusion reigned. It took a while for him to come to grips and wrap his thoughts around the possibility. Panic levels rose enough to paralyze him as he rationalized.

Hollywood could easily create a movie that showed magic and space travel that appeared to be real. However, he was a long way from a movie set. One second, Brad was in a farm cellar. The next moment he was traveling through time and space. It took a while to wrap his mind around the concept, but he had to face reality. Clement had brought him to various times and places and allowed Brad to interact on a limited basis with random people to verify their location and date. Their first stop was a souvenir stand in Niagara

Falls in 1988, and the next was at a supermarket in Dayton, Ohio, in 2010. After three more random locations, Brad had enough.

Time travel was real.

Clement had taken Brad to the university. When asked where they were, he replied, *"Some things he had to see for himself."* Now Brad found himself on a bench seat in Canada.

"Virginia Kincaid is the one with the green backpack. She starts this whole disaster with her experiments. In one timeline, I've even killed her to avert the end. It didn't work."

Brad stared at Clement in shock, and his hand twitched for a set of cuffs. "You're serious?" As an FBI agent, hearing this confession rocked him. As a person, it made him nauseous. "You killed a kid?"

"I was out of ideas, and everything I tried to do *always* resulted in the same thing. It was one of the hardest things I ever had to do, making me physically sick. Virginia was the same age as my oldest son. However, it was one person versus seven and a half billion people."

Clement shrugged. "From what I can tell, large events are tough to change. Almost impossible. Someone else just took her place and performed the same work with the same results. That particular timeline didn't work, so I abandoned it."

"What causes this disaster?" After traveling through time and space, Brad had given up on any pretense of disbelief. There was no possible way for him to have been subjected to a hoax this large.

"I have spent a great deal of time learning as much as I can on this subject. But, at the end of the day, I'm a farmer at heart. I have a great deal of trouble trying to understand quantum mechanics. I'm okay with admitting it is beyond me. I have noticed it's easier to return to a specific point in time and a location that I have been to before. When you bend a strip of metal, it creates a weak point. The second time you bend it, it's easier, and so on. At the quantum level, space bends and twists when it's manipulated. Doing so again at the same coordinates seems easier, like bending the metal strip."

While still trying to grasp certain aspects, one question came to mind. "Do you meet yourself? What about paradoxes?"

"When learning about traveling and how to move about, I messed up several times. I met myself often until I learned how to enter alternate timelines. Every time you make a choice, an alternate timeline is created. In one timeline, the girls decided to go straight to their class; in this one, they went for drinks first. There is almost an infinite number of choices at all times, creating an infinite number of possibilities."

He tried to follow along, but Brad had to interrupt. "There's an infinite number of worlds?"

"Far as I know, there is only this world, but with infinite variations. As to paradoxes, I don't worry about them. If a paradox were possible with time travel, it would have already sorted itself out."

"So, the old adage of you going back to kill your own grandfather?"

"Then, I would cease to exist. Right?"

Smiling at the intellectual dilemma, Brad thought he had him.

"That is one test I'm unwilling to try for obvious reasons. I suspect someone else would have found the meteorite, and this situation would still be happening. However, I wouldn't *then* be able to travel in time to kill my grandfather, so that it couldn't happen."

Brad chuckled at the twisted logic and stood as well. "This is conundrum territory." He didn't know the exact moment it happened, but he believed.

If I'm insane, I'll have to sort it out later.

"Okay, let's see if we can discover anything new with the stone complete."

Brad frowned, not understanding. "Where to now?"

"Forward."

Clement placed his hand on Brad's shoulder, and the twisting pattern of time embraced them both.

Chapter 16

 Brad had thought moving forward through time would be like a long, looping water slide at a park, with events and images that steamed past at Mach speed. That wasn't the case. A white radiance traveled all around and even through him. He sometimes saw geometric shapes in the nether, or they resembled wisps of smoke. No two forms or images seemed to repeat. There was a vague sensation of movement, but he couldn't confirm it. *Maybe everything else is moving, and I'm staying still?* He had no basis for comparison. Moving forward through time felt like he was in a bright white room with an elevator. He knew he was moving but couldn't prove it.

Clement retained his grip on Brad's shoulder and tried to explain. "When I travel backward in time, everything switches to shades of gray imagery. I suspect it is related to photon wavelengths, but I'm unsure. It turns bright when we go forward, and a white light permeates everything."

Brad looked about. "How come we can talk while traveling?"

Clement shrugged. "I hadn't tried before since I was alone. I know all the energy and synapses happening in our brain, the firing between neurons is happening at a quantum level. We're moving through time and space. I'm sure it is all relative."

Unsure if it was supposed to be a joke, Brad remained silent.

Clement continued. "I know I was a farmer and grew up in a different time, but I've spent a lot of work catching up with technology and reading. The internet works, and I've learned what I can."

Brad's sense of moving through time had slowed, and the brilliant white light flickered all about them faster and faster. The pressure steadily increased on his mind the longer they attempted to advance. It was like swimming upstream, and suddenly, the current increased to such a degree that they could not progress further.

"This is beyond the point where I could go before." Clement dropped them out of the time stream. They stood on the lawn in front of buildings resembling warehouses mixed in with offices. There was a definite chill in the air, and the leaves on the trees had turned gold and red.

"This is the TRIUMF building in Vancouver, British Columbia. They have one of the world's top particle accelerators. We're approximately three days away from the end."

The building was four hundred feet long, and the dark brick appeared new. The front steps led up to a glass-paneled entrance that rose two stories. A few people walked past the windows on the second floor. It resembled a dozen campus buildings he had seen throughout the country.

Brad rubbed his eyes and winced. The headaches were about to start again, and he began to get twitchy. "What do you suggest to stop this from happening?"

Clement took a few steps away and turned to look at Brad. "I'm not too certain. But I *am* sure of one thing. Unless you get this under control, you won't even be able to help yourself."

Brad became defensive. "I'm fine. Don't worry about me."

"The world doesn't have time, but we certainly do."

Brad took a step back as Clement stepped forward. Not liking where this was going, Brad looked about, but there was no backup. "What are you talking about?"

"Do you want to help save the world?" Clement's eyes bored straight into Brad's. "Seriously, want to help?"

"Of course I do. Why?"

"You need to help yourself first. I'll ensure this doesn't become an issue or a future problem. There's too much at stake. Just about everything, in fact."

Before Brad could raise his hand or move, Clement grabbed his shoulder. Everything turned black as Brad lost consciousness and his knees buckled. He was out cold before Clement guided them through the quantum realm.

~

Once again, Brad woke in the cabin. He wasn't sure how much time had passed. Holman wasn't sure what time *was* anymore.

Brad groaned as he grew aware of the headache. It felt like he was in a bass drum that pounded with every heartbeat.

He quickly patted his pants pockets, only to find them empty.

One eye cracked to look at the chair beside the bed. Brad saw his wallet and the same tin cup filled with water. Nothing else.

"You have to be kidding me."

A panic set in as Brad swung his feet onto the floor. Everything was the same in the cabin except for the kitchen table. It was loaded with food, supplies, and a pile of clothing folded neatly on a chair.

The sun was about to set by the light coming in through the window. The last time he was here, it was the middle of September. Today the air contained a hint of frost, and he revised the date.

Late October? He wasn't sure, but there was a definite chill.

When he stood, his head spun, and he reached for the back of the chair to keep his balance. It took a few seconds to focus and realize he wouldn't fall. Brad studied the supplies at the kitchen table—everything from flour to fresh fruit, a loaf of bread, and various other items. The bottle of pills was absent.

On top of the bowl of potatoes was a note.

There is plenty of time for you to heal and fix your problem.

See you soon.

Clement

"Son of a bitch." He crumpled the note and threw it across the kitchen. "When I said I wanted help, I was thinking of a doctor."

Brad picked up the tin cup of water to bring with him as he stepped outside. It did little to soothe his headache, but it felt good. The sun had sunk below the treetops, disappearing in a few minutes. He could barely distinguish a group of large birds walking across the field's far edge.

Are those turkeys?

Brad's hand shook while bringing the cup to his lips, and some spilled down his chest. After decades of dealing with junkies and addicts, he knew he would be in for a rough time.

As his mind began to work on the problem, he grinned. If the cabin and this moment in time were a prison, Brad knew where the key was kept.

"If a farmer can use it, so can I."

Inside the kitchen, Brad opened the trap cellar door. He felt the cold, damp air, and an earthen smell filled his nose, but it was too dark below. The lantern sat on the kitchen counter, but Brad had no lighter or matches. The cupboards held plates and bowls, and he found another tin cup and two ceramic mugs. The two drawers had various utensils, cooking spoons, and a large hand-carved wooden ladle.

He didn't find anything to start a fire, but Brad found a gray stone on the mantle after checking the woodpile and then over at the fireplace. Remembering a television show about survival, he suspected what it was.

Next to the cabin, Brad grabbed the ax embedded into a stump and returned to the kitchen.

Even if this doesn't work and I can't get the stone to work, I still want a fire. The temperature had dropped when the sun went down, but he couldn't see his breath.

Once he moved the iron kettle, the ax made quick work of the dried wood, and Brad had a bed of shavings and kindling in the fireplace. He added paper strips from the crumpled-up note and gently laid it on top. When the ax head glanced off the stone, sparks leaped out.

Perfect. It's flint.

Brad struck the ax head sharply with the flint again at the right angle. A series of sparks danced over the paper and kindling, but nothing caught hold.

It took twenty minutes of hard work before a spark smoldered. Ignoring the pounding headache, Brad blew and gently coaxed a flame to life. Excited, he slowly fed small twigs, bark, and branches, then split wood once it had caught.

His hands shook, and sweat beaded across his forehead when he dropped the ax. It was pitch black outside, and the fireplace was the only light source. He carved a thin stick and held it in the flames until it caught. Moments later, the lantern was finally lit.

In the cellar, Brad brushed spiderwebs off his face as he made his way to the corner. Last time he was sure they didn't walk through any.

"Lucky me."

He wasn't surprised to find the table was empty.

Brad waved his hand through the air and trailed his fingers through the dust. Frustrated, Brad kicked the leg, and it slammed into the wall. Even though Clement mentioned he "bonded" with the meteor fragment, he couldn't call the stone forth.

He was trapped.

Chapter 17

Special Agent Brad Holman sat in the surveillance car outside Silver Falls State Park entrance in Oregon and patiently waited. He sipped his cold coffee and cracked the window for fresh air. While it wasn't his first stakeout, it was his first alone. Despite knowing he was right, doubts ran through his mind. If he guessed wrong, a life would be lost.

Earlier that same day, the FBI field office received a call from the Oregon State Police to assist with a kidnapping case. A seven-year-old girl was forced into a white Toyota Land Cruiser in a Portland suburb. A quick-thinking crossing guard wrote down a partial license plate before calling 911.

Thirty minutes later, all hands from the field office worked with the state police to surround the suspect's home. With an abduction or kidnapping, especially with children involved, no one was worried about jurisdiction, and the FBI would work with law enforcement on all levels.

A detailed search of the house and property turned up nothing. However, the FBI's full power was now tasked with finding everything they could on a fifty-four-year-old white male, Samuel Greene, and they tore his life apart to find clues.

While the field office started their work, Brad joined the forensic teams as they slowly walked through Samuel's house. Brad wore latex gloves and checked each book on the shelf in the living room. It didn't take too long before noticing a pattern of survival and outdoor living guides. He also noted several framed pictures of camping and hiking scenery on the walls throughout the house.

The single-car garage had abundant fishing gear, tackle boxes, and outdoor camping equipment along the rear wall. If anything from the collection was missing, Brad couldn't tell. While searching the garage, Holman called the forensic team over. Empty 9mm ammunition boxes and two empty twelve-gauge cartons lay in the bottom of a garbage can.

An immediate update went out to all law enforcement, stating that the subject may be armed. Brad found a box of MREs stashed on a back shelf in the garage. The rations resembled military issue, maybe from a surplus outlet.

I'm just missing the direction of travel. The puzzle pieces are all there.

Once he found the FBI special agent in charge and liaison officer to the state police, Brad filled her in on his findings before going to a state police patrol car that blocked the driveway.

Brad got behind the wheel with the state trooper's permission and searched the mobile data terminal (MDT). Soon he scrolled through the sparse record history of the 1994 Land Cruiser. The owner had three speeding tickets and a few parking fines. After scanning the speeding ticket information, Brad called the trooper over.

Tapping on the display screen, he asked, "Where is the 214 North?"

"I figure about thirty minutes east of Salem."

"How far is that from here?"

Closing his eyes, the young officer thought. "If you take the I-5 south, it would be under an hour. Give or take."

"Thanks. Can I find an internet search engine on your MDT?"

The state trooper leaned over, hit a few buttons, and granted the FBI agent access. The officer watched, curious as to where this was going.

Two hours later, Brad found himself alone outside the Silver Falls Park welcome gate in an unmarked Ford interceptor. Brad's reputation was already growing in certain FBI circles, and the SAC authorized Brad to go but to remain in contact.

The state park had over nine thousand acres and more than twenty-four miles of walking trails. If someone with survival wilderness training skills could get inside, they could avoid detection and hide for months.

An hour after the sun had set, headlights approached the gate. Brad sat up straight, and the fatigue vanished as he opened the keeper on his holster. It took a moment to confirm, and Brad picked up the phone. "This is Special Agent Holman. I have the suspect's vehicle at my location. Requesting support and aerial surveillance."

"Support en route."

After he disconnected, Brad switched off the vehicle's lighting system, started the Ford, and followed at a distance. It didn't take long to discover they were headed toward the RV camping area. Various signs pointed the way along the winding roads.

While trailing the vehicle, Brad's phone chimed as he received a text message. A lady who had reported her daughter missing, Elizabeth Anne Gibson, age seven, confirmed she never came home from school. The next text came through: a picture of a little girl in a white dress and dark hair in a ponytail posing for her school picture.

"Hold on, Elizabeth. Everything will be okay."

The white Toyota pulled into the RV campground and drove into the overflow area before finding a distant and vacant spot. A few campers were set up at the north end of the campground, but the Toyota was the only one parked in the overflow area.

Not wanting to alert the suspect, Brad used the last RV camper as cover and turned off the engine. The lights were off inside the trailer. They must have gone to bed early. Once out of the car, Brad pulled on his blue windbreaker. FBI was written in large white letters on the back, and he softly closed the car door behind him.

He pulled the slide half-inch on the Glock 22 to confirm a round in the chamber. Ready, Brad carefully walked along the tree line toward the Toyota. There was enough moonlight to navigate, and the lack of clouds helped. Brad didn't need his flashlight to show that the Land Cruiser was empty. The vehicle pointed to a break in the trees and a wide path. The sign designated it as one of the many horse trails within the state park.

Brad had to slow the pace as soon as he entered the pathway. The trees made it extremely difficult to navigate along the trail, and it took a while to acquire his night vision.

The route was covered with wood chips, making his progress reasonably silent. Brad tried not to jump at the noises with his pistol aimed low along his right leg. At one point, he heard scratching, but it was high in a tree. He hoped it was just a raccoon.

The light evening breeze made the leaves rustle, and it helped mask any noise. After fifteen minutes, a light flickered off the path, fifty yards past a massive poplar tree. It was just a glimmer, but it moved within a small area.

Basic training from Quantico had the recruits complete a forty-eight-hour survival and wilderness first-aid course. However, Brad had always felt more comfortable within an urban environment. There was something disturbing about being in the woods that he couldn't put his finger on.

Thoughts of discomfort were thrust aside as he focused and moved with a heel-toe movement. He checked each step for branches or twigs not to give away his position. Brad breathed through his mouth, slow and steady, to calm his nerves and control his racing heartbeat.

Brad peeked around a wide trunk fifty feet away to get a view. The man had lashed ropes to various branches across a small clearing and set a ridgeline. He had erected a shelter with a dark-colored tarp, which resembled a lean-to more than a tent. Brad searched for any sign of Elizabeth but only noticed a few large bundles under the tarp.

I'm not sure if that's the little girl or camping equipment.

Without an option, Brad moved closer until he confirmed that the man was Samuel Greene. Despite the beard, he resembled his driver's license picture. Slowly, he brought his pistol into a ready position.

With two slow, steady breaths, Brad was about to run into the clearing when his cell phone chimed with an incoming text message.

Immediately Samuel dropped into a prone position as he turned off his lantern. The after-glow danced before his eyes, destroying any night vision.

Seriously? Fuck!

He darted behind the large tree, and Brad tried to remain perfectly still while his heart threatened to burst from his chest. After a full minute of silence, Brad slowly shifted to get a visual of the target.

The first round took Brad through the right shoulder and spun him around and back. A second round quickly followed, but it struck the tree next to his head. Had the first bullet missed, the second wouldn't have. As he fell, he was showered with bark and wood pulp. The shots echoed throughout the forest and made his ears ring.

Brad remained on his back despite the burning agony in his shoulder, lying perfectly still. Blood blossomed across his shirt and jacket, pooling under his shoulder.

Samuel chuckled after a minute of silence and got to his feet. "Rookie."

The wanted man turned on his battery-powered lantern and walked over. Samuel kicked Brad's feet and slung his rifle. "Time to get a shovel."

Samuel shook his head and chuckled once again before turning back to camp. Brad's Glock 22 rose in his left hand, and the tremble didn't affect his aim. Two rounds slammed into Samuel's side, and a third went into his head.

After being shot, Brad's pistol was flung backward into the dirt. By luck, he landed with his left hand on the grip. Otherwise, he wouldn't have had a chance.

The small arms fire sounded completely different from the long rifle and would hopefully draw more attention. Campers may come to investigate, but there were no guarantees. The sound of a body landing in the mulch didn't carry far, but it still brought a grimaced smile to Brad's face. *Fuck you, Sam.*

A wave of agony coursed through his body, and it came close to rendering him unconscious when he sat. However, he still had a job to do. Screaming in pain, he staggered to his feet and tucked his right arm inside the jacket to hold it secure. Below the tarp were bundles of gear, and Elizabeth lay tied and gagged under a blanket. She was alive but unconscious.

Brad found a large survival knife, and the sharp blade made quick work of the bindings, freeing the young girl. A red bandana was used as a gag, and he pulled it over her head and tossed it to the side. Elizabeth didn't stir.

"Almost over. Hold on." Brad placed two fingers on her neck and waited. "Good, you're going to be fine."

Her pulse was strong, and she was breathing. More than her captor could say. She didn't appear to have any wounds—just knocked out. Relieved, Brad collapsed with his back against a tree. He fumbled with his left hand to get his cell phone out and eventually made the call. Medical help would arrive soon.

Brad updated his supervisor about the girl and his condition, but the pain and blood loss took their toll. The cell phone fell to the ground, and he lost consciousness.

~

Eighteen hours later, Brad woke in the recovery room at the hospital. Despite the blood loss, the surgery had gone well, and a full recovery was expected. The bullet had entered just below his collarbone and had gone straight through.

As he recovered, several visitors congratulated him on finding the child, even the girl's mother.

Soon as he was released from the hospital, Special Agent Bradley Holman was honored in a ceremony by the Deputy Director and awarded the FBI Medal for Meritorious Achievement. It was bestowed to agents who risked their safety and were wounded in a suspect's apprehension and saved a life while on duty. The fact that the suspect died in the encounter didn't bother many people.

While he recovered, Brad was on desk duty until the surgeon cleared him to return to work. Not looking forward to the three-month recovery, Brad threw himself into physiotherapy. He quickly recovered with oxycodone and other pain medication and was cleared to be active from desk duty within twelve weeks.

Unfortunately, oxycodone is one of the more addictive painkillers available, and Brad found he could not operate without it. Obtaining the painkiller was ridiculously easy, and over the next twelve months, he learned he couldn't function without it.

Elizabeth was saved because of his efforts, and his application to become a supervisor was quickly approved. He was posted to the Phoenix, Arizona, field office with his qualifications and track record.

However, Brad had a problem, but he figured he had it under control and could stop at any time. He resigned himself to minimal drug use to feel normal and avoid withdrawal.

Unfortunately, it slowly took over his life, and he could no longer function without the drugs. He had thought he could quit anytime, but it was too hard. Brad had expected to pay the piper but didn't realize it would be this soon.

Chapter 18

After closing the cellar door, Brad sat on the bed and stared at his hands, defeated. The fire took the chill out of the air and warmed the cabin. He knew what to expect over the next few weeks or so. He had dealt with addicts over the years, and when they went through detox, they went through hell. He would find out firsthand.

If the pounding in his head was any indication, he had already started the descent. He couldn't remember how long ago it was since he had popped any pills, but it had to have been close to eighteen hours. His hands shook, and he had trouble focusing. After finishing the cup of water, Brad fell back on the bed and closed his eyes.

"I hope this is over quickly."

Two hours later, cold sweat and a churning stomach woke him. Brad barely made it outside before vomiting on the grass. He stood hunched over, with hands on his knees, but another round of retching almost caused him to collapse.

Brad made it back inside and threw a few logs on the fire. He quickly searched the kitchen again, hoping to find the pills, but they were not there. Moments later, he passed out on the bed.

Over the next three days, things grew steadily worse as the symptoms and fatigue set in. Every waking moment was a form of torture. Any food was almost immediately thrown up, and he could only keep down a little water.

Brad stumbled into the kitchen like death warmed over on the morning of the fourth day. An empty tin cup clutched to his chest, and he reached for the water pitcher only to find it was empty. He ran out of firewood two days ago and was now out of water.

Despair overwhelmed his sense of being, and any semblance of strength flowed like a burst balloon. Brad crumpled to the kitchen floor, wishing he had never gone down this path. Tears rolled down his cheeks and through the stubble before trickling off his chin. His head rested on the seat of a chair, and he waited for death. Every part of his body ached and was weak. Brad hadn't eaten properly for days. The thought of food made his stomach churn as he grew weaker.

Hours passed to summon enough courage and strength, but eventually, Brad stood with the empty water pitcher and shuffled outside.

The sun was overhead, and it had snowed during the night. A light dusting covered everything, turning the fields and trees into a winter landscape. He squinted against the bright onslaught as he shuffled off the porch rubbing a week-old beard.

Brad's mental image of a well, with a circular wall of bricks, a peaked roof, and a rope on a hand crank, was shattered. Before him lay a pile of flat fieldstones formed into a stepped pyramid. Boards covered the opening, and a wooden bucket rested on the ground with a coil of rope tied to the handle. The other end was connected to a flat rock the size of a loaf of bread. The cord was wrapped around the stone several times and tied with a simple but effective knot.

Brad lowered the bucket once the boards were removed, but it bounced off the bottom after fifteen feet. A dull *thud* echoed off the stone walls. After peering over the edge, his frustration grew when the bucket sat atop a layer of ice.

"Seriously?"

He raised the bucket a few inches and dropped it to break the ice. Nothing happened, except he wondered if the container would be destroyed first. Using his Glock or explosives seemed a viable alternative.

Brad yelled, "Why couldn't you have left me here in August?"

Angry at Clement for putting him in this situation, Brad looked around for a way to break the ice. It was too deep for him to use a branch. His eyes rested on the other end of the rope, tied off to the rock. Quickly he brought up the bucket and then picked up the stone. It weighed almost six pounds, and it should work. Hand over hand, he lowered it to a foot above the ice and let go of the rope.

"There we go."

Brad grinned when the rock smashed through the ice and into the water. A warm glow blossomed through his chest, and momentarily put a bounce in his step. He brought it up and down a few more times. Switching ends of the rope, Brad lowered the bucket and hauled the freshwater with pieces of ice shards. Not waiting for the tin cup, he tilted the pail and drank deeply. Water spilled across his chest, but Brad didn't mind. It was cold enough to set his teeth on edge, and like a sponge, he absorbed as much as he could.

Exhausted, Brad filled the pitcher and returned indoors. Soon as his head hit the pillow, he was out. Two hours later, Brad still had a sense of accomplishment when he looked at the cold, empty fireplace. Grabbing the ax, Brad went outside and stared at the woodpile. He hadn't used an ax previously but knew staring at it wouldn't get it done. How hard could it be?

The first blow hit the log's edge, and the blade narrowly missed his foot. The next swing was more controlled, but the ax head bounced.

"This is going to take a while."

After thirty minutes, he gathered what small amount he had split and carried it inside. Brad's shoulders burned, and the soft skin on his palms was torn and blistering. Despite the exhaustion, lighting the fire came easier with practice, and a spark caught on a piece of birch bark with little effort. A lighter or matches would have been simpler, but wishes didn't get the job done.

The persistent headache ramped up again with his efforts, but it wasn't as bad as the first night. After a few mouthfuls of stale bread, Brad washed it with fresh water and barely returned to the bed before passing out.

Day by day, Brad grew stronger, and the simple chores of gathering water and keeping the fire going became his world. It took five days before he had an interest in food. It was minimal, but it was there.

Brad wasn't much of a cook but had learned a few things over the years. After dicing the carrots and potatoes, he threw them into the iron cauldron. The onions had begun to sprout, but he wasn't that fussy. In they went. The mushrooms had turned to mush, and Brad threw them away. After poking around in the cupboard, he found ceramic jars of salt and pepper; simple, but they would work.

Cooking over a fire was a new experience, like everything else, and Brad watched the pot like a mother hen, stirring and adding wood several times an hour.

As the soup was simmering, Brad caught a whiff of himself and knew what was next. There was no hope of saving this clothing, and the best bet was to burn them outside. With a sigh, he turned to the pile of clothing Clement had left on the chair, and he grabbed the bar of soap. He knew how cold the water would be, but it was necessary.

Brad's screams carried a mile into the woods, startling the wildlife. He was wrong. The water was on the verge of freezing and cold enough to make his teeth chatter. But he was clean.

~

It took Brad eight days to be somewhat functional. He tired easily, and tremors wracked his body, but they grew less frequent with time. The following weeks showed Brad how far he had fallen as he improved and became his old self.

After four weeks of living in the cabin, two things surprised him. One, he actually enjoyed splitting wood. The physical activity took his mind off the situation and placed some muscle back in his body. Although he didn't want to leave the immediate area, he walked the perimeter of the fields twice daily. The exercise kept him warm and helped him relax.

The second revelation was that he craved meat. The only source he could find were the turkeys that scratched at the ground in the far field every morning. While the supply of oats, potatoes, onions, and carrots filled him, he *needed* protein. The birds never got closer to the cabin than two-hundred yards. There must have been squirrels and other creatures in the woods, but Brad only found tracks in the fresh snow.

When he was a boy, his uncle had taken him hunting for rabbits with a .22 rifle. They had walked through the woods for almost a full day and didn't see one rabbit. Brad remembered a picnic lunch by a stream and his uncle suggesting they would have better luck fishing. Once a year, they went for a hike in the woods carrying rifles but never shot anything. When he was twelve years old, his uncle passed away. Brad had always treasured those moments and the time they spent together.

Wish I had that old .22 right now. Even my Glock would work.

Brad figured it was late November, with the snow almost a foot deep. It could have been December. There wasn't any way to confirm the date. Brad's beard was nearly half an inch for the first time since college.

The barn's roof collected the most snow, hanging over the edge like a crested wave frozen in time. The tree branches and twigs piled high with the white powder turned the landscape into a winter wonderland. While there were sunny days, it never melted, and the ground had frozen solid. The rock trick for the well stopped working when the ice grew inches thick. Brad had a moment of panic before realizing there was an easier method. He scooped fresh snow in the bucket and left it by the fire to melt. It was much easier than having to draw water from the well.

Despite many searches in the cabin, Brad couldn't find any weapons for hunting. He had long since explored the loft and the small sleeping pallets. It was empty. He set his mind on a bow and arrow or even a crossbow. Not knowing how to use them didn't seem to matter. He had the time to practice.

One place he hadn't explored was the barn. It was larger than the cabin, with a peaked roof and a covered side garage. A broad set of double doors took up most of the front, with another door near the roof's peak. Farming equipment and tools were stored under the overhang. An old wheelbarrow, shovels, and rakes leaned against the wall. Long chains and a leather harness were hung next to a two-man rip saw. Everything rested on iron square-head nails driven into the boards. Brad lifted a long-handled rake off the wall and gave it a few swings. He doubted he could get close enough to a turkey to use it.

An old cartoon he had watched as a kid made him think of the wheelbarrow. *If I turn it upside down and use the rope to pull out a stick, maybe I could trap a bird.* Brad gave up on that idea. He didn't know what to use as bait, but the thought made him chuckle.

As he walked through the deep drifts toward the barn, a breeze swirled the powdered snow into ridges. Flakes melted on his cheeks and stuck in his beard. The wind had sculpted the flat landscape into a series of frozen waves. He had no choice but to avoid the deeper drifts past his waist.

Opening the double doors was challenging with the piled snow, and he had to stomp and kick enough away to slip through.

Two horse stalls were to his right, and a larger pen was built on the opposite wall. A chicken coup rested inside the enclosure. The rest of the barn was empty except for several hay bales stacked along the rear wall. A wooden ladder attached to the central support post led to the loft, where more bales were stacked near the edge.

"It isn't much, but it was all mine."

Startled, Brad turned around to see Clement leaning against the door. "I'm unsure if I should thank or punch you."

"I need you to be fully functional." Clement looked him up and down. "You look better in my old clothes."

Neither mentioned the weight loss or the hollowed look on his cheeks. However, the bounce in his step wasn't faked, and Brad knew he was on the road to recovery.

Sighing in resignation, Brad asked, "Are you just checking in on me, or are we returning to work?"

"I'm not too sure. I wanted to talk to you first to see how you are doing."

Brad understood and shrugged. "It was rough for a while. Very rough. But I'm on the road to feeling normal again."

Clement stared at him for a moment, then nodded. "Okay, let's get started."

"Just like that?"

"If you need more time, then let me know. Be honest with yourself. But if you are ready, yes, just like that."

"Hold on." Brad raised his hand in the air. "I have a pot of soup that will be ready soon. I was also looking for a way to catch a turkey to cook."

Laughing, Clement asked, "How about we return to your apartment, and you can shave and shower? We can hit a steakhouse for dinner. If you are up for it?"

Brad's mouth watered at the thought of eating meat. "Yeah, forget the soup. I'm ready."

Instead of reaching for his shoulder, Clement smiled and extended his hand. With a firm grip, they shook.

"Thank you." Brad's smile was genuine. The recovery process wasn't a method he would have recommended to anyone, but the farmer had a different style. Most importantly, it worked.

The two men were enveloped in the timestream as the snow gusted into the empty barn and quickly filled their footprints.

Chapter 19

"The first problem I ran into was myself," Clement explained as he pushed the empty dinner plate away from him. "When I found the meteor, I went back to the barn to get the shovel. Then I saw myself walking away from the stone when I returned."

Both men arrived at Brad's apartment in Phoenix, and he cleaned up and changed in record time. A hot shower was one of the most wonderful feelings he could ever remember. However, the thought of a good meal came in second. The warmer Arizona weather felt wonderful and warmed his bones after the winter chill. Dressed in a dark suit and tie, Brad was ready. Clement fit in one of his dress shirts, if a little tight across the shoulders, but he passed on the tie.

Brad finished the last bite of his steak and leaned back in the chair. His eyes closed to savor the moment. It was probably one of the best meals he could recall, and he was too full. The steak house was in downtown Washington DC, and despite the dinner hour, it was relatively empty. The dim lighting and quiet atmosphere were perfect for conversation.

"I started digging the stone out of the ground, but it was too deep, and I couldn't get it out. Then my alternate self arrived, and we worked together. That was when the accident happened."

Brad fished out his wallet and dropped enough cash on the table to cover the bill. Even if they could easily skip out on the payment, he didn't want to be *that* guy.

"I was down in the hole, and the other me was prying it loose with the shovel when the blade slipped off the stone and caught me across my forearm."

Clement rolled his right sleeve back to reveal a sixteen-inch scar on the inside of his arm. Clement continued. "Once my blood went across the stone, everything changed. My second self disappeared, and time stopped. I didn't know I created a time bubble like you were just in. Time seems to carry on normally within a small radius, about half a mile circle, but outside, no time passed in the real world."

"So, I was there for over a month, but no time passed in the real world?" Brad was having trouble wrapping his mind around the situation. "Isn't the FBI wondering where I am and why I haven't reported in?"

"No. Right now, we are a week before you cut yourself at work. I try to avoid overlapping when possible. It makes things less complicated."

"You mentioned various timelines. How does that work?"

Clement grabbed the salt shaker and upended it, making a small pile on the table.

"If I made a river, with all the creeks and streams flowing into it, it would look like this." Clement turned the salt into a thin line, with random branches running to the sides.

"Each creek or stream is an alternate timeline, with the river being the main branch. If I go and explore an alternate timeline, there is the possibility that I can change it so that it becomes the *new* main timeline. Changing key events at the junction point causes the main flow down the alternate path."

Clement redirected the salt, so the main path had altered, and it was now the main river.

"If that timeline isn't viable or doesn't flow in the direction I want, I can go back and change it. However, all timelines and variations show that the black hole is created, and everything we know ends soon. All attempts to alter the path result in the same outcome."

Clement swept the salt off the table onto his empty plate. "That's why you are here. I need help, and we are running out of time. Are you ready to start?"

"Ready as I can be."

Once outside, they headed into the rear parking lot of the restaurant. Clement wanted to make sure that they were out of sight. Clement brought Brad into a time-stream, and they left Washington behind. Everything turned black and white, and the familiar swirling energy streams flew by and even through them. No matter how many times it happened, Brad would never get bored watching the kaleidoscope display.

Eventually, they stood on the sidewalk outside Graziella Fine Jewelers. Brad wasn't sure what city he was in, but it was still warm, and the sun had just risen. The window display showed various rings and necklaces on white discount signs. Inside, they were greeted by a middle-aged man behind the counter. He wore a pin-striped suit and tie, and a short, neat beard, which contrasted against his lack of hair.

"Jack! Nice to see you again."

"You as well, Mr. Wallace. How is the ring? All good, I hope?"

Shaking his hand, Clement turned to introduce Brad, then he added, "No problems. I need to order another ring with the same specifications as mine. Here's the money upfront, and the other envelope contains the stone."

Clement pulled two envelopes from his pocket and handed them over. Jack picked up a ring gauge from behind the counter and asked Brad, "Which finger would you like?"

Unsure of what was happening, Brad chose the ring finger on his right hand. Jack quickly had him correctly sized. "Thank you, it will be ready in two weeks, I still have the mold from the first one, so it will not take as long. Is that okay?"

"That will be just fine. Thank you."

The two men stepped outside and walked around the corner before Clement grabbed Brad by the shoulder. Everything turned a brilliant white for a few moments before letting go. They stood in the same spot outside the jewelry store. However, the sky was overcast, and it looked like rain was coming.

"There are some advantages to time travel." Clement grinned.

"Just a little easier this way." Brad agreed.

Once inside, they were greeted by Jack. "Perfect timing! We just finished polishing it up. I'll get the ring. Try it on, please."

Jack returned and held the band out to Brad. It was a wide-banded gold ring without any embellishment. Inset was a small piece of the meteorite.

The inside of the ring concerned Brad the most. The stone chip protruded inside the band, and the edge that stuck out was quite sharp.

"I'm sure it will be perfect. No need to try it on right now. Thank you very much, Jack." Clement held up a hand, forestalling Brad before he tried it on.

"Thank you, sir."

Jack shook their hands and wished them a good day.

On the way out of the store, Clement turned to Brad. "Just put it in your pocket. Don't put it on yet."

Once outside and out of view, it took them only a few moments to travel back to Clement's cabin. "Follow me."

Clement led the way into the cellar. Instead of lighting the lantern, he pulled an LED flashlight out of his pocket.

"Wish you had left me one of those," Brad muttered as they returned to the table.

"What you're about to go through took me a hundred years to figure out. Don't panic. I'll be right here with you. Okay?"

Brad swallowed. "Got it."

"Take out the ring and put it on."

Brad slid the ring to the first knuckle, then stopped. "You know a sharp piece of stone is sticking out on the inside?"

Clement smiled. "I know. Mine's the same way."

Brad tried to slide it the rest of the way, but the point dug into the back of his finger.

"Need some help?"

"Sure. Does it hurt?"

Clement shook his head and grabbed hold of the finger. "Okay, on three. One, two …"

Without waiting for "three," Clement jammed the ring deep into Brad's finger. "Jesus Christ!" Brad jerked his hand back as the stone cut into the knuckle and flesh of his finger. Blood dripped onto the dirt floor, but he didn't notice.

A door opened in Brad's mind, and it was like a blind person seeing or a deaf person hearing for the first time. He was instantly aware of having an extra sense—an ability to see time. Brad reached out with one hand to feel the quantum realm at his fingertips. He could not just sense time in a linear direction, ticking along at its standard rate, but also manipulate it. Each layer of energy was a path, a possibility—the fourth dimension. Time.

It's the power of the gods.

Everyone has an innate sense and can reasonably and accurately judge how much time has passed. Brad's perception of the quantum state grew, and he could now see an ability to move forward or back in time and temporarily suspend it. Bend it to his will.

"What I can see and do, are you the same way?" Brad looked around, but not at the cellar. His mind saw various time possibilities. He just wanted to reach out and tweak it.

"Hold on, don't do anything yet." Clement forestalled Brad from doing anything. "Yes, I can see what you are experiencing as well. Watch what I'm doing. Then it's your turn."

Clement knelt in front of the table and concentrated. With a gust of air, the meteorite appeared. Brad had finally seen how Clement reached out to call the stone to their location. It was hidden in the space that exists between all things. The stone was close to everything at once but out of reach simultaneously.

"I'm not sure exactly where it was, but I guess it was in a different universe or dimension. I can call the stone to us from anywhere." After he stood, Clement asked, "Can you send it back to where it just was?"

"I'll try."

Brad was unsure, but he had an idea and trusted his instincts. Brad placed both hands on the stone, and energy flickered through his body, like holding onto a low-voltage wire. The sensation funneled through the ring as a contact point, making the hair on the back of his arms and neck stand on end. There wasn't any pain, but the current filled him like a charging battery.

Brad used his new abilities and tentatively parted the curtain of time around the stone. He then wrapped that same curtain around it. When he relaxed the hold on the energy, the opening snapped closed. The rock was hidden in nothingness. It was everywhere and nowhere at the same time. Even with his eyes closed, Brad could still feel the connection. This moment also convinced Brad, beyond any doubt, that time travel was real. What he could now see and feel could not be faked.

Clement patted him on the shoulder. "You did great! Once in a while, you have to contact the meteorite physically to recharge. Your abilities are not infinite but decline with use. Otherwise, you draw energy from yourself when traveling through time. It can be exhausting, and there's a price to pay."

"Oh." Brad stood and dusted the dirt off his pants. "That part doesn't sound good."

Clement shrugged. "It isn't too bad. We start to age. The effects are reversed once we have contact again. The good news is, far as I know, we'll never get old."

Immortal?

When Brad thought there were no more surprises, he was hit with this. "We have to deal with the black hole first."

Clement nodded. "That's the catch. Ideas?"

Brad grinned as he began to dissect the problem. "We need some intel, and since we can't hire out, it's up to us."

Chapter 20

Brad has worked as a custodian for the past two months at the University of British Columbia. He emptied garbage cans throughout his shift, cleaned the floors, and picked up after the staff and students. His efforts to remain undercover had been frustrating, but they needed to gather information on Dr. Virginia Kincaid. Brad also ensured there were no attempts at sabotage on the particle accelerator.

After lengthy conversations with Clement, Brad didn't have enough information to start the investigation. So, he relied on what the FBI had taught and ingrained in him. The first step and reasoning for reconnaissance were to gather more information on the operation.

People could die if they went into a situation without knowing the dangers. Right now, they had almost nothing. The next step was to find a baseline "normal" pattern, determine what is different or changing, and then place their efforts there.

Creating a job opening for the university was a simple matter of time-hopping. They dropped a lottery ticket in the wallet of the former janitor with the winning numbers. The sixty-year-old man pushed a mop and emptied garbage for over thirty years at the campus, and he was glad to retire early. Brad made it clear that he didn't want to be part of killing anyone in an attempt to alter a timeline. That was a dark path, which he didn't want to tread. There had to be other solutions, and they would find them.

Brad still considered himself an FBI agent and would follow the rules, at least the moral laws, as long as he could. If something happened that might change those rules, he would handle it case-by-case. However, everything he learned at Quantico didn't cover time travel or the universe being consumed by a black hole.

The other applicants for the custodial staff position had bad luck, from a flat tire to a follow-up phone call that stated the job was already filled—*thank you for applying*.

"I can travel through time, and the first thing I get to do is mop floors for a living." Brad chuckled.

He couldn't help but talk to himself while he worked. The halls were empty, and he had to laugh at the situation. Brad swirled the mop in the bucket before placing it in the squeeze press. When he pulled back on the handle, the excess dirty water streamed into the large yellow bucket. The days of wearing a suit to work were gone. Instead, he was dressed in light gray overalls and steel-toed boots.

When Brad glanced down the hall, his hand twitched toward a holstered pistol that wasn't there.

Someone just walked across my clean floor!

Shaking his head at the absurdity, Brad retraced his steps and cleaned the footprints to the lounge. Once finished, he stored the mop and bucket in the maintenance room before heading to the Center for Comparative Medicine across the street.

The university didn't have many support staff, and he had to clean and maintain the two buildings. He did get full access to the TRIUMF building that housed the particle accelerator, but the downside was the other building he had to clean. Brad had a new appreciation for the cleaning staff at his field office in Phoenix.

The weather in British Columbia was pleasant, and the warm breeze hinted at rain, but for now, stars blanketed the night sky.

Clement appeared beside him as he crossed the empty road. "How are you doing?"

"Nothing is happening. I haven't noticed anything irregular. Everything is boring, in fact."

"Do you think we give up and try something else?"

Brad paused with one foot on the sidewalk, hands in his pockets. He felt like quitting the janitor cover, but it was essential to get information. "The event is still a full seven days away. We may as well see how close we can get before the black hole starts."

Clement held out a hand. "I'm worried about that. If we get too close to the actual singularity, odds are we won't be able to escape it. The quantum field would pull us in, and we die along with everyone else."

Brad's mind kicked into overdrive, and he discarded ideas as soon he entertained them.

"How close to the event do you think we can be and get out safely?" Brad had an idea but wasn't sure how to implement it. "What if we're far from the university itself?"

"The quantum realm would be warped and unstable close to the black hole. If we were far enough away, we *should* avoid its effects. The timing would have to be perfect. I think so, anyway."

"Okay. I need to return to my apartment, get a suit and clean up, and return to work with the FBI. As much fun as this is, it isn't going anywhere."

~

Brad straightened his tie as he walked down the corridor and knocked on the office door before entering.

"Stephanie, I need some help from the NSA. At least, I think they would be the agency to ask. I'm fairly sure the FBI doesn't have what I am looking for."

Stephanie's mouth dropped. "I didn't know you were back from Boston so soon. Did you fly?"

Brad mentally kicked himself. He had forgotten that she had arranged his flights. "Yes, sorry I didn't let you know. It was unexpected. I need small and self-contained surveillance equipment with broadcasting capabilities to a remote location for recording. At least eight units to one receiver. Is that possible?"

Without breaking eye contact, Stephanie scribbled on a notepad. With a stern look, she turned to the computer monitor. Brad could almost feel the chill in the air from ten feet. He must be more careful and allow Stephanie to do her job. After a series of clicks on the keyboard, she looked up. "I suspect it can be done. NSA can do it. How soon do you need it?"

"An hour ago, if possible."

"Come back in twenty minutes. I will shake the tree and see what falls."

Brad was already dismissed from her mind when she turned her back to the door. Stephanie typed away with one hand and reached for the phone with another. Brad hoped she would get over it soon.

Brad realized he had forgotten his gun and jacket at a desk in Boston. For him, months had passed subjectively, but it was only a few minutes in this timeline.

With little effort, he concentrated on the time currents which surrounded him. Brad phased into what he called a slipstream of quantum energy or just the quantum realm. He used it to move from Washington to Boston in zero time—an instant. Clement explained how time and space were related and the same thing. When he moved in time from one spot to six months in the future, he not only shifted through time but space as well. Earth was not in the same position in its rotation with a six-month duration difference. Spatially, the radius of the earth is ninety-three million miles to travel around the sun once per orbit.

So, when they time-hopped six months into the future, they did so while landing on a planet 584 million miles away, in location, from where they left. Not only was the planet orbiting the sun, but the galaxy was moving as well. Such implications boggled the mind, and Brad wasn't sure who exactly could comprehend the math and science behind the ability the stone granted.

He arrived in the hallway outside the offices in the Boston field office. Brad timed it so he wouldn't run into himself and Clement. His past-self wouldn't understand yet what was going on, and the last thing he wanted was for someone else to run into *both* 'Brads' simultaneously.

The suit jacket was still draped over the chair, and he found the drawer key in the pocket. He slid the holster clip on his belt, and the weight was reassuring. The letter opener was still on the floor, and he placed it on the desk. There wasn't any blood on it, and he couldn't help but wonder how that simple instrument had changed his life.

Everything was different since he was last here, and Brad questioned why he remained with the FBI. The only answer he could come up with was duty. The oath he swore when he became a federal agent still applied, which meant something to him. The stakes were higher now, trying to save everyone on the planet and not just US residents.

In subjective time Brad hadn't been gone long. The screensaver had not even timed out. The unfinished email with his updates and reports was on the screen, waiting to be sent. With a glance at the emails to refresh his memory, Brad sent them before logging off. He was back in the Hoover building as Stephanie walked into the conference room, which he took over as his office.

"Mr. Holman, the NSA expects you at Fort Meade in Maryland. I'll have a car and driver ready for you downstairs in one minute."

"Thank you. I'm on my way. No need for a driver. I'll be fine."

Her brow furrowed, and her lips thinned. Brad couldn't say for sure whether in disapproval or concern, but he had a good guess. Stephanie abruptly turned without waiting for a reply and closed her office door. If the hinges allowed it, Brad was sure it would have slammed in her wake.

He tried to forget about a quirky assistant. Too much depended on the next attempt. He would make it up to her later if there *were* an afterward.

Once in the Chevy, Brad headed east on US-50, and in just under an hour, he arrived at the NSA building in Maryland. The traffic was heavy by eight o'clock in the morning, but he made excellent time.

A particular prejudice rose in Brad when he looked at the NSA building. It was nine stories tall and shiny with darkened windows, making it look like a fortress. The structure was sleek and modern—Brad knew where the budget went first—but he saw what looked like the most massive parking lot in the world surrounding the building. The Hoover building in Washington was an ancient relic, in sorry need of repairs and updating, compared to the NSA headquarters.

Unsure of where to park, Brad drove toward the front doors, looking for a sign pointing him in the right direction. At the front crosswalk stood a middle-aged man with a short beard and sunglasses. The man wore a green hoodie, jeans, and a dark blue backpack over one shoulder. He caught Brad's eye, and with a wave, he pointed for him to pull over. Despite the man's age, an image of a full-time online gamer leaped to mind.

The man opened the passenger door, placed his backpack on the floor, and climbed in. "Just drive around to the far parking area."

Brad thought this was a little too cloak and dagger, but he needed their help and couldn't complain. Out loud, anyway. He was unsure of how they operated, so this could be normal.

It took a few minutes to get to the far lot under the direction of his new passenger. He had never seen a parking area this size at any mall or airport. Brad studied the NSA agent out of the corner of his eye and followed his directions.

"Just pull into this spot."

The space was at the far edge of the lot, over a quarter-mile from the building. After backing in, the agent opened the backpack and showed Brad a sleek black case about the size of a box of tissues. His thumbs flicked open the two stainless-steel latches revealing eight small black boxes inside and a larger red and blue box.

One of the small black boxes easily slid out of the bracket, and he pointed to the side. "Pull this tab to activate it, peel this back to place it. It's a sealed unit that will run and transmit for five days. Do *not* try to open it. The acid failsafe will be released, destroying everything inside. They are one-time use only."

Once he replaced it, the larger red box filled his palm, and it looked more substantial. "This is the relay. It must be within five hundred feet of the cameras to transmit to the receiver. All images and videos will be relayed to the home unit for storage. The receiver can be anywhere."

As he scanned the equipment, Brad asked, "How far is *anywhere*? Range?"

"Anywhere in the world. The home unit can be in Australia if the cameras and relay are set up properly. It will work just as well as from five feet or thousands of miles away. Everything is paired with the relay and receiver."

The receiver slid back inside, and the lid closed with a snap. The NSA agent left the case on the front seat once he stood beside the Chevy with his backpack.

"Okay, thanks. One last question. Why are we in the back parking lot?"

He raised his eyebrows and shook his head. "My car is back here, and it's a ten-minute walk. When you are done with the equipment, destroy it. Even you G-men can't fuck that up."

After slamming the door, the man headed toward a blue Honda Accord in the back row.

What an asshole.

Brad drummed his fingers on the equipment case on the drive back to Washington. Too bad he couldn't relocate the car with him.

I hope this works because we need the information.

Brad was ready to start his plan and hopefully get some answers. One thought nagged him. *If the other side of the world isn't far enough, there isn't any hope.*

Chapter 21

"Do you think this will be safe? Can we get away in time?" Brad paced back and forth. He was worried about the possibilities, and he wasn't the only one.

Brad and Clement met in a small apartment they had rented for a year in Vancouver, just a few minutes from the university. It served its purpose as a base of operations, but Brad still couldn't get over the price of a two-bedroom apartment in that city. It may be the most expensive place in the world to rent, and he couldn't fathom buying a home in this area on his former salary. The building mainly catered to students, but each unit had the essentials, and most importantly, it was already furnished.

Brad sat at the kitchen table and held the equipment from NSA. "We would be gone and back to a safe location. Once the event happens, we grab the receiver unit and go. Should be near-instantaneous."

"If we do this, I suggest we get about as far away as possible from the university, like on the other side of the world."

Brad offered, "South Africa?"

"Hold on, I'll check."

Clement's image blurred and flickered back into focus within a split second. The difference was Brad could see him slip into a timestream and reappear at the same moment he returned.

"Madagascar, the east coast is about as close as we could get unless you count Antarctica. I'm doubtful of cell reception there."

Brad agreed. "Can you secure a place there and return the supplies we'll need to your farm? I'll set up the cameras and relay unit."

Clement opened the black case and held the red receiver unit. "How do I set this up?"

"Hit the button on the side to link to a laptop. Once we are linked, we'll need to confirm the feeds. After, I'll join you for three days while we watch the countdown to the event. Then we slide back to the farm and go over the footage."

"Hopefully, we will get some information. I'll leave you the address at the cabin."

Brad gathered the equipment. With a final look around the apartment, he ducked into a timestream.

Hopefully, I'll be back soon.

He moved forward as far as he could, through the bright white twisting nether within the quantum realm, before hitting the invisible wall. Getting closer to the event was impossible. Brad wasn't sure if he could look ahead or sense the black hole, but he could feel the effects that rippled through the quantum realm. Timestreams and eddies of matter led to a vast area of nothingness.

Brad ceased to be worried as he grew more confident and practiced moving through time. The void ahead brought up a fear that reached from the depths of his being. It was death personified, and not even light could escape its grasp. The future didn't go beyond and straight into a lifeless reality. That part of the mission still scared him. Facing a primal force of the universe is not an everyday occurrence.

Arriving outside the TRIUMF building, Brad used his security passkey to enter the front doors. He could have appeared within the building but wanted to avoid any issues. There wasn't any point in getting close to the equipment from the quantum realm unless they couldn't help it. There was still too much they didn't know.

Only the cleaning staff and a roaming security guard would be inside at one o'clock in the morning. After weeks of working inside, Brad knew all the security personnel, so he wouldn't be bothered by them if he was caught. He could always step into a timestream, but he was as close to the event as possible, and he didn't want unwarranted risks, especially at this location.

Brad installed two cameras at traffic congestion points. One was placed in the control room for the particle accelerator and another in the mechanical control room. The last camera, with a view of the front entrance, was installed outside the building at maximum range.

The cameras were small, about an inch and a half square, and black, making them hard to see when placed properly. Before activating the system, Brad found the roof's central point and installed the relay box beside the air-conditioning units.

Brad double-checked the cameras and ensured they were activated and functional before stepping into the quantum realm to meet Clement. They wouldn't get a second chance with the gear. It had to be perfect. Brad dropped off the surveillance case at the cabin and found a note on the kitchen table with the address for their meeting.

The kitchen was fully stocked and ready, including a laptop and charged battery packs. Not wanting to bring a weapon into a foreign country, Brad removed the shoulder holster and left the pistol on the back of a kitchen chair. He felt rather odd about seeing modern technology in the cabin. It seemed out of place. He loaded a small pack with the essential gear and entered the quantum realm. Within a moment, he had relocated to the other side of the world.

Antananarivo was the capital city of Madagascar, over four thousand feet above sea level on the island. With over a million people, Clement had no problem securing an Airbnb rental for the week.

Unsure of the location, Brad stepped out of the quantum realm downtown, on the edge of a residential subdivision and business core. Like a blast of air from a sauna, the humidity punched him in the face, but it wasn't just the heat. Brad was also tired. The abilities drew energy from himself, and he needed to recharge as soon as possible from the stone.

Downtown traffic was almost non-existent compared to Washington, and Brad had no problems hailing a taxi and giving him the address. The city could have been anywhere in North America.

The tall buildings and residential areas were modern and well-maintained. One significant difference Brad noted was the sheer abundance of tropical plants. They were lush and green, growing everywhere roots could find purchase. Iron-wrought gates and a stone fence to a property were covered in thick vines, and a small tree grew out of a crack halfway up a building.

After fifteen minutes, they pulled up to a quaint cottage in the suburbs of Antananarivo with a white picket fence. Green vines grew along one side of the small home, with bright pink flowers. Several birds the size of sparrows hid inside the fauna as the taxi pulled into the driveway.

Without any cash, Brad placed the fare on his credit card and tripled the normal rate as a tip. He might as well be generous if the world could end in a few days. As he walked to the front door, Clement opened it and waved him inside.

"The place is rented for the week, and we're all set up."

A laptop for the cameras sat on the small kitchen table. Brad quickly paired the receiver unit with the computer and installed the program from the USB drive. Within a minute, the system was up and running. With a few clicks, Brad cycled through the various footage from each camera. He confirmed it was recording, and each unit broadcasted a clear and crisp image.

Brad smiled. "This is pretty amazing."

Clement couldn't help but agree as he filled a kettle for tea. Madagascar was eleven hours ahead of Vancouver, and the outdoor camera showed it was dark at three in the morning. Their current local time was two o'clock in the afternoon.

"We have sixty-two hours until the black hole arrives. I would suggest we not use any abilities this close to the event. Already, we are closer to it happening, in subjective time, than we were able to jump." Clement offered tea, but Brad declined. He preferred coffee, but first, he needed to rest.

Brad mentioned how he felt after jumping from Vancouver, despite the fatigue not lasting long.

"We both need to connect with the stone again soon but wait till we are back at the farm. I don't want to chance it now."

"Sounds good. I'm going to sleep for a bit. This time zone hopping is giving me incredible jet lag." Brad yawned as he hung his jacket on the back of a chair and found an empty bedroom.

He had three days to rest before the action.

If this wasn't the calm before the storm, I don't know what else qualifies.

*****

FBI Director Matthew Adams reviewed the senate intelligence committee's briefing report that he would deliver for the afternoon session. Too many items had yet to be declassified, and the update would be brief.

The director had a large corner office with a walnut conference table at one end. Eight bookshelves lined the walls behind his desk, made from the same wood as the wainscoting, a dark oak. The two leather armchairs facing his desk were comfortable, and he preferred to sit in one so he could put his feet up on the other.

As he finished reading the last few pages of the report, two women were arguing in the reception area. Their voices steadily increased in volume, and it was going downhill fast by the tone. Adams tossed the paperwork on his desk. There wasn't a chance he could concentrate.

With one hand on the handle, the director paused. He recognized his secretary, Angela, as one of the voices. She was protective of his time, and unless the president came knocking, she wouldn't let anyone disturb him when he asked for fifteen minutes of quiet time.

When he cracked the door, Angela was out behind her desk, ready to physically block the other woman from entering. The other woman was Stephanie, and she saw him as the office door opened.

"Director, I need to see you *now*. Call your dog off."

"Are you serious, you little—"

The director stepped in between the two women. "That's enough. Stephanie, go inside my office and sit down. Angela, it's appreciated, but I was nearly done."

Angela muttered under her breath as her eyes bored a hole in the back of Stephanie's head. Neither woman would forget this moment.

Adams closed the door and sat. "I suggest you apologize on the way out. I wouldn't want to piss her off more than you already have."

"No time for that." Before handing them over, Stephanie waved three typed pages with photographs. "Supervisory Special Agent Brad Holman can either fly like a superhero, or there is a spaceship that can beam him around."

Adams scanned the pages, and the bottom dropped from his stomach. The first picture showed Brad Holman in the Boston field office foyer as he went through security. He had taken a flight to catch the thief. A computer report confirmed Holman had logged in, along with date stamps and email confirmations.

The second photo and report showed him in Washington on the Hoover internal security camera on the fourth floor. The date and time stamp was within a minute of the Boston confirmation. Thirty seconds later, Brad Holman was logging out of the computer in Boston, then *back* in Washington for Stephanie's first-hand witness report.

"Now he is in Antananarivo, Madagascar! Or someone that looks exactly like him just used his credit card. I knew something was up when he was here in Washington when it wasn't possible, so I did some digging. If someone could please fill me in, it would be appreciated. Does he have a twin?"

The last screenshot of agent Holman in the back of a taxi was taken from an internal security camera halfway around the world. Stephanie had access to resources that rivaled the NSA. Adams made a mental note never to cross her.

Stephanie's foot tapped on the floor as she perched on the edge of the chair. Adams read the report twice. The sinking feeling in his stomach had just bottomed out as the implications whirled through his mind. A cold sweat beaded across his forehead.

"Are you feeling well, Director? Your complexion is pallid."

He coughed into his sleeve to cover his reaction. "Yes, I'm fine. Thank you, I'll look into this when I can."

"But that just isn't possible for—"

"I'm going to look into it. Thank you for bringing it to my attention." Cutting her off would be the only way he could get in a word. He knew how efficient Stephanie was and had to redirect her energy quickly. "I want you to continue to monitor his actions and report to me *directly* every two hours."

Stephanie nodded. "Yes, sir."

Adams walked her to the door. "I have work to do, but I'll be in touch when I know more information. Thank you, Stephanie. Good job."

Once Adams sat behind his desk and placed his head in his hands, he closed his eyes. The disbelief and implications of what he had just read rocked him. The potential of what Brad Holman may have unlocked could destroy everything. It was too much power for one man if it was true.

Can we take that chance?

When he opened his eyes, Adams had made a decision. He activated the intercom. "Angela, reschedule the committee briefing and have my driver ready. Make sure the president's time is cleared and ready to see me in thirty minutes. Priority Alpha-Zulu."

A direct and imminent threat.

Adam slid his suit jacket on and tucked the reports into an inner pocket. He was about to witness the intelligence community and the United States' full resources react to the president's next order based on the meeting and his recommendations. However, with the three pieces of paper, Adams knew the commander-in-chief would err on the side of caution.

Chapter 22

 While in Antananarivo, they were confined to the rental home. There was zero chance Brad would see the famous Lemur Park or the beautiful island.

There was little to do but stare at the laptop and rotate through the various camera feeds for two days. Brad absently noted the university hadn't replaced the janitorial position in the TRIUMF building. To his relief, Clement had taken over the kitchen and meals, and he enjoyed cooking. The pot roast fell apart with a fork, and Clement brought his brazing torch to make crème brûlée. Brad had never eaten so well and was in serious danger of gaining weight.

Despite the laptop recording, they had taken shifts to watch the feed for forty-eight hours. Brad had experience with stakeouts and long hours of nothing happening compared to sitting in a car or alleyway—this was luxurious.

Bored, Clement suggested that they get out. "There's a farmer's market a three-minute walk from here. Fresh vegetables and fruit would be good."

Brad agreed. "I think we can take a little break. We still have a full twenty-four hours. A stretch and fresh air would be good."

Brad had dressed in slacks and a short-sleeved golf shirt, while Clement wore jeans and a T-shirt. An afternoon rain shower had finished an hour ago, and once they stepped outside, the humidity assaulted them. Within seconds Brad's shirt clung to his skin, but the sun felt good as they walked uphill to the market.

Their cottage rental was in the rural section of the city, with many cabins and parks. They passed a high-school soccer team performing drills before a game. The blue and red jerseys popped against the green mountain backdrop as they practiced on the field.

The elevation of the city provided stunning views of the mountains, farmlands, and distant villages. Some homes had cattle tied up on the front lawn, with chickens and geese wandering freely. It was a different way of life, but Brad thought the city was peaceful and relaxing.

Contrary to the quiet country, the market was hectic, with vendors selling everything from jewelry to bananas. Guides offered tours with the lemurs to zipline runs through the jungle canopy. Even in the rural setting, they catered to tourists. Brad waved off several locals waving pamphlets in his direction, and one young lady offered her "services" for a fee.

They quickly loaded a cloth bag with fresh fruit. Brad didn't trust the quality of the meat, and Clement wanted to buy a live chicken for dinner.

"I don't think we have time to deal with a chicken. I'll get you three next time."

"Deal." Clement nodded. "I did see a recipe I wanted to try."

They turned to leave the market when Brad darted to a far booth. The FBI agent handled the displayed bottles and talked to the young man behind the counter. Brad tried not to lean on the stall. It was made with haphazard materials—a rusted six-foot piece of tin acted as a roof, and the sides of the three-walled structure were made of cinderblocks and random bits of lumber. The counter was constructed with discarded wooden fruit crates. Brad couldn't be sure whether the young man behind the counter spoke English, but it was clear what he wanted.

The man reached into a rather sizeable marine cooler filled with ice and pulled out two large bottles of Three Horses Beer. The weather had changed, and clouds rolled through with a brisk breeze, but it was still humid.

Clement joined him and leaned close to whisper. "Do you think drinking after your recovery is a good idea?"

"I'm good. Do you have any money?"

The farmer gave him a strange look but handed over the cash to pay for the pilsners.

Brad didn't waste any time and set a rapid pace returning to the rental. Clement almost had to jog to keep up while carrying the groceries and beer. "Is there something I should know?"

Brad didn't turn his head or slow. "We'll talk once we are inside."

Before Clement could put the bags down, Brad had locked the front door behind them, and he quickly went around the house and made sure the windows were closed and the curtains were drawn.

In the sitting room, Brad turned on the old radio to full volume. A local music station played 1950s big band music, which filled the home with a trumpet solo, and Duke Ellington's voice. Satisfied with the precautions, Brad whispered in Clement's ear. "We were being followed to the market and watched. There were also two people watching our place. They didn't look like locals. I could see them studying us when I got the beers."

Clement quickly moved to the laptop and checked the timer. "Twenty-three hours, thirty-two minutes."

Brad glanced at the retro clock on the wall that resembled a white daisy and packed a small bag. "Sunset in six hours. I suggest we move just after dark and go to ground somewhere close. So that we can run out the clock."

"This is your area of expertise, but it sounds good. There's time for me to cook a good dinner. You can pack a back, and I'll cook."

Brad loaded a backpack with food, two bottles of water, and a change of clothes for both.

"I would feel more comfortable with my Glock right now."

Clement shrugged and continued to prepare a salad. "If things get that tough that you need a gun, we will leave. We can always recreate this attempt in an alternate timeline."

Knowing it would be a long night, Brad made a pot of coffee before sitting behind the laptop. They used the kitchen table as an office desk as the stakeout continued.

Brad watched the feeds for movement or someone sabotaging the equipment in or around the particle accelerator. They still had a few hours before anyone would arrive at TRIUMF to start their day.

"Can you watch this while I look around the house?" With his adrenaline levels and the coffee, Brad couldn't sit still for long. Without waiting for an answer, he checked the windows to see if they were being observed.

The single-floor home was compact, with a sitting room, kitchen, and a short hallway that led to the two bedrooms and a single bathroom. The sliding door off the kitchen opened to a small deck with a bistro set. Brad had enjoyed his coffee while looking out at the elevated views and the sunset the night before. If it weren't for the end of the world looming, it would have been quite pleasant.

The rental home lacked any personal effects or anything he could use as a weapon. He quickly discarded the frying pan and an old lampstand.

At Clement's shoulder, Brad whispered, "Keep up the normal appearance. I can't see them out the windows, but I doubt they have left. I have an idea, and we should be good once it's dark. I'll get the equipment ready."

Clement nodded and continued to cook a large meal while the radio blasted Sinatra.

~

Even though Brad knew it was coming, he still flinched when the front window broke. The glass shattered, and shards flew all over the living room floor. A split second later, the flashbangs went off. It filled the small house with a million-candle light flash that would stun and blind anyone temporarily with an ear-piercing bang. Immediately following the flashbangs, the front door was assaulted by a tactical battering ram.

"Go! Go! Go!"

A group of men rushed into the house. Their combat boots sounded like thunder as they stormed each room and called out orders.

"Clear!"

"Covering."

"Kitchen clear."

"Check the bedroom."

Closets were flung open, and the beds were flipped. Anywhere a target could hide was searched.

Brad's best guess was a CIA special operations division or mercenaries as they followed orders. Either that or they contracted out. Only one government worldwide would be interested in what agent Holman was doing, and it wasn't the Irish.

"All clear."

One man swore in French. "Secondary sweep. Check everything."

Two men checked for false walls and the attic space. A third man pulled the stove and refrigerator out and checked the cupboards.

Nothing.

Moments later, one man in the kitchen called out to the others. The Kentucky accent was easy to pick up, further solidifying his suspicions. "Sarge! Over here. It looks like they climbed down and left off the patio."

The kitchen had great views, but the drop was seventeen feet. A knotted rope from bedsheets was tied to the railing and reached the ground.

Brad heard their boots on the patio. Mile after mile of dark, black countryside lay below them, with no indication of a target. The men talked in hushed voices, too low to make out, and then Brad heard them leave. They tried to slam the front door behind them, but the latch and frame were broken.

Brad brought his finger up to his mouth and gestured for silence. Clement nodded and remained still. There was barely enough light to see, but they heard a floorboard creak above.

A full hour after sunset, Brad began the preparations. Clement was adamant about not using their abilities until it was needed. The black hole distorts the quantum realm enough that any use may jeopardize their efforts. After all his attempts to discover what happened, Clement had never been closer and didn't want to take any risk. After the event, they needed to make a clean break with the cameras' information, or all the work would be for nothing.

Brad descended the balcony rail with the knotted bedsheets and caught the full backpack and the laptop. Clement soon followed. A kitchen knife was used to pry the wood lattice panels away from the deck's base. Once inside, they made quick work of the plywood sheets and pulled a board out from the supports. After squeezing past the opening, they pulled the lattice and panels back in place. You couldn't tell it was forced unless you knew where to look. The ground sloped away from the front of the home, and they had enough room to stand under the kitchen. The height rapidly narrowed toward the front, where they crawled on their hands and knees. Brad plowed through the cobwebs before settling into a place partially hidden by two support beams directly under the front sitting room.

When Brad served warrants, an early morning entry into a home was best when the majority slept or were at their lowest energy. It gave law enforcement an advantage in reaction time and helped ensure their safety. Even a slight edge could make a difference. With all the efforts to place them under observation, Brad had a hunch that the surveillance team would escalate from observers to assailants. In the worst-case scenario, Brad was wrong, and they would spend an uncomfortable night under the home while counting down the clock.

The maneuver had paid off, and they had approximately nine hours left before the black hole destroyed the world. Brad wouldn't have any problem waiting, despite lying in the dirt with the joists of the home inches above his nose. He was almost comfortable in the dark gloom.

The assault team begged the question. *Why?*

Slowly the hours passed, and he didn't have much to do besides think. For some reason, the United States turned on him. The government believed Brad had to be dealt with because he was a threat. He didn't think they were going to arrest him. The team was there for one reason. For that to happen, they must have known about his new abilities.

Somehow, he slipped up. Brad wasn't sure where, but he will have time to consider it. While they waited, Clement breathed deeply with his eyes closed, and Brad was sure he nodded off a few times. For a pair of time travelers, time *did* pass, but slowly.

Every tick and creak of the home stilled his breath. Over the hours, Brad listened intently, and his nerves became frayed. When the couch springs shifted above, his eyes grew wide. From the expression on Clement's face, he had heard it as well.

Brad's stomach twisted in knots at the ten-minute mark, and a sheen of sweat beaded his forehead. Knowing the black hole chain reaction destroys the world would upset anyone. Brad sensed time *bending*, and it would obliterate everything on the planet and possibly their corner of the solar system. Energy surged from the quantum realm, pushing like an ocean subjected to the tides, and despite their efforts, it would overwhelm them.

Death seemed unavoidable, and Brad struggled not to groan at the nightmare.

Clement grew nervous, fidgeted, and stretched more often. Brad wasn't the only one to sense the destruction. Once, he looked at Brad and raised his eyebrows, fear in his eyes. The event was getting closer to reality.

Brad opened the laptop at the two-minute mark, hoping to see what was happening at the Vancouver TRIUMF building. When he opened the lid and hit the power button, the laptop startup sequence and a series of beeps began. Soon as that happened, Brad knew he had made a mistake and tried to cover the speakers, but it was too late. The floorboards creaked right above them.

Brad whispered. "Get ready to get out of here. I'll see you at the farm."

Clement was about to respond when a round, fired six feet away, exploded through the living room floor. The gunman, who waited silently for the last nine hours, vented his frustration by unloading his magazine. Brad jumped and nearly banged his head on a floor joist as Clement clutched the backpack.

Brad was ready when another bullet blasted through the floor, but he still twitched. The round was closer to the kitchen's rear door, and they could see two beams of light piercing the crawlspace's gloom.

The floor creaked and shifted as the shooter moved.

Thirty seconds.

Rounds were fired at an increased pace in a random pattern. The last landed an inch away from Brad's feet in the dirt. Suddenly, the countdown in his head was completed.

"Now!"

Brad felt the well of quantum energy rise like a tidal wave on the other side of the planet. As the force built, they felt the pull as they dove into the timestream and attempted to return to their base of operations—the cabin.

They battled against the undertow quantum currents, quickly depleting their energy levels. Fear lent him strength, and Brad dug deep to bring them both back. Previously, there was never a sense of direction in the quantum realm, but all that had changed. Brad felt like a leaf in a strong current, going over rapids, and headed for Niagara Falls. The sensation was making him nauseous and disoriented.

The usual twisting nether of black and white no longer hurled passed but spun in all directions. The black hole bent space as gravity absorbed light and all matter. As a result, the damage was visible in the quantum realm. Forked lightning flashed around them, and when two flares overlapped, it resembled a network of webs. Golden cracks in the fabric of reality stretched into infinity.

Brad's mind was being ripped apart, and his throat was raw as he screamed in pain. The quantum energy tugged at them from all directions. They couldn't last much longer. Knowing it was almost over, he grabbed hold of Clement's shoulder.

A ball of gold lightning struck Clement and chained him to Brad. Instead of disappearing, the light flared and continued to grow. Something shifted in Brad's mind, and he could now see ghost images floating around him.

Other Brads and Clements spun together across the quantum realm. Every couple screamed in pain as reality sundered. Brad couldn't worry about the variations as Clement slumped into unconsciousness. He grabbed the other shoulder, and with one last effort, Brad parted the quantum realm punting them out of the fabric of space and time.

The stress and energy took their toll, and Brad's eyes rolled back. His screams were abruptly cut off as the tear in the quantum realm sealed behind them.

Chapter 23

 After being ejected, Brad floated in a vast ocean of emptiness and couldn't feel his body. He was without form and part of the void as his mind pieced itself back together.

Slowly, external stimuli made him more aware, second by second. Pain wracked his body, and it felt like his bones were on fire. The agony became unbearable, and Brad's hands tried to hold his head together. He could not do anything but rock back and forth on his knees. He didn't have the strength to scream and prayed for death.

"Ride it out. It'll soon pass!"

Clement yelled beside his ear, but his voice had a strange echo. He gripped Brad's shoulder, but it did little to reassure him.

"Almost done. You can do it."

There was little doubt that God existed as he went through hell with the sensation of molten steel flowing through his veins.

However, as predicted, Brad felt relief within a minute. It felt like his ears popped from an altitude change, and suddenly, the pain was gone.

As his heart rate calmed, Brad tentatively opened both eyes.

"Are you okay?" Clement whispered.

Numbly, he nodded. "Feel free to kill me if I ever go through that again. Seriously."

Clement helped him stand and guided Brad to a chair near the cabin's front door to recover. He had appeared on the grass, an arm's length from the porch. As he grew more aware of his surroundings, Brad wiped the sweat from his face and looked at Clement. "What happened? When are we?"

The timeline they had established for the farm wasn't in existence. The fields were overgrown, and the cabin was in a high state of disrepair. Boards had fallen off the exterior walls, and the wood was weathered. Weeds had grown through the porch floorboards, and birds had nested in the rafters, unchecked for years.

"I arrived and went through the same thing fifteen minutes before you appeared. It seems we missed our target location." Clement collapsed in the second chair.

The weariness had left, and Brad felt good enough to stand. He stepped out onto the lawn and examined the exterior of the cabin. The corner roof had caved in, with apparent age or as the result of the weather, Brad couldn't tell. The inside looked the same, but a thick layer of dust covered everything. It looked like a raccoon had crawled inside to tear the kitchen apart, searching for food.

"We're in a different timeline?" Brad seemed unsure but ventured a guess.

"Try and look for yourself."

Brad concentrated and tried to slide into the quantum realm to estimate their position.

Nothing.

He tried once again, but the ability was gone.

"Same here. We're burnt out. Notice anything else?" Clement asked.

Frustrated, he had a closer look at Clement. Brad's jaw dropped. Most of Clement's hair was now white, and the lines had deepened on his face. He appeared to be twenty years older, if not thirty, with a receding hairline.

"I'm guessing I look how I feel. But bad news for you. You have aged and not too well. Your hair is now pure white and thinned with age."

Brad felt the same age inside but realized things had changed when he looked at his hands and arms. "How old am I now?"

Clement winced. "Mid-seventies, possibly eighty. I think it affected you more. Sorry, but I have no idea why."

"Nothing we can do about it for now." Brad paced back and forth on the porch, then gestured to the property. "I'm guessing we are sometime after you have initially found the meteorite?"

"Sometime after, yes, but I'm not too sure. I had come back to the cabin after finding the stone. I experimented with it for a long time and tried various things. I even sent this area back in time. After looping the immediate cabin, it aged. We may be back in that actual time, to where I initially found the stone. Not sure. It's just a guess."

"So, we could be here after you left or before you found the meteor. Is there any way to check?"

Clement's shoulders slumped, and he looked his age. "We can walk into the city and find out the date. It's only twelve miles one way. I'll also check where the meteor landed, but that may not tell us anything."

He looked at their clothing, and Brad wasn't sure of that idea. They had changed in Madagascar, and both wore jeans, running shoes, and T-shirts—not period-appropriate.

"What happened to the equipment and items we had stored here?"

"They would be in another timeline, but not this one."

Clement led Brad into the kitchen, where all the items from the pack were spread out. "We have the laptop and the receiver unit, two bottles of water, a few sandwiches, and a small bag filled with cut-up mangos."

Brad had thrown two T-shirts and a few pairs of socks and boxers in the bottom of the backpack. The clothing was to cushion the food and computer. He hadn't packed for an extended stay or survival.

"Let's see if all this was worth it." Clement tapped the computer.

Brad sat at the table, eager for answers. The computer booted up and showed eighty-eight percent left on the battery. There was no way to recharge the batteries, and it would be a few centuries before that could happen. However, they were lucky it worked at all.

Brad scrolled through each recorded camera feed, one at a time, trying to spot any clues and irregularities.

The camera with the exterior building angle only showed people coming and going throughout the day. It couldn't give any details on anyone from the recorded distance, but there was an overall view of the entire complex. Brad skipped ahead to the final hour and fast-forwarded through the footage. Everything looked ordinary until static distorted the video in the last five seconds before a black screen suddenly appeared.

They quickly scanned the remaining footage with the same results. Everything happened as expected, and a black screen ended the recordings.

"If there is anything for us to see, it would be in the lab." Clement pointed to the remaining file. The last footage showed the interior control room of the particle accelerator. There wasn't audio, but the image quality was outstanding. Brad had installed the camera on a wall filled with technical equipment. It gave them an unobstructed view.

Brad watched Dr. Kincaid direct the technicians to prepare for the experiment throughout the day. Her hair was in a ponytail, and she carried a clipboard in one hand with a pencil tucked behind her ear. Brad noticed the skirt under the lab coat showed quite a bit of leg. *Keep focusing, old man. Don't get distracted.*

Virginia moved from member to member of her team and referred to her paperwork and checklists. All staff calmly moved through their procedures and checked equipment. To all appearances, everything looked normal. Once everyone stood ready, Dr. Kincaid placed her glasses on her head and began the countdown.

"Holy shit." Brad sat upright in the chair at the one-minute mark. His eyes bored into the laptop as he absorbed the details.

A figure in a white lab coat side-stepped into the scene and stood next to the camera. The figure turned, and a hand covered the camera lens. They couldn't see any features, just a mid-torso close-up view of the lab coat and a hand as it approached the lens. The camera was pulled off the wall and placed inside a pocket.

Next, a brief flash of light shone through some material, and blackness again took over the footage at the final moment.

End of the signal.

Brad reviewed that final scene one more time before shutting down the laptop. They had to conserve what remained without a way to recharge the battery. Brad slumped forward on the table with his head in his hands as he realized their efforts didn't reveal any answers. After a deep breath, he turned to Clement. "What do you think?"

Clement shook his head. "It appears someone knew of the surveillance, and whatever happened, they knew they were being watched. Clearly, they didn't want to be observed."

"How would they know about the camera? With all that technology on the wall, there isn't a way anyone could see it ahead of time. Not without recording them."

Clement leaned against the kitchen counter. "Unfortunately, it could be someone else's problem. We are stuck here in the year seventeen-eighty-three. Unless you know of a way out that I don't?"

Brad stood and shook his head. "Sorry, I wish I did."

Clement gazed around the cabin. Brad knew the disarray and repairs needed to be done if they stayed.

"I'll start cleaning up if you can get some firewood ready?"

He wasn't surprised at Clement's idea. Without their ability to travel through time, there wasn't a choice. This was now home.

"No problem."

As the sun began to set, Brad stood at the pile of logs. The weeds and grass had grown tall, and the bottom logs could no longer be used as firewood. They had retained too much water and started to rot.

The ax head had rusted, but it would still get the job done when Brad ran a thumb over the edge. With a few practice circles to warm up, he tackled the job. The difference in his age became apparent as Brad tired quickly, and his grip frequently slipped. Previously, he could split a log with one swing. Despite the dry wood, it took him several attempts to get through one eight-inch round. As Clement cleaned, dust clouds billowed out the front door. While Brad rested to catch his breath, he tried to feel the quantum realm and locate his abilities but had no success.

With the chill in the air, and by Clement's best guess, it was either late April or early May. It would be colder at night than during the day, but it shouldn't be too bad. Buds had already started on the trees, and the grass would change soon from the brown of winter to a lush green. Spring would arrive, and the farmland eagerly waited. Clement had mentioned that a late snowfall wasn't uncommon at this time of year. It was better to be prepared for a long duration at the cabin.

As the pile of split wood slowly grew, Brad knew they had narrowly escaped death on two fronts. The gunman could have randomly shot them while counting down the clock and the black hole. Both options seemed a quick end compared to what now awaited.

Living out the rest of his days on a farm and dying of old age looked likely. With the age spots and wrinkles on his forearms, that could be any day. Starving from lack of food or an infection could kill them.

As he lowered the ax and scooped an armful of split wood, a tear trickled down his cheek to land on the ground. Unless they found a way out of the past, he would die of old age hundreds of years before he was even born. Now Brad had all the time in the world, and he wasn't sure he wanted it.

Chapter 24

 Clement and Brad based their days on survival while avoiding expending calories needlessly. The small amount of food they had brought was rationed, but it went quickly. Fortunately, Clement had experience foraging in the woods and providing roots and mushrooms. Dandelions had sprouted, and as Brad discovered, the whole plant was perfectly edible. A white springtime flower the size of his thumbnail had a pleasant aroma to supplement the greens and was plentiful. The flora never filled him, but it supplied minimal calories and nutrients they needed.

After a week, both of the men were tired of eating plants. They would constantly snap at each other as their patience was stretched. After their evening meal, Clement pushed back the kitchen chair and headed to the door. "Clean up. I'll be back in the morning."

Brad ran a hand over the thick white stubble on his chin and didn't have a chance to reply. The door had already slammed shut. Clement accepted his fate rather well but was withdrawn and kept to himself when they weren't arguing. He would certainly talk if there were chores, but he seemed quite content to remain silent for long stretches.

Brad had taken over a sleeping pallet in the loft. Once they patched the roof's corner, the attic space was usually a nice warm spot that he claimed as his own.

An hour after sunrise, Brad returned from the outhouse when Clement walked across the western fields with a turkey over one shoulder. Brad grinned at the sight.

Son of a bitch.

"Do you have any idea how badly I wanted to kill one of those? How did you do it?" Brad called out once he got closer.

"Practice." Clement tossed the big tom at Brad's feet. "I'll show you how to clean it after plucking it."

With a running shoe, Brad poked the dead bird. There wasn't any sign of a gunshot or wound, but the neck was twisted several times.

"Deal." Brad readily agreed. He was sure they were slowly starving to death. His pants were loose after just one week of the new diet. He carried the turkey to a tree stump and started plucking.

The bird lasted seven days. They rationed portions, and the carcass was used for a broth once the meat was gone. Clement added edible forest roots and plants. No part of the turkey was wasted, and anything remaining was turned into compost.

The next day Clement showed Brad how to make a fishing line by slowly pulling the threads out of an extra sock. Individually the material was too weak, but once several strands were braided together, they had a solid line eight feet long. Clement produced an iron nail from the barn and placed it in the hot embers of the fire. Once it had turned red, he pulled it out with tongs and gently shaped the glowing metal with a small hammer. Under his gentle ministrations, a pointed hook with a single barb emerged.

He dropped the nail into the tin cup of water to cool and smiled. "That'll work. My father used to make hooks for me when I was young. His were much better."

Outside, Clement removed a sheet of bark off a log and rolled it into a cone. He collected earthworms and grubs under the rotted logs and stones and carried them inside the container.

"Ready?"

Brad was excited at the chance of food and something different. When Clement gathered the equipment, he eagerly followed. A small trail led into the woods behind the cabin, and they followed it for almost half an hour. The mosquitos were vicious, and Brad would have sworn some were the size of birds.

"I haven't been here in a long time. I used to bring my sons fishing at the pond when they were little."

Clement didn't talk about his family, and despite the years, Brad could tell it still pained him. Clement would open up if he wanted to; Brad wasn't going to pry.

The path resembled an animal trail through the woods, but it was wide enough that they didn't have to hack through the bush.

After thirty minutes, the trees thinned, and Brad entered a large forest clearing.

A creek drained into a long pond, and the frogs stopped their chorus when they came closer. Tall reeds grew along the banks, and the surface rippled from a light breeze.

"This would be a nice place if it weren't for the mosquitos." Brad repeatedly batted away the insects. They preferred him over Clement.

"This place used to be full of trout." Clement was lost in memories as he slowly looked around. Not wanting to bother him, Brad stayed back.

"Anyways, stay away from the edges. I think the fish can see us with the water this clear." Clement snapped off an eight-foot branch from an elm. His knife made quick work of the twigs, and soon he had a flexible fishing pole. The makeshift line and hook were tied to the end, and Clement used a four-inch piece of cedar as a bobber. With an earthworm as bait, he moved behind a bush and flicked the line into the water.

Almost immediately, Clement laughed and pulled out an eighteen-inch rainbow trout. He tossed it to Brad. "Grab a thin bendable stick and put it through the mouths and out the gills."

The fish flopped and squirmed on the grass, dancing in its desire to return to the water. Brad struggled to get it under control. Every time his running shoe pinned it, the fish shot out the side. It was still slippery and had plenty of fight left. Brad pulled a long thin branch off a tree and threaded the trout down its length.

Clement's mood changed over the next hour. The dark cloud over his head vanished with every catch. The simple act of fishing worked wonders, and he grinned like a young boy. Brad had never considered fishing fun or something he would like to do. However, his mouth watered as he kept adding fish to the stringer.

Within an hour, they had nine trout hanging from a long branch that Clement tied off. The last was barely a pound, and the largest was over three.

Brad lifted the catch and chuckled. "I guess we don't have to worry about the ministry. I seem to have misplaced my fishing license in another century."

Clement winked. "That isn't our problem anymore. Before we head back, I'll clean up in the creek. There's a little pool up ahead."

They each took a dip in the cold water before heading back. Brad wiped the water from his beard and hair and wished he had a towel and soap. He would have to come back for a more thorough cleaning. After catching a whiff of himself, he knew the walk would be worth it.

"We can have one for lunch and have some for the never-ending soup and smoke a few."

At the cabin, Clement showed Brad how to clean the fish and prepare them for different meals. Meat doesn't last without refrigeration, but it would keep when they smoke and dry it out.

Brad eyed the laptop after placing the largest trout over the coals for the mid-day meal. It sat on the kitchen table as a constant reminder, and despite their efforts, Brad didn't find anything to help them. There was only five percent battery power remaining.

"We may as well have one last look." Clement pulled out a chair, and they sat. "The charge is almost done."

Brad leaned over his shoulder. "We can't have the laptop discovered in the future. Once we finish it, we'll have to dispose of it properly."

Clement brought up the last feed of the control room. They have watched it dozens of times and didn't learn anything new.

Brad rubbed his chin with a thumb and index finger, an old habit he couldn't shake. His frustration peaked when the battery flashed at two percent, and the laptop warned it would shut down.

Brad's shoulders slumped, and he officially gave up.

"This is ridiculous." Brad walked to the front door and paused. "Even if we found something, it isn't possible to do anything about it. Bury it in the cellar, I guess."

As the door slammed behind him, Brad finally accepted his fate. No one was coming to save them. Being aged from the previous attempt to discover an answer, he would only have twenty years remaining if things went well. Realistically, it would be five to ten years if he was lucky. Physically, he was seventy-five years old. Decades ahead of where he should be. Brad had no illusions about living until he was over a century. Death is also a form of escape, one he no longer fears.

*****

Clement stood when the door closed, and he almost followed Brad outside. The laptop beeped with a low battery warning again, and he sighed with one hand poised on the lid.

"Maybe Brad has the right idea." False hopes can lead to disaster.

The last video had frozen, and Clement leaned close to the screen. His eyesight wasn't the same as it used to be, but the video had paused just before the hand covered the camera lens. Clement backed the footage up, frame by frame, focusing on the palm. He chuckled in the empty cabin as the computer shut down permanently. Despite the situation, Clement was suddenly cheerful.

"The light at the end of the tunnel isn't a train."

But some information he had to keep to himself.

Time was a fickle mistress.

Chapter 25

Three weeks passed, and Brad and Clement focused on survival, often living meal to meal. Clement could forge consistently with the spring weather, and despite the tightening of their belts, they did well. Lack of food was a situation the farmer had previously dealt with; without him, Brad wouldn't have made it beyond the first week.

Jeans and running shoes wore rapidly and wouldn't last much longer. Their T-shirts were worn and ripped from the abuse. Modern clothing couldn't stand up to the hard physical work. Before bed, they washed their clothes and hung them to dry. However, they didn't have any replacements, and it clearly showed.

As Brad dressed one morning, his shirt ripped across the chest. "This isn't any better than a rag."

"Mine isn't much better." Clement poked a finger through a large hole across his shoulder. "I'll walk up to the next farm. They raise pigs. I'll try to negotiate a deal since we have no money."

"Do you want me to go with you?" Brad hoped for a change of scenery, even if it was another farm.

Clement was firm. "Not a chance. They know me, but not you. My age difference and what I wear now might not go over well. We shall see."

Brad didn't like it, but he understood. "How far is it?"

"Without a horse, I'd say forty-five minutes. I should be back in a couple of hours."

"Okay. I'll start taking down the dead elm beside the barn. Good luck."

Clement soon left, and Brad began the chores around the cabin. After several trips from the well, the large iron kettle was filled with water. He coaxed the embers to life and added the kindling and split wood to boil water. Clement had a large supply of soap on hand that he had made from the ashes of the wood fire and rendered animal fat. Time-consuming and messy but essential.

Before tackling the dead tree, Brad cleaned the bedding and towels. The progress through the thick trunk was slow but steady. Thirty years made a difference, and he had to rest. Throughout the day, Brad kept an eye out for Clement while keeping busy.

When Clement failed to return by nightfall, he expected the worse. Brad kept busy the next day, making snare traps for the game trails. After watching Clement make the snares, he figured he had it down, except for the actual execution. A few hours later, Brad gave up and picked edible plants to cook with the last rabbit on his way back to the cabin.

There was no sign of Clement by sundown. Something had happened. Hopefully, he wasn't dead. The next morning, he would begin the search.

~

After a breakfast of smoked trout and broth, Brad took stock of what he could use for weapons. He decided on one of the larger kitchen knives and a long staff he cut from the dead elm. Brad held the ax in his hands, contemplating bringing that instead, but it was too slow to swing and unwieldy. Maybe if he were younger, but not now.

Brad ensured that the kitchen fire was banked before leaving. It was a simple rule that Clement insisted on, and after learning how difficult it could be, Brad complied. With the kitchen knife in his belt, he planted the staff into the ground with each step. The double-rutted driveway began past the barn and curved uphill.

During his previous stay, he had never ventured off Clement's property. He couldn't walk far while initially recovering, mostly because he associated the place with a haven and didn't want to leave. He understood the reasoning for getting clean of the drugs, regardless of whether he enjoyed it.

The cabin and the fields were in a valley, and the farther he walked uphill, the elevated view lay before him. The gentle plume of wood smoke rose from the chimney before disappearing in the morning breeze. The picturesque setting made him wish he had brought a camera or a phone, not that he had a way of charging such items.

The road was hard-packed, made by wagons and horses over the years. Brad wasn't a woodsman but could not see any trace of Clement. Maybe if it rained and the ground was muddy.

It was a twenty-minute walk to the edge of the property he arrived at the main road. The road was twenty feet wide and well maintained, with the trees and brush cleared back from the shoulder. The brief walk winded Brad more than he cared to admit. He remained healthy for a man in his mid to late seventies but had to take a moment to catch his breath. He hadn't thought to ask which direction Clement was traveling, and as he studied the path, he couldn't tell.

His knees cracked as he knelt to find a footprint in the smooth dirt. There may have been signs of a bird or a leaf, but nothing else stood out. In the movies, a tracker could glance at an overturned pebble and tell you the direction and how long since someone passed.

"Oh, look. Three people came by eight days ago, and the man had a limp." Brad chuckled.

If I guessed the wrong path, it wouldn't help matters any.

"I thought you were going to stay here."

Brad used the staff to stand as Clement approached from the north. The bend in the road hid him from sight until the last moment. He carried two large bundles wrapped in linen and had a leather backpack over one shoulder.

"Where have you been?"

Clement frowned. The lines on his face looked deeper than usual, and his hair had turned a uniform gray.

"I went to my neighbor's property. We talked about this. What happened?"

He could tell by the tone of the farmer's voice that he thought Brad was losing it. "You've been gone two and a half days. I was fairly sure you were dead."

Clement appeared confused, and he cleared his throat. "What are you talking about? I've been gone maybe two hours. Ninety minutes."

Brad held his hand out and stopped him. "For me, you've been gone over two days. For you, it appears only a few hours have gone past. And …"

Clement raised his eyebrows. "Yes?"

"You also have aged. I would say easily another ten years older since I saw you last."

Clement wasn't shocked. "I can feel it. There is no way that a little walk like that should have winded me or made my knees hurt."

Brad carried a pack as they made their way to the cabin. He noticed something odd and confirmed it once they were inside the building. He knelt next to the fireplace and held his hand out. There was nothing but cold ash inside.

"I banked this less than an hour ago. It should still be going."

Clement sat at the kitchen table. "It seems this whole situation may not be over quite yet. I went to my neighbor's home, and it was empty. It's been that way for years. There wasn't any food, but I grabbed a few things that would be useful. I couldn't find any livestock, or I would have brought some back."

"There's a time distortion happening around the farm. I don't know what that means or how." Brad joined him at the table and tried to make sense of the facts.

"The quantum disturbances released from the black hole's creation, coupled with its effect, had done something when we moved through the time stream." Clement shrugged. "I'm only guessing, but it sounds reasonable."

Throwing his hands up in resignation, Brad paced in the small kitchen. "We just don't have enough information."

Clement agreed, then added, "We have some clothing now and spices. Including lots of salt."

The thought of seasonings perked Brad up. While filling, at times, it was like eating cardboard.

"Never thought I'd be saying this." Brad smiled. "How about we go fishing?"

Chapter 26

Clement stood in the doorway, watching Brad kneeling in the dirt and pulling weeds. The soil was good, but they had to stay on top. He had taken a quick break from the afternoon labors. His back burned from the uncomfortable position, and the hot summer sun baked him through the thin brown cotton shirt. The wide-brimmed hat blocked the heat, and without it, he would have been burned to a crisp. Clement had woven the pond reeds into headgear for them both.

The primary field north of the cabin had transformed over four and a half months. It took three weeks of work to get an acre ready for planting. The seeds were carefully nurtured and watered when needed. Sprouts grew in the fertile soil, with the weather cooperating, and men fretted over each shoot as if their lives depended on it—it did.

The late July sun was powerful, and they watered the crops daily. Barrels helped collect rainwater from the cabin and barn roof to supplement the well. Clement had seen that water source run dry many times.

They completed the intensive work in the morning before the temperature rose, leaving the light, menial tasks for the afternoon. Although, weeding and watering seemed anything but light work. Backbreaking, painful, and repetitive, but not easy.

Two of the three clay jars from the neighbor's home contained seeds Clement guessed were turnips he grew for his pigs. The third jar was a mystery, but he planted them anyway. They grew fairly quickly and were already three feet tall, with a pointed green leaf. Clement guessed they were beans, and so far, but Brad thought squash. It turned out that Brad was correct, but Clement was loath to admit it to the city boy. The door slammed behind Clement as he crossed the field.

He carried a pitcher of water and two tin cups. Brad straightened with a little difficulty after gaining his feet.

"At your age, you need to drink plenty of water." Clement handed Brad the pitcher.

"I think we are easily the same age now, physically anyway."

Brad wiped the sweat from his brow and rubbed his hand through his white beard.

Clement still shaved every few days. He couldn't get used to having whiskers. They both could easily have been eighty years old. His back and knees certainly felt the age.

The well water was cold and refreshing.

"How are the squash plants coming along?"

"Beans. And they're doing good." Clement knelt and checked the soil. "We'll need to water the turnips again tonight. They are thirsty in this heat."

When he heard a thump, Clement quickly stood. Brad had dropped the water pitcher and tin cup and gasped for breath. A shaking hand pointed toward the barn as the water soaked into the soil, forgotten.

"Jesus Christ …" Brad trailed off as they watched in disbelief. Clement echoed the sentiments as he tried to process the image.

Translucent visions of horses flickered in and out of existence one hundred yards away as they slowly proceeded across the lawn, crossing the barn. Many things don't have an explanation, like UFOs and ghosts, to name a few. Despite living for centuries, Clement had never learned about the afterlife, but before his eyes were something he couldn't explain.

Apparitions.

One second, they were visible, and the next, they were gone. When they reappeared, the horses were in a different position. The images paused in front of the barn before moving toward the cabin.

Clement walked toward the horses and glanced over at Brad. "You can see them, right?"

"Yes."

The closer they came, the more details became apparent. On top of the horses were men in military uniforms. It had been a long time, but Clement knew who the images were. "This is the local militia. They patrol the area. It's hard to tell, but I may have met them before."

Clement walked right up to the man in front, but he couldn't make out any further details. They phased in and out of sight, and they could see straight through them.

"It's like watching a hologram. Do you think they can see us?" Brad waved his hand in front of the man who dismounted.

Nothing.

"I don't think so." Adrenaline coursed through his muscles, and Clement felt like dancing. "It's quite possible there is no such thing as ghosts."

Five men walked across the field and headed to the woods on the north side. Brad muttered for them to stay out of his garden as they followed.

Clement thought the soldiers had disappeared for good, but they flickered back into sight at the edge of the woods. Clement figured out where they were headed as he hurried to catch up.

He yelled, "I know where they're going, another fifty yards through the trees."

Clement walked through the images, and Brad followed. They stopped halfway up a hillside on the other side of a rather large rock.

I haven't been here for a long time, but I'll never forget it.

"This is where the meteor fell!" Clement's thoughts whirled, and he could barely contain the excitement. He realized he shouted, but it was warranted. The soldiers were *new,* and the implications revealed that things were not over. Yet. Certain events had yet to happen that had already occurred. He would only have one chance.

The militia soldiers circled the impact area, and Clement thought a young man stood inside the pit. Suddenly, they disappeared except for one man, who rested against the limestone.

Clement stared intently as the last man sat. Quicker than the blink of an eye, he flickered solid and in full color before fading into a ghost image.

"Brad, I want you to return to the cabin and watch them from there. I'll join you in a bit," Clement whispered.

"What is going on? Do you know?"

"I have an idea, but there isn't time. I suggest you run. *Go!*"

Without waiting to see if Brad followed his instructions, Clement took off through the woods. He ran as if a hungry bear were on his heels and was several decades younger.

After a hundred yards, Clement turned east and followed the ridgeline. He was on track for intersecting the road off his property, but he wasn't in the physical shape he once was. His age and abilities had slowed him, but there wasn't time, and Clement pushed through. Clement's toe clipped a fallen log and caught the edge in his rush, landing hard. A buried rock ripped through his worn jeans and slashed his knee open.

Swearing, Clement climbed to his feet and continued without regard for his safety. Too much depended on this moment.

It would not come again.

Thirty yards later, he stood beside the road, hidden behind a cluster of birch. He gasped for breath, ignoring the blood that ran down his shin and filled his shoe. Clement placed his back against the trees as if in ambush and waited.

His efforts paid off when the horses walked along the dirt road. The mumbled conversation as the men spoke reached his ears, and a grin deepened the lines on his face. Injuries were forgotten as Clement peeked through the trees and watched men ride in a single file. Their images were solid, with only an occasional flicker of a ghost overlay. Two men ate apples, and the juices rolled down their chins.

Clement waited until they rode past and studied the bearded officer that trailed behind, lost in thought.

He whispered while leaning around the tree. "Captain O'Sullivan. Over here."

The mare glanced his way, but her rider didn't respond. Clement tried again, a little louder. "Psst. Brandan, over here."

Startled, the officer halted and squinted in his direction. "Mr. Wallace? Is that you?"

"It's me, Brandan. Make sure your men go ahead. I need a private moment with you."

Clement could tell the patrol captain was confused, but he called the second last man. "I'll be with you in a moment. I have to take care of business."

The last trooper in line raised his hand as an acknowledgment and followed the others. After dismounting, the captain held on to his horse's reins and stood to get a better look at Clement.

"Sweet Mother of God! Clement Wallace, is that you?" Brandan's eyes widened as his jaw dropped, taking in the image of the aged farmer. "What happened?"

"Rest assured, this is me, and right now, I'm not at liberty to go into any details. I do need something from you, though."

The captain's brow furrowed at his request. "What is it you need? I don't have any money."

Clement shook his head and smothered a grin. He had missed the Irishman, who redefined the word tight. "No, not that. I think you picked up something while you were in the woods. I need to see it."

"I don't understand what you are talking about …."

Clement smiled to put him at ease. "Unless I'm wrong, you have gained some weight since you saw me last. I think you know *exactly* what I'm talking about."

Slowly Captain Brandan O'Sullivan nodded. "Yes, I found something."

"Please. I need to see it, and then I'll return it to you. Right now, there isn't *anything* else in the world that is more important. Trust me."

Brandan studied his face and clothing. His eyes narrowed when he looked at the worn-out running shoes. The patrol officer took a deep breath and slowly nodded. He lifted the uniform jacket, removed the stone fragment he found in the woods, and held it out to Clement.

Hope rushed through his veins as he reached for the meteorite. The fragment was cool to the touch, and until that moment, Clement wasn't sure he could interact with the stone. It was the same size if he had placed both fragments together. It was whole, and Clement not only held the meteor fragment in his hands. He held the last chance to escape.

"Hand me your knife, please."

The captain drew his small blade and handed it over, hilt first.

Nodding his thanks, Clement took the knife and plunged the tip into the palm of his left hand, reasonably deep. Immediately, the blood pooled, and he cupped it in his palm. He wiped the blade on his pants and handed it back. Clement held the meteorite against the cut, covering one end in blood.

A jolt of electricity flickered through his body. The current started at his hands and traveled to his feet in a split second. An echo or warmth flared in the gold ring before disappearing. The pain was brief, and he relaxed his clenched jaw and grinned. Although significantly weakened, his heart raced once he identified a familiar ability.

Clement held the meteorite fragment out for the captain. "Take this back."

Brandan looked at Clement like he saw a ghost and numbly followed the instructions. Placing the knife back in its sheath, he moved like an automaton with pale skin and jerky movements.

"You don't look nearly as old as you were a second ago, Mr. Wallace." The Irishman's voice was barely above a whisper.

"Captain Brandan O'Sullivan, I need you to listen to me. You must follow my instructions *to the letter*. Do you understand?"

The officer had trouble blinking, but he managed to nod in agreement.

"You are never to mention meeting me or what just happened. You will continue as planned, but don't tell me any details. I don't want to know."

"What *did* just happen?"

Clement ignored the awe in the Irishman's voice.

"You can never know, and you will never attempt what I just did. *Everything* depends on that. I'm on the level, and I hope I can count on you."

Clement shook his hand and covered his right hand with his left to hide the grip. The patrol captain understood and stepped forward, toe to toe, as they shook. His left hand reached around and patted the farmer on the back. "You can count on me."

"Thank you. You're a good man. It was nice knowing you."

"Good to know you as well, Mr. Wallace. May God be with you."

Brandan mounted, tucked the stone under his uniform, and rode to catch up with the patrol. He never looked back.

Chapter 27

Brad paced back and forth on the cabin porch as he waited. After months of survival and worrying about food, something had changed. Were the ghosts real? Where had Clement gone? Is he still alive?

Soon after Brad returned, the ghosts mounted and rode up the hill past the barn. The farther away, the more real the soldiers became. Brad even saw flashes of color before disappearing around the bend. Faint noises from the horse hoofs on the hard-packed trail echoed through the trees.

When Clement walked down the trail and toward the cabin grinning an hour later, his step had a definite bounce.

"What's going on? What was up with the ghosts?"

Clement didn't answer but proceeded into the cabin with a nod to follow. After lifting the cellar door, Clement quickly descended and moved to the small wooden table in the corner. Brad followed, just a little more slowly. It was dark, and it was hard to see. Apparently, he had horrible night vision for his age and many other issues.

"Almost there ..." Brad heard the strain in Clement's voice. Suddenly, the familiar concussive wave knocked Brad back a step and pushed Clement into a seated position.

"How?" Tears rolled into his beard as Brad helped Clement to his feet. He wasn't the only one crying.

The meteorite was back with energy flickering through its depths. Clement didn't waste any time and laid his ring and hand on the stone. After a moment, he sighed in relief.

"Much better. Your turn." Clement's age had been stripped away as his voice was robust, firmer.

Brad placed both hands on the meteorite. He drank deeply of the energies like a sponge. The hidden door opened in his mind, revealing his quantum abilities.

"How did you do it?" Brad performed a quick knee bend and was pleased to discover it was pain-free. His eyesight had improved as well. He felt like a kid again.

"Let's go upstairs, and I'll try to explain."

Brad wrapped the stone in a curtain of quantum energy and allowed it to disappear. It felt like he had regained the use of a limb he didn't know was missing.

My back no longer hurts!

Brad felt whole once more and eagerly followed Clement to the kitchen table.

Clement said, "I believe *you* were the nexus point. After the black hole was created, we both were tossed around as the quantum energies were released, and I tried to bring us back to our other location. You *also* tried to bring us back, but we went into an alternate universe that overlaid ours. The reality was twisted."

Brad tried to understand, but this explanation was beyond him.

"When I went farther away from you, time distorted, aging me in the process. I started sliding out of the reality you created."

"How did you free us?"

"The local militia found the meteorite fragment when they checked out the initial crash site. I followed the ghost images to the edge of the affected area, and I took a little charge from the fragment. Just enough to call forth the large stone."

The knot of tension Brad had carried with him for months disappeared. "Okay, we can travel again. However, we're back to the original problem. How do we stop the black hole from ripping apart our reality?"

Clement shrugged. "Investigations are more up your alley. What would you like to do?"

Brad thought about it for a minute. "I do have a few questions that you haven't answered yet. How did you know where the two fragments were stored?"

Clement stared at his ring. "I just followed the fragment through the decades. I don't know why, but I cannot change history where the meteor is involved. I couldn't just go back and grab the fragments in a past timeline. I had to do it in the current reality or the present time. Once I found the journal, I read it in the undertime to find out where it was stored."

Following along, Brad nodded, and he got up to pace. It felt like he was questioning a witness once again. Although he thought Clement held something back, he wasn't sure, but it couldn't be essential, or he would have mentioned it. "Tell me about Fort Knox."

"Not much to tell, I just read about that location, and when I arrived, I just walked in and got it."

"What about the gold bar? Why did you leave it on the road?"

Clement looked confused. "What gold bar?"

Brad felt he was on to something and leaned forward over the back of a chair. "A gold bar was found on the road outside of Fort Knox. That was the initial reason I was called in. The same fingerprints on the bar were found on the metal chest where the fragment was stored."

Clement drummed his fingers on the tabletop and shook his head. "Sorry, I don't know anything about that. I did pick one to hold. I'd never seen that much gold before, but it was too heavy. I didn't have any use for it and just took the fragment and left."

Brad sat and closed his eyes. He could almost hear the gears in his head as he digested this new information. "How did you figure out the other half of the stone fragment was in the Cheyenne complex? That was an obscure reference from President Ford."

"President Bower updated the journal. He wrote down the location of where it was. Looking back at Ford's entry, I knew exactly where to search."

Brad knew this information was important but couldn't put it together. Yet.

After he read the journal, it was given to Director Adams. The FBI director would have passed it to the president, and after *that,* a new entry was written. Brad had read the book several times. There was no final entry from President Bower. But a few answers were obvious since he was dealing with time travel.

Something had changed in the past, but I don't know what it was right now. Has the future changed?

Brad shook his head. He didn't know the answers.

The future couldn't be changed because the past hadn't changed. "I need to think about this for a little bit. How about we head back to my apartment and get cleaned up? I need a shave, and we both could use a haircut."

Despite it no longer being white, Brad's beard remained, and he tugged at its length.

Clement chuckled. "A hot shower would be good. I miss that the most."

"Let's grab some things and head out. I have an idea or two."

Despite this being considered an alternate reality, neither wanted to leave any technology in this time period. Just in case, the laptop and everything from the future were removed.

~

After a quick shower and change of clothes at Brad's apartment in Arizona, Clement led him through the quantum realm, returning to Boston.

"I've been coming here for a while." Clement showed Brad the building. It was an older part of the city that some might have considered run-down, but the area was slowly being rejuvenated with new stores and condominium conversions.

They stopped outside a low red-brick building on a busy street corner. A red and white barber pole attached to the front of the store still worked, and when they stepped inside, a bell jingled overhead.

An hour later, Brad looked in the mirror and felt better. A large pile of hair lay on the floor at his feet. Outside, he rubbed a calloused hand across a smooth face and short hair. "Much better. Never liked a long beard."

"They help in winter, but otherwise, not for me either. Okay, what's our next step?"

Brad said, "I would like to go back in time and see if there is an anomaly *before* the TRIUMF building is built. It would be easier to deal with the event if there was an outside source that may be the cause."

"Do you want me to go with you?"

"I was hoping you could set up a base of operations. I'm thinking of funds and private property. A day before the event, the government tried to kill us again. I want to avoid that if possible. If we survive, I'd like to be able to disappear."

"No problem. Backup plans are good. What area are you thinking?"

"Who owns the property where your farm used to be?"

Clement laughed, and a hand gestured in a broad circle. "Look around. Do you see the coffee shop across the street? That's where the barn was."

In disbelief, Brad looked behind him at the barbershop nestled in a small strip plaza. "This is where your cabin was?"

"Yes. In part, that is why I like to come here." Clement grinned. "Plus, Jimmy gives a great haircut."

"Okay, my big idea isn't happening now. I'll meet you back at my apartment in an hour."

Clement walked down the street and turned into an alley before allowing the quantum energies to transport him. Brad glanced at the various people that drove or shopped and couldn't help but wonder how they would react should someone disappear in front of them.

Magic?

Maybe that is how the idea of magic and illusions started. Someone had found a meteor, and they could do magic with their abilities.

Brad turned into the same alley before he stepped into the timestream. Soon the familiar pulsing vortex of black and white images streamed by as he traveled back in time. His destination was Vancouver before the university was built in 1900.

The black hole happened regardless of the captain at the helm, and Brad hoped to understand the area. It didn't take long for him to be reasonably sure nothing significant happened here. A large forest of primarily cedar trees covered what would eventually be the university grounds. A light mist blanketed the woods giving everything a glimmering shine. One of the largest trees Brad had ever seen dominated the area. It was over two hundred feet tall and easily thirty feet in circumference. The pine cones on the forest floor were twice the length of a football.

Brad smiled at the vision of the cabin he could build from just one tree. After that, the environmentalists would most likely hang him. Brad wasn't willing to invest one hundred and twenty years of living in the "now" to determine what happened at the property. If there were some information that would narrow it down, he would consider it. In ten-year intervals, he jumped forward and witnessed the university's growth and the forest diminish in equal proportions as civilization expanded.

I'm not too sure what I'm doing. Everything seems normal.

Out of ideas, Brad dropped into the quantum slipstream and arrived at his apartment in Phoenix.

There was no sense of homecoming when he arrived. It was rented as a place to sleep when he was promoted and transferred to the Phoenix field office. He had spent most of his time at work or in the gym.

The apartment had a large kitchen overlooking an eating area next to the living room. The bedroom and bathroom were down a short hall inside the front door. The open concept of the layout appealed to Brad, and it suited his needs at the time. The furniture was some of the finest Ikea had to offer, and it served his bachelor lifestyle.

Clement sat at the small table next to the kitchen, sipping a hot cup of tea with piles of papers arrayed before him. It had only been a few hours since Brad checked the university grounds, but that wasn't how time travel worked.

Clement's hair was longer by a few inches, and his tan had faded. The brown suit and tie made Clement appear older, but Brad knew the stone prevented that from happening. It seemed odd to wear the outfit, but he appeared comfortable.

When he stepped out of the quantum realm, Clement wasn't surprised. He gestured for Brad to join him at the table and handed a sheaf of paperwork. "For some reason, I won the lottery several years ago. Half was put into the name Brad Sheppard. You now own a few thousand acres in Wyoming, south and east of Yellowstone National Park, and a condo downtown Washington DC."

When he saw the balance in his bank account, Brad was shocked. "This is too much! What about the person that was supposed to win the lottery? How can this be good if we change the timeline for us to win?"

"I've already looked into it. A single man won the Powerball lottery and died ten months later with no relatives, so the government took his estate. I gave him several million, so he would be happy for the rest of his life."

Brad thought hard on a reason to disagree with this logic, but it made sense, even if it made him uncomfortable.

"We won the money twelve years ago, so if we need to travel back that far, the funds are still there. Anything we need before that, we will need to buy something to liquidate back time. We can set up a base of funds going back a few hundred years that way if needed."

Clement handed over a secondary pile of papers with a wallet on top. Brad found a new driver's license, credit cards, a passport, and even a birth certificate for Bradley H. Sheppard.

Brad's stock photo for his identification was the picture the FBI used when he was promoted to supervisor. "You had left your ID behind. I used that picture."

"Thanks. These IDs look good. They are well done." Brad had seen several dozen fake identifications. These were of a quality that he hadn't seen before. They would easily fool him.

"They are legitimate. I went back in time and started working at the DMV in Casper, Wyoming, for a few months and then made the IDs. There are legal records now, and we have a full background history for both of us."

Turning the paperwork around showed Clement Robinson was his new name, with all the same paperwork to back it up as Brad now had.

"I found it much easier to respond and work with your first name. Unless you join the military, the last name isn't used as much or as necessary. I also have a house in downtown Boston. I'm done living in a cabin, especially since running water and electricity make life much easier."

After Clement ran through the accounts and properties, Brad was impressed with the detailed work. Brad Sheppard and Clement Robinson had a thorough history, from school records to paying taxes, stretching back over three decades.

Once the information session was over, Clement asked, "What's next?"

Brad had thought about the options during countless hours of gardening and fishing. He had run through many variations, always arriving at the same answer. "Everything you have done to avoid the black hole doesn't work."

"Correct. What do you have in mind then?"

Brad slid the new wallet inside the front pocket of his jeans and smiled. "I think it's time for us to go back to school."

Chapter 28

The Doctor William Riddell Centre was a building at the heart of the University of Regina. It's a hub of activity for the students and faculty with the student employment services, food courts, the student union, the Owl bar, and the restaurant, all in one large, sprawling place. Students who must complete a mandatory cooperative placement as a part of their course curriculum would find their assignment through the student employment services.

Ginny sat in the student services lobby, reading the brochures on the table. Most of the information dealt with student placements and other programs offered as jobs. Several other students sat in the waiting area as well.

She had her hair back in a ponytail and wore a large school sweatshirt under her puffy blue jacket. Mittens and hats were stuffed in her pockets. Winter had hit early in Regina, and another snowstorm blanketed the city. Her cheeks were still glowing from the brief walk from her apartment.

"Virginia Kincaid?" A man in a blue sweater leaned out of the office door and smiled in her direction. His gold nametag stood out in contrast. He was reasonably handsome with his short dark hair, stubble, and a deep tan—despite it being October.

"Right here." She made her way through the maze of student legs and chairs.

The placement officer gestured for her to enter. "Come on in, please. Take a seat."

The office was small, with a desk occupying most of the room. Three shelves on the wall contained information for courses, future studies, and various financial services available to the students. Two black plastic chairs faced the desk, and she chose the closest one. The computer monitor took up half the desk space and blocked any view through the narrow window.

Closing the door behind her, he sat. "You're on time for your appointment, a rarity here. Give me a second to pull everything up."

He typed in the information she had filled out on the mandatory forms. "Okay, here we go. You're here for your choices for the co-op portion of your physics course?"

"Correct."

He paused and tapped the blank portion. "Do you know what area you want to specialize? That will help with placement."

Ginny blushed and felt awkward. "Not yet. I'm open to suggestions."

"Don't worry. It's more common than you think."

Ginny didn't feel relieved when she heard the answer, far from it.

"I have one position left for SNC-Lavalin for a reactor core physics as a co-op position. Unlike some other positions, this one has a wage of twenty-five dollars an hour. It also includes flights and accommodations for the four-month assignment."

Her mouth opened wide at the possibilities, and she tried not to squeal. That wouldn't be professional.

This would be perfect!

Ginny couldn't find time for an occasional job with her course load. The extra money would come in handy and take some pressure off her parents. The scholarships were good, but they could always be better. "Where's the placement?"

A few clicks on the keyboard brought up the information. "Toronto area, Ontario. Looking at your courses and qualifications, it seems you check all their requirements."

"I would like that very much."

You can't be serious. Ginny tried not to grin.

Having grown up in a rural town in Saskatchewan, she wanted to see the rest of the country and Toronto in particular. After hearing about other students' nightmare positions for their placements, this sounded like a dream.

"There's a matter of a background check that they require. Anything I need to be aware of that may raise any flags?"

Ginny shook her head and smiled. "Nothing at all."

He continued to type for a minute. "I've temporarily taken the posting for that position down. It's held for you, pending approval from your department head."

He stood and stretched out a hand. Ginny tried not to bounce out of her seat as she shook. Ginny glanced at his nametag. "Thank you, Mr. Sheppard. I'm looking forward to this."

"My pleasure. Keep your grades up, and you'll have plenty of opportunities."

*****

"How did it go?"

"Good. You were right. Virginia jumped for that chance and position."

Brad pulled the sweater over his head and collapsed on the couch. The apartment in Arizona had turned into a makeshift headquarters building, and instead of jumping to the next day of work, Brad returned to brief Clement.

One problem with the black hole as part of Dr. Kincaid's experiments was their lack of expertise. Brad readily admitted that it was beyond him even if he enrolled in the courses and took fifteen years to study the subject. That was Clement's case as well. Something went wrong during the experiment, but they didn't have the knowledge to aid or troubleshoot.

But, instead of trying to halt or sabotage the experiments, they were now trying to do the opposite. Give Virginia Kincaid every opportunity to reach her full potential.

Her parents had found great high-paying jobs, and Virginia received a full scholarship to the university. Handing out choice assignments for the cooperative portion of her physics program was Clement's idea. Brad had agreed and jumped farther back in time.

His stellar references and background made him easily chosen for the position.

The last two years at the student employment center weren't as bad as Brad thought. It took him a while to learn the ropes, and when the appropriate time came, it was a simple matter of redirecting Virginia's case to his file. The ability to jump forward through the weekends, summer breaks, and holidays added to barely fourteen months of work, which wasn't that horrible.

Brad would return to the apartment to shower and change, then head back to work the next day. One side effect of the meteor was his ability to go without sleep. By his best guess, he hadn't slept in over a year. The energy cost to stay awake was low, and it didn't force him to recharge from the stone more than usual.

"I'll continue to feed her some good assignments. With her courses, she has a few more years of co-op placements. Besides, next year I get an extra week of holiday at the university."

Grinning at the absurdity, Brad pulled out a meal from the freezer and threw it in the microwave. He could go without sleep, but his stomach let him know it needed fuel.

"Those things are horrible."

Brad shrugged. "You get used to it."

Clement closed his notebooks. "I'm ready to go up-time. I'm done studying for the technician position."

They figured having someone on the inside working in and around the experiment would be much easier to understand and see what could go wrong. It would be more reliable than relying on a hidden camera to record near the end. Although Clement could easily slide and modify the test results for his qualifications, he would need to perform the job.

They agreed that anything closer than the five-day mark was considered too risky.

"The main goal is to discover what happened during their first experiment and who is funding them. Virginia received another grant just after their first trial." Brad sat to eat at the table and read the titles for Clements's course. *Electro-Mechanical Technician, Nuclear Ventilation, and HVAC Systems.*

Clement closed the *Radiation Safety Training* notebook and nodded. "I'll look into the funding and see where that goes." He placed the paperwork and books in a backpack and added, "I'll come back and leave you a note here at this time location. Take care."

Clement stepped into a quantum realm while Brad finished his meal. It wasn't long before the note appeared.

Details on the unknown benefactor for the grant to continue research: *Offshore holding shell corporation – Heinemann*

C

Brad wasn't sure how to start an investigation in the corporate financial world, but he knew someone exceptional in that area.

Chapter 29

 Brad adjusted the shoulder holster and buttoned the suit jacket. It had been a few years since he had last worn a pistol, and it felt strange. There wasn't much call for being armed at the Canadian university. He clipped his photo ID on the breast pocket, and after a quick once over, he was ready.

After a brief knock on the door, he entered Stephanie's office. As usual, she was scanning between the different computer monitors.

"Special Agent Holman. How can I help you?"

Brad made sure to arrive at a proper time, just after he started the case and back in Washington. He didn't want to create a new timeline or run into himself. With Stephanie's attention to detail, Brad figured she was the one to raise the red flags. He trusted his gut on that, and it made sense.

Clement had mentioned that he ran into himself once, but he didn't discuss the encounter. All in all, Brad was reasonably sure that that would be something he would want to avoid. One comment in passing could disrupt years of work or alter a specific outcome.

"I have the name of an offshore holding company, possibly a shell corporation. Heinemann is the only name I have."

Brad wasn't sure of the exact date when Dr. Kincaid's team got the research grant to continue her work, and he wasn't ready to tell Stephanie about that in case he was giving out information that hadn't happened yet. He was juggling facts of events that may or may not have occurred in his head. In a nutshell, thinking of it gave him a headache.

"Do you know of any of their dealings? That will help trace them. You follow the money."

It sounded easy when Stephanie mentioned how to accomplish it, but it was beyond him.

"They may be issuing research grants. Unsure of any other details."

"Okay, that isn't much. I'll see what I can find."

"Thank you."

As usual, Stephanie had turned back to the computer and dismissed Brad from her mind as she focused on her next task.

Brad was sure that he wouldn't be going back to work for the FBI. The bureau had been his life, and he had focused on that exclusively. When they betrayed him, when his *government* betrayed him, it made him reevaluate. There were better ways to serve his country. He had given everything and risked his life on too many occasions for the FBI, and right now, he used them to accomplish the mission. Nothing else. He was a great investigator and had brought closure to many cases, but someone else would always be ready to step into his place. Brad could *still* apprehend the bad guys, but this time he could use his abilities to help. There wouldn't be any way they could avoid being caught.

However, that's a possible future, and he wasn't sure there would be one right now. The black hole would annihilate everything, and despite all they did, it seemed unavoidable. With Brad's guidance and the opportunities Virginia had, he failed to make any changes in the timeline.

Clement and himself would be the only people to survive the black hole. They only had to stay back-time and avoid the future.

It was time to discuss quantum gravitons and the effects of radiation from an event horizon in a vacuum with a resident expert.

~

Brad worked out a deal for one shift per week to maintain his position within the student employment services with an appropriate caseload. His cited reasons were for personal health, and that wasn't questioned. His job became superficial during Virginia Kincaid's last year at the university.

She was on track to graduate with top honors from the University of Regina with her Ph.D. in physics. She researched for a full year while writing her thesis.

The Dr. John Archer Library was the primary research building on the university's campus, with the world's best resources at hand. The central computer and research room had wide white columns that rose forty feet in a grand abstract curved design. The ceiling window panels were in a framework that allowed the outside light and gave an illusion of great height.

In one of the computer station cubicles, Virginia was working. Brad had a hard time referring to her as Ginny. She had long since outgrown her childhood nickname and had turned into a beautiful young woman.

"Virginia. How are you doing?"

When she looked, a smile stretched across her face. "Mr. Sheppard! Nice to see you again. I'm doing good. What brings you to the library?"

Brad pulled over a chair and sat. "This will be hard to believe, but I'm looking up various ways of collapsing a black hole."

Virginia smirked. "So, you know what my thesis is all about. So, when you look up information on the subject, you *just* happen to run into me?"

"Okay. Yes, you're right. This isn't a coincidence. I was talking with a friend who works in Vancouver about black holes. Long story short, I said there was, no doubt, a way to destroy one. He disagreed."

"Sorry, Mr. Sheppard. Your friend is correct. As of now, there is no way we know that would destroy a black hole. One theory would be to stop all matter from entering it, which may cause it to stop expanding, and eventually, it would collapse on itself."

"And let me guess, the technology for this to happen does not exist?" Brad had no illusions, but he asked.

"Even if technology were advanced enough to do so, it would be impossible. To stop a black hole, you would have to be close enough to it, but you are subject to the forces it exerts by being close enough to it. Gravity, radiation, and so on.”

“Thank you for spelling out my doom on the bet.” Brad chuckled as he stood. “Thank you for your time. I don’t wish to hold you up. Nice to see you again.”

“You too, Mr. Sheppard.”

“Just call me Brad. Good luck with your studies.”

At his desk in the student services building, Brad found a note from Clement. They had created a message system to arrange a meeting, and with their abilities, the location also included a date, time, and year. He locked the office door from the inside, entered the quantum realm, and arrived at his new condominium in Washington, DC, fourteen days before the black hole was created.

The condo was three times larger than Brad’s apartment in Phoenix. Clement had arranged for it to be furnished, but it wasn’t precisely to Brad’s taste. The fact that a farmer from the 1700s preferred glass and chrome and a modern flair he found amusing. Brad knew he could change the décor should he use the condo. First, he had to ensure there *was* a future before worrying about such details.

Clement had just removed his jacket and put the kettle on for tea. It didn’t take long for them to catch up. After working with the particle accelerator for a few years as a radiation technician, Clement discovered nothing except an appreciation for farming. Clement had also continued to check the future, and none of their efforts had affected the outcome.

Brad tapped his gold ring on the glass table while mulling over an idea. “What if we bring Dr. Kincaid into the problem and show her that time travel is possible? Show her what's going to happen. Virginia is one of the world's leading experts in quantum mechanics. I don't doubt she would have more insight than a farmer and an FBI agent."

Clement paced the living room. "I'm not sure. For all we know, that's maybe why the event happens."

Frustration levels continued to rise. Nothing they seemed to do worked at stopping the black hole from forming.

"Tomorrow, they will experiment, resulting in the double black hole. *The Double*. It will also last point four-six seconds. That time triples the duration of any other black hole created by anyone else."

Brad stopped tapping the ring, and an idea formed. "Somehow, they get more funding based on tomorrow's experiment. What if I can sabotage it? Then they don't get the funding, and they won't be destroying the planet in two weeks."

Clement stopped pacing and grinned. "We have nothing to lose. I'll bring you in as a VIP guest. There are always dozens of them around."

"I'm going to recharge with the stone. I don't want any other issues."

"Good idea, I'll do the same. I'll bring you through security tomorrow."

"I'll wear a suit and shave. No point in being recognized as the former janitor all dressed up."

Brad felt good about the plan to take direct action and ignored the voice inside his head that thought it wasn't a good idea. *What would my subconscious know anyway?* Laughing to himself, he got ready.

Chapter 30

 A jump to a downtown New York shop fitted him for a new pin-striped, blue suit and matching tie within a few hours. The polished shoes completed the image. Despite any misgivings, there were no issues with the credit card for the alias. With a final look in the mirror, Brad nodded. The custom suit would be a perfect disguise many wouldn't see past. After a quick stop at the cabin to recharge from the meteor, Brad arrived at the university.

Clement met him at the front door of the TRIUMF building, signed him in, and clipped a visitor badge on his suit pocket. Clement seemed out of place in a white lab coat, and his photo ID looked like he grimaced for the picture. "We have a few minutes. I'll get you set up in the viewing area."

It seemed a lifetime ago when Brad worked here as a custodian, and he had that same strange feeling adults had when visiting their grade school. Everything seemed smaller and not quite as they remembered it. Then again, he had only worked here for two months, but a lot had happened since then. *Years have passed for me, regardless of the subjective time.*

The particle accelerator's central control room was packed with computer equipment and display screens. The actual cyclotron was mainly used to produce medical isotopes and research for other companies that could afford the price tag associated with its use.

There were two areas for the visitors. The general viewing was on top of a catwalk above the large work area, and the second was roped off behind the technical support with half a dozen seats.

"I have to go and help with the startup monitoring sequence. I'll get you when it's over." Clement moved to his station, and a keyboard emerged from a hidden compartment. Soon he was busy and paid Brad little attention.

Brad sat on the lower level and watched as everyone bustled about at work stations, checking readings on displays and getting ready. He should have expected it, but he was surprised to see Dr. Virginia Kincaid enter. She wore a white lab coat with a skirt underneath. She looked youthful with her hair tied up, and the glasses were new.

She hadn't seen him since the meeting in the library, which happened fifteen years ago for Virginia. That would make her forty-one years old now.

She's matured into a beautiful woman.

He tried to keep his mind on important things and avoid looking at her legs, but the short skirt did nothing to help keep his eyes from wandering. Six people were on the catwalk, and one other joined Brad in the roped-off area. Almost twenty people filled the control center, moving like a well-orchestrated dance routine. Despite the hustle and energy in the room, they didn't bump shoulders.

Dr. Kincaid went to each monitoring station and confirmed they were ready. She turned to her audience and cleared her throat with a last look at her checklist. "Okay, we are about to proceed. We're ready to see if we can monitor Hawking Radiation as a possible energy source and establish quantum fulgurations stability and—"

Dr. Kincaid stopped and stared at Brad. She frowned and appeared to be confused. Brad could see when Virginia remembered him, and a huge smile brought life to her eyes. He couldn't help but grin in return as she blushed. "Sorry, and with their relationship with the event horizon. The procedure will occur too fast for the human eye to follow, but we will be showing still frames on the monitor after it has occurred."

With a final smile at Brad, she returned to supervising the experiment.

Brad studied everything around him, looking for a way to throw a wrench into the works to halt the experiment or sow chaos. It had to be done while he was in the under-time. He couldn't let Virginia distract him from the task at hand. Too much would ride on the outcome.

After everyone confirmed they were ready for the experiment, they had a countdown from ten, just like a New Year's Eve party.

Brad slipped into the timestream on the count of three but didn't travel forward or back. Everyone stayed in position, frozen, as Brad stood. Virginia remained mid-step, and several had funny faces as they counted down with the team. When Brad traveled backward through time, everything had a black-and-white twisting pattern, turning a brilliant white forward.

With the time-stop, everything was a subtle shade of red. The floors, walls, people, everything was tinged like he wore rose-colored glasses. Clement was also frozen in time, but had an orange outline instead of the same uniform red color.

An effect of the quantum abilities? Brad wasn't sure.

As he looked at the computer monitors, Brad realized he had no idea what they represented or how to influence them for a negative experiment. Brad knew of a maintenance room in the hallway that allowed entry into the cyclotron housing area. He never had any occasion to go in there for any work. It was off-limits to the custodial staff.

Once in the hall, he stopped at the security door and paused. It was locked with a passcode required on the LED screen. It could take days to stay in the quantum realm until someone entered the room. There had to be a more straightforward solution. He thought to try the original plan and abandoned the door. Brad returned to the control room and went over to the connection wall to the particle accelerator. When he wanted something to stop working, the easiest solution was to unplug it.

A large metal box appeared to be a junction for the control room with many wires. The next problem, Brad didn't know which one was which.

"Someone should label this mess."

Randomly, he grabbed a cluster of cords resembling a power plug for a computer but eight times the size. The quantum world exploded as he pulled and twisted the thick black cables.

When Brad's hand wrapped around the cord, a lightning bolt struck him in the chest. At first, there wasn't any pain, but that quickly changed. A visible blue and white arc of energy flickered the length of his body while the other end connected to the cyclotron's metal panel. Instead of quickly dissipating, the intensity steadily grew. He tried to let go, but the muscles in his hand wouldn't respond.

It felt like the recruit training at Quantico when he was a test subject for the Taser demonstration. Only a million times worse. His nerves were on fire, and his jaw had clenched tight. He tried to scream, but it only came out as a whimper.

After what seemed an eternity in the quantum realm, the energy heaved, and Brad was tossed back several feet when it exploded. He was hurtled past the seating area and into the hallway.

He slid six feet on his back before bouncing off the wall. After struggling, Brad shook off the discomfort and realized he would be fine. The pain dissipated, and he would be fine besides the growing lump on his head. The red tinge remained in the time-stop.

"What the hell was that?" There was an echo in his voice, and the experience left him feeling groggy. He had worse hangovers and ignored the discomfort. Brad resumed his seat in the control room, but there were differences.

He was the only one present.

All the technicians, Clement, and even Dr. Kincaid, were gone. He checked his sense of time in the quantum realm, but it was scrambled and not working correctly.

I'm in the right location, but when?

Brad stepped out of the quantum realm into real-time and felt his chest. There wasn't any damage where the electrical arc had struck. The only injuries were a dull ache around the gold ring and a bump on his head.

He walked across the hallway toward the staff lounge from the control room. Brad slipped on the wet floor two steps outside but regained his footing. The dress shoes had little traction. A strange feeling of déjà vu made him glance over his right shoulder down the hall.

A man in gray overalls mopped the floor with his head down. He was relatively large, with short dark hair. The wet mop flicked side to side as he walked backward. The janitor never looked up and remained focused on the task at hand.

Shit! That's me.

After hours of discussions with Clement over paradoxes and disrupting a timeline, the last thing he wanted to do was meet himself. Gingerly, he stepped across the hall and into the lounge, grabbed a water bottle, and quickly slid into the quantum realm. Since he recalled the footprints on the wet floor, Brad re-oriented himself in the timestream. The memory acted as a calendar date; from there, he moved through the white light and returned when he disappeared.

Everyone had moved, but only very slightly as he sat. In subjective time, he had disappeared for less than a second. Hopefully, not enough time for anyone to notice, especially with the countdown still on.

"… one!"

Everyone cheered when the experiment ended, and the data poured in through the sensors. One of the younger technicians shouted excitedly and pointed at the overhead monitor. "Check it out!"

Virginia gasped as the information was revealed before confirming the visual and data results. The central monitor above the workstations showed a thermal image of the black hole.

Instead of one black hole being created, *two* images were on the monitor, mirroring each other. The cheering resumed again, but Brad could hear Dr. Kincaid the clearest. "We have a double event horizon lasting almost four seconds!"

The colored photo on the wide-screen monitor looked like two inkblots facing each other, with a broad color spectrum of energy surrounding each image. Brad wasn't sure about their size, but they were supposed to be larger than typically produced.

Brad placed the water bottle on the floor and clapped with everyone else. He caught Clement's eye, and they shrugged. They would talk shortly.

Suddenly his face was buried in blond hair as Virginia's arms wrapped around his chest. "Mr. Sheppard! I'm so glad you were here. It's good to see you again."

Brad couldn't help but grin at her excitement. "I'm fairly sure it is safe to call me Brad now. I, however, must insist on calling you Doctor. It seems you are doing quite well. Congratulations, Doctor Kincaid."

Virginia blushed, and Brad wasn't sure, but he hoped it was from the experiment.

"Thank you! How are you here? Do you—" Virginia was cut off as she was congratulated by three executives from the elevated viewing area.

"I'll see you later. Go enjoy your success."

She flashed him a quick smile and mouthed *I'm sorry* before she was dragged off again. After returning the visitor pass, Brad went outside, and soon enough, Clement joined him. The lab coat was gone, and he was dressed in his jeans and T-shirt. Brad could tell by the look on Clement's face that he was worried.

"Something happened." It wasn't a question. Without saying anything, Clement knew.

"When I tried to interfere, electricity hit me while I was *in* the quantum realm. It knocked me off my ass and shot me backward through time."

"Mother Mary." Clement stepped back in shock as he struggled to comprehend. "Far as I know, that's impossible. Either that was time keeping events on track, or it resulted from the particle accelerator. I know the accelerator is shielded, and what happened isn't possible."

"Possible or not, it happened. It sent me back, and I landed in the same location, but back-time. I saw myself in the hall, but he didn't see me."

Clement shook his head. "We just don't know enough about the physics and machinery used. Even if we went back and tried to learn for decades, I'm sure it would be beyond my understanding."

Agreeing, Brad added, "Same here. So, is it time for plan C?"

"Your call. But I think it's the right decision. If not, we can always try and make adjustments later."

"Hopefully, things won't get worse."

Clement laughed. "What could be worse than the whole planet getting sucked into a black hole?"

Chapter 31

 Brad entered the Vancouver International Airport from the parking garage and rode the motorized walkway into the main terminal., Native paintings and sculptures were displayed throughout, giving Brad a sense of being in an art gallery. He took a moment to appreciate a beautifully decorated fifty-foot totem pole followed by twelve-foot tall painted wood carvings. As airports go, this was one of the nicer ones. Despite the bustle and lineups for security and gates, the high windowed roof and open spaces made it feel less crowded.

The lounge was restricted to those who upgraded their flights or paid for the privilege. Many didn't want to hang out in the general area and wished for a quiet space. Each major airline had a private waiting room, including finger foods and an open bar for the patrons.

Bypassing security and the ticket checker for the Air Canada lounge wasn't an issue for someone who could alter time. Inside, Virginia Kincaid reclined on an oversized leather couch while typing on a laptop. Her carry-on luggage sat at her feet, along with the empty laptop case. A half-eaten sandwich and a bottle of water sat on the side table.

Virginia had kicked off her running shoes and sat with her legs crossed. She wore track pants with the UoR logo along the pant leg and a matching gray hoodie.

Before sitting on the other end of the couch, Brad unbuttoned the suit jacket. He waited for Virginia to notice him. After a minute, he gave up. "It looks like you're rather busy."

Virginia nearly fumbled to keep her laptop from spilling while turning white like a ghost. A range of emotions flickered across her face before her eyes narrowed. "Hello … yes, I *am* busy. Either I have a stalker problem, or this is the strangest coincidence imaginable."

Brad didn't want to upset her. "First, I guarantee I'm not stalking you. I'm here because I need a quick conversation about your work."

Virginia said, "How can I help you? I don't have too much time before my flight."

"I have a simple question that you should be able to answer." Brad cleared his throat. "Is time travel possible?"

Virginia placed the laptop in the case and leaned forward, elbows on her knees. "Yes. That's the quick answer, without getting complicated."

Somewhat shocked, Brad echoed her answer. "Yes?"

"There are two ways to time travel. First, we are traveling through time as we sit here. In a linear progression forward, at a one-to-one ratio. The second method involves moving an object on the external curve of a gravitational source. Time dilation occurs. Farther from a large mass, like the planet Earth, time will be slower than an object on the ground. The change in time isn't significant, but there's a difference."

Despite being in just one direction, Brad never thought about being *normal* as traveling through time. Her statement solidified any of his misgivings. "What do you think about traveling through time, like stepping through a door into the past or future?"

"Impossible. First, if there were time travelers, they would already be here. Wouldn't they?" Virginia laughed. "We've talked about this many times at the university. Trust me. It hasn't happened."

"How open would you be to find out the truth?"

Virginia looked skeptical and stood to leave. "Sorry, Mr. Sheppard. I have to be going. I have several meetings to try and secure another grant and funding to continue the research."

Holding out his hand, Brad implored. "Please. One more minute, then I won't bother you ever again if you wish."

Virginia pushed her glasses on top of her head and nodded.

"Could you please pass me your water bottle?"

Not understanding, she handed it over. Brad could tell Virginia was prepared to run should this go awry. "What's going to happen is *not* a trick, and please remain calm. Okay?"

Virginia looked unsure. "Okay."

Brad smiled and casually tossed the plastic bottle in the air five feet before them. Simultaneously, he laid his left hand on Virginia's shoulder.

Virginia's eyes followed the container, and she instinctively put her hand out to catch it. She gasped when the bottle stopped in mid-air and hung suspended. The water inside the bottle remained still.

Everything had a red-colored tinge, and she turned to Brad in shock. Virginia didn't notice his hand on her shoulder. "How did you do that? That's an amazing trick!"

"Look around, don't panic. It isn't a trick."

Virginia glanced at the lounge, and the background humming noise of the airport and other passengers was absent. Everyone in the waiting area was frozen in mid-motion. The passengers, the bartender, and the waitresses had turned into statues.

"Oh, my God!" Virginia had trouble breathing despite the assurances not to panic, and she rubbed her eyes and blinked several times. Brad tried to be sympathetic. It wasn't every day the laws of the universe changed for one person. Virginia broke contact with Brad's hand when she stood, and the noise, color, and movement resumed like someone had hit play on a paused movie.

The water bottle fell to the floor at her feet. Turning to Brad, she could barely formulate words. "How? What the actual fuck is going on?"

"Time travel is possible, Virginia. There's a huge problem that I'm trying to fix, and on the whole, it isn't going too well. Please sit back down."

Brad picked up the water bottle before passing it over to Virginia. She tossed it a few inches to see if it would stay. It fell back into her hands. After doing that a few times, she gave up.

"If it is a trick, it's a perfect one." She quietly scanned the lounge to see who else may be in on the prank.

"Sorry, it's real. We have all the time in the world. Would you like me to explain?"

Taking a quick sip, she nodded.

"Put your shoes on, grab your things. Don't worry. We can be back here in a second if you like."

Brad knew she could not sit still for long and thought walking would help. Virginia looked at the information board for her flight. "That would be good. I can't miss my flight, though. I board soon."

"I promise. Just take my hand."

Brad waited, and after a moment's hesitation, Virginia picked up her things and placed her hand in his. "Okay, I'm ready."

Brad pulled them into the quantum realm and straight into a time stream without warning. Virginia screamed and crushed Brad's hand as the twisting nether of black and white images flickered by them.

"Relax, we're traveling backward and to a slightly different location. As far as I know, we are suspended in a quantum state."

"How can we talk? According to what I've read, this makes no sense or is even possible!" Virginia quickly moved past her fears and reached out to touch a tendril of quantum energy as it passed, but her hand went right through it. She tried to see everything at once and make sense of the imagery.

"You'll break your neck if you twist it too much. Almost there." Brad squeezed her hand to reassure her.

Once Brad stepped out of the quantum realm, he landed on a freshly cut lawn at the side of a country road. A white church stood on the edge of a field in the town. The area was filled with acres of wheat that stretched to the horizon. A warm summer breeze blew in from the south, and the chirping birds were unusually loud as they dove from view into the grain. Plumes of pollen swirled in the air before settling.

It was late evening when Virginia was ready to board her flight in Vancouver. The sun shone in the morning sky moments later, and the seasons had changed. She shuddered as the whole experience crashed on her at once.

Virginia dropped her bag and gasped. "How did you do this?"

Brad didn't expect the punch in the arm after Virginia swung, and it stung. "What was that for?"

"How did you do this?" She repeated her question and gestured to the buildings, fields, and homes.

"Time travel is real. It's that simple."

Virginia stood outside the Lutheran Church in Yellow Grass, Saskatchewan. "This looks like where I went to church as a little girl. Before my family moved to Regina."

"Hold on. Just watch."

Virginia stood shoulder to shoulder, holding Brad's hand when the church doors opened, and a crowd left. A couple walked out with a little girl holding her father's hand, and the woman had a baby on her hip as they descended the steps. They were the first family out, and soon the others followed as they headed home.

"That's my parents and baby brother, and me. We were always first out because I always had to go to the bathroom, and we didn't live too far," Virginia whispered, lost in memories. Tears rolled off her cheeks as she watched most of the town empty out of the church. Her family walked across the street and entered a small white bungalow.

Brad tried not to notice her soft hand in his, and she didn't let go. Virginia closed her eyes and took a deep breath of the country air. "I'm ready to go somewhere and talk about this. There is no way this could be a hoax. Unless I'm dreaming."

"You're awake. I know the place to start my explanations. It's a little rustic, but it isn't that bad."

Brad wrapped the quantum energies about them, and the church faded to a memory. The destination was becoming a pleasant refuge and growing on him for some strange reason.

Chapter 32

"So, you're telling me time travel is *actually* real?"

Brad grabbed a handful of hay off the floor and tossed it in the air. It landed in a beam of sunlight shining through the wooden slats of the barn. "It's hard to believe, but yes. It's real."

"How?"

"It started in 1783 ..." Brad led them over to the hay bales on the barn's end, and they sat while he went through the familiar story. It felt strange to be on the property wearing a suit, but Virginia seemed comfortable in her track pants and sweatshirt.

Once he was done, Virginia brushed her pants clean. "Can I see where the meteor landed?"

"Of course, it isn't far."

Virginia occasionally stopped to look at the scenery as they crossed the main field. When Brad arrived at the hole in the ground, she didn't hesitate to jump into the depression and measure the area. Virginia brushed the dirt aside and examined the results of the impact.

"I thought the damage would have been more extensive for a stone of that size." She held a hand for Brad to help her out. "Can I see the meteor?"

Virginia appeared to accept the new reality as they crossed the field toward the cabin. He expected everything from flat-out denial to conspiracy theories. Refuting the evidence is hard, especially when seeing and feeling it.

Brad wasn't surprised to see Clement in the cabin. He had lit a small fire in the kitchen and sat at the table waiting. Despite knowing one of her technicians worked on the project to gather information, she wasn't shocked to find Clement.

"Nice to see you here, but how did you know where we are?"

"I checked a few other places, but it's easy to figure out where Brad would go." Clement stood and gestured for her to sit.

Virginia had to ask. "How did you know the *time* we would be here? Besides just the location?"

"As far as I know, this place exists only because we created it. It's not part of actual history but based on the farm I owned."

Virginia looked shocked. "You mean that you've created your *own* dimension?"

Clement shrugged. "I consider this more of an alternate timeline that we never pursued. While we are here, it exists. If we stray too far from this place, time behaves strangely."

Brad remembered the ghost images. "It's somewhat overlaid with reality but separate if that helps."

"This changes the theory of relativity and how we even think about the universe and natural laws." Virginia rubbed her eyes, still finding it hard to believe.

"Except you can't mention this to anyone." Clement wanted to make sure it was clear and insisted her silence was one of the conditions.

"I don't think anyone would believe me anyway. Can I see the meteor now? I think I've been pretty patient."

Brad chuckled at her enthusiasm, lifted the cellar door, and lit the lantern with a piece of tinder from the fire. Soon he battled the cobwebs as he crossed the cellar floor. Virginia kindly allowed him to lead.

Brad knelt in front of the wooden table and concentrated. The concussive wave knocked them back a step and startled Virginia let out a little scream. That moment was quickly forgotten as she walked over to the stone.

"Is it safe to touch?"

Neither Brad nor Clement mentioned how they bonded to the stone, and they didn't want that to happen with Virginia. Circumstances happened to throw them together on this matter, but they figured adding a third to the equation would be too much. The secret of the rings would stay with them as long as required.

"Go ahead." Brad leaned forward and placed both hands on the meteor to show her it was okay to touch. As she placed her right hand on the stone, Virginia waited for something to happen, looked at Brad, and shrugged. She was disappointed the stone was just that for her—a cold, dark rock in a farmhouse cellar.

"The universe is infinite in size and, therefore, infinite possibilities. Right now, I have no idea what this meteor is or its properties." Virginia was disappointed.

Brad guided her back to the kitchen. Clement hid the stone behind the quantum curtain before joining them.

"Knowing what will happen, I won't continue the experiment. That way, we can avoid any black holes."

Clement cleared his throat. "I hate to say this, but we have previously tried a few variations of that scenario. Time doesn't like to be altered."

He didn't want to detail some of his previous attempts to change the timeline. Virginia had been bombarded with information, and Brad was reasonably sure she didn't need to know about Clement's drastic effort.

"History and the future do *not* like to be changed, and the project still goes forward with the same results whether you are involved or not."

Brad tapped his ring on the table while they began a brainstorming session. After an hour, the initial excitement wore off, and Virginia had trouble staying awake. It would be the middle of the night for her, and she didn't have the stone's abilities.

They relocated to the condo in Washington, DC, and Virginia slept in the spare room while Brad and Clement jumped six hours ahead.

When she woke and rejoined them, Brad handed her a fresh cup of coffee. "I had a feeling you would be getting up about now."

"Thank you." Virginia had a sip, and they sat around the dining room table. "I had time to think about a few things."

Clement nodded. "Do you have a solution?"

She reached for a pad of paper and a pen and sketched. After a minute, she flipped it around so they could see. Pointing at the first diagram Virginia had drawn a rotational black hole. It looked like a bubble in the middle of an old record, with everything spiraling inward. "A magnetic field around a black hole aids matter to be consumed by the event horizon. It draws and accelerates particles inward. The *Synchrotron* effect."

Next, she drew a picture of the globe on an axis tilt and continued. "The Earth rotates, and the liquid metal inside the planet causes a magnetic field. Black holes have no magnetic field generated, but the particle accelerator magnets may aid it and draw in the matter exponentially. The mass of the black hole could outgrow the area, and instead of consuming just small particles, it will take in *all* matter."

"So, if we can shut down the magnets in the particle accelerator, this would stop feeding the black hole?" Brad looked at the diagrams and knew he was lost.

"Yes, then the normal gravity of the planet will cause it to break up and evaporate."

Clement asked, "How do we shut down the magnets in the accelerator without disrupting the experiment?"

Virginia drew a circle on the paper and then an arrow going the other way. "Reverse the polarity in the cyclotron. Get as close to the event as possible, then flip the polarity on the last section."

"Due to the event's disruption, we cannot get within three days." Brad didn't want to relive diving away through time after the black hole went off.

"That would mean it's bending time and space in a curve to the quantum level. There isn't enough study available to say if that's normal." Virginia shrugged.

Brad mentioned. "I couldn't get into the control area during your last experiment last time."

Virginia grinned. "I know the passcode for the door. Inside has too much technical equipment for the cleaning staff to be around."

Brad had briefed her on his custodial position and the months spent learning at the TRIUMF building. He had never run into Virginia due to the shift differences. It was something he wanted to avoid. Brad couldn't sit for long and paced while thinking about the possibilities.

Virginia looked at them both, concern on her face. "Right now, I don't even have funding to continue the experiments. I was off to a startup company in California to see about a grant."

"How much were you looking to get?" Brad had no idea of the dollar amount to operate the experiments.

"Anywhere between fifty million to one hundred million would set us up for years."

Clement shrugged. "How about we give you the money so we can move forward?"

Virginia's jaw dropped. "Holy crap! Are you serious? How can you have that much money?" She trailed off as she realized she was talking to time travelers and that much would be effortless to accumulate.

Brad had sent the FBI on a hunt to investigate and find out who supplied the funding grant. He didn't want any trails to lead back to himself. "Virginia, do you know how to make an offshore shell company?"

"I don't, but I know someone who can—my father. He handled the accounting for the farmers in my hometown, but he landed a job in Regina for an accounting firm. He ran it for many years and has just retired. There isn't anything that he doesn't know about accounting."

"How about we stop by and set that up? I want the grant to remain hidden so that the money won't come back with my name. Then we can jump forward, check out the particle accelerator, and see if we can reverse the polarity. We don't need to be closer than three days, but we can check if the black hole still comes into existence from the quantum realm without getting close."

"Sounds good. I'm ready." Virginia finished her cold coffee, then stood, and Brad touched her shoulder. Instantly, they were sliding within a time stream, traveling through a black-and-white storm of images. Clement followed, and Brad was excited to try something new. They both were.

The three arrived in Regina, Saskatchewan, and they met up with her father at his office under Virginia's direction. Her father was still head of the accounting firm before his retirement. George Kincaid didn't resemble the mental image of an accountant. He stood six-foot-five inches, and when they shook hands, Brad had to make sure nothing was broken from the firm grip.

"Dad, this is Brad and Clement. They want to pay for my research grant but wish to remain anonymous so that nothing can be traced."

George peered at them through his black-framed glasses and nodded. "As long as there is nothing illegal, I can help."

His voice rumbled into the baritone range, and he studied the two men with his daughter. Poppa bear was protective of his cub.

"No, sir. We want to avoid all scrutiny from any in-depth investigation. That's all."

The large man turned to his daughter. "Do you trust them?"

Virginia chuckled. "Of course, Dad, or I wouldn't have brought them here."

Slowly he nodded. "Good enough for me. Okay, I'm going to need some information first. It may take me a few days. I'll need to call in some favors."

Neither Brad nor Clement needed to know the details, and they wanted to give Virginia some time alone with her parents. They jumped two days forward after supplying the information required.

George Kincaid was true to his word, handling the transactions and setting up the accounts with the utmost discretion. When they arrived to pick up Virginia, they could see tears in his eyes as he hugged his daughter. He was a good man.

Virginia had a few tears in her eyes as they left his office.

Brad squeezed her shoulder before moving up-time through the quantum realm and white light to the university particle accelerator. They were just outside the three-day window for the event. As agreed, they arrived at night when the chance to run into anyone was low.

Virginia led them to the maintenance door and punched in her security passcode. A long corridor stretched to either side and ran the length of the hall. It was filled with servers and computer equipment designed to help the cyclotron and monitor results.

Virginia turned to the right and led them to the end of the corridor, where the magnetic controls were arranged through a twelve-foot control board. The command center was the size of a car.

"This is the magnetic control unit (MCU), and it electronically controls the particle accelerator and sends information back to the control room for monitoring."

Flipping a series of switches at one end, Virginia pushed in a long flat section of the panel, and Brad heard a muffled click. A keyboard emerged in a whirl of internal gears, and a small screen flickered to life above it.

Within a minute, she finished and pushed the keyboard back into the housing unit. "I just turned off the sensors and switched the polarity for the last R-34 section of the cyclotron. The control room monitor will read everything as correct."

Clement looked around at all the equipment and shrugged. "Only one way to see if it was successful."

"I'm ready if you are." Virginia turned off the light.

Brad brought Virginia with them as they stepped into the quantum realm. Slowly they moved forward up-time to the event. Brad gave Clement a thumbs-up sign when they passed the old barrier. They were in new territory.

Clement grinned. "This is good so far."

Brad gave him a wink as they moved forward.

"Do you guys think this worked?" Virginia slid her hand into Brad's and gripped tight.

When a white light completely engulfed them, Brad hit the same familiar invisible wall. The barrier wasn't gone but had just moved forward in time. This new barrier felt different than the previous one. Brad struggled to push forward, and Clement did the same.

"We have to get closer," Brad spoke through clenched teeth as he strained. "Any information may help."

It could have been an eternity or a split second as they battled their abilities against the forces of the universe. However, their efforts were rewarded as the blockade fractured against their onslaught.

"Yes!" Brad cheered, and Clement laughed as they raced forward into the future.

Unfortunately, their joy was short-lived.

A blue arc of electricity struck Brad first, then arced through Virginia and grounded in Clement's chest. It flickered up and down their bodies, chaining them with a current of power. It was similar to what Brad had previously experienced, only fifty-fold. It held him immobile, and then the pain started. Virginia didn't have any abilities, and she was knocked unconscious immediately.

The agony could be felt at the cellular level, freezing them in place. Brad couldn't tell how long the moment lasted—time held no meaning.

Brad screamed and retained his grip on Virginia's hand. The mind-numbing pain filled every thought, and there was no escape.

When the explosion of energy traveled along the length of the blue electrical current, it was almost a blessing. One type of torture was exchanged for another as the force hurled them *backward* through the black-and-white twisting nether of time. Brad lost physical contact with Virginia as they were flung head over heels.

Someone yelled, and Brad wasn't sure who it was. It could have been him. The pain had scrambled his brain. "No!"

Clement and Brad tried to reach her, but it was too late.

Virginia's journey in the quantum realm was cut short as she was suddenly ejected from the timestream. Faster than the blink of an eye, she vanished from sight.

Brad was disorientated and became nauseous as they struggled to pit their abilities against the fundamental law of the universe. Relief arrived when their minds couldn't cope with all the stimuli, and they shut down. Travel throughout the realm was only possible with conscious efforts and the stone's power. A brief golden nimbus surrounded them before being ejected from the time stream.

Chapter 33

Brad rolled onto his hands and knees, swallowing several times to keep from vomiting. By the sounds of it, Clement wasn't as successful. A warm summer breeze blew in his face. Thankfully, he was upwind.

After what they had gone through, they were lucky to be alive. Clement swore under his breath, and Brad opened his eyes. He had double vision, and then slowly, everything came into focus. Neither had the energy to spare, and they focused on recovery.

Brad knelt on all fours at the edge of a clearing. The grass was damp under his fingers, and he could feel the moisture seeping through his knees. Cedar trees clustered together on the far side. The morning sun had just cleared the treetops, and a chorus of birds sang from the shelter of the thick branches. No cars or planes could be heard—only Clement trying to empty his stomach again and the wildlife.

Brad tentatively reached out with his senses, and to his surprise, he could still sense the quantum realm, which meant his abilities were still there. As he struggled to his feet, vertigo threatened to unbalance him. Brad recovered within a few minutes, and he helped Clement to his feet.

"This was still better than last time we were punted across the timelines." The pounding headache made Brad wince with every word.

Wiping his mouth on the lower half of his T-shirt, Clement agreed. "Barely."

"Can you sense *when* we are? I have my abilities, but I have no sense of direction."

Clement concentrated. "I'm having problems pinpointing anything. I can safely guess we are far from any civilization."

"What do you think happened to Virginia? How will we find her?"

The image of her being kicked out of the timestream replayed in his mind. He couldn't help but groan. *I was responsible for her.*

"She doesn't have our abilities. I don't know what happened, but I imagine she's fine. Most likely lost between three days from the event happening and wherever we are currently."

Brad surveyed the field and raised his hands in the air in frustration. "Okay, let's figure out where and *when* we are. I think our best bet is to find Virginia. With her ideas, we were closer to the event, and with her, I think we stand a better chance of stopping the black hole from forming."

"Agreed. There was definite progress."

Brad pulled them both into the quantum realm and held them there in an attempt to become orientated. A quick trip fore-time showed no change to the scenery except for a slight shift in the tree line and the weather.

Clement frowned. "I think we are *much* farther back than we think. That was a jump of approximately one hundred years. Let's keep going."

This time Clement joined Brad, and they both went into the white brilliance, heading to their future. While traveling, Brad sensed time was not passing in its usual manner. In subjective time they could be back in a particular place within half a second, and no one would be aware they had left. However, this specific journey seemed to stretch on without end. Brad signaled Clement to halt their efforts when it was clear they both neared the end of their patience.

After stepping out of the quantum realm, neither was surprised to discover they were still in the clearing beside the woods. The wood line appeared slightly closer, although Brad wasn't sure. *Are the trees different?* It wasn't easy to tell.

Clement didn't have any answers. "I know we traveled forward in time, but it doesn't appear that way. We're like a hamster on a wheel."

Brad smirked at the analogy. "I want to try something else. We haven't done this outside the cabin, but I guess there is no reason why it shouldn't work here."

Brad knelt, held out his hands, and concentrated on parting the curtain of reality. He tried to call the stone from where it usually remained in its quantum state. Instead of the meteor appearing instantly with the concussive force of air, something new happened.

The air above the ground shimmered and distorted like a heat wave above hot asphalt. The gold ring on his finger pulsed, and a warmth spread throughout his hand.

Surprised, Brad relaxed and started to let the energies dissipate.

"No, keep going!"

Brad refocused at Clement's insistence, and soon the shimmering in the air resumed.

"Do you see it?" Brad yelled with excitement.

Through the ripples, they could see the meteor. It was like viewing the stone at the bottom of a pond. Despite the distorted image, it was recognizable. After a minute, the view solidified, and the wooden table came into focus. Not only was the stone clear, but the damp smell of the cellar made Brad's nose twitch. The former FBI agent reached out a hand into the large opening.

"I can feel the cool cellar air. This isn't just an image."

"This may be our only way out of here." Clement glanced at Brad. "Are you willing to take it?"

It didn't take Brad long to reach the same conclusion and nod in agreement. "I'll hold it open. You pull me through. Ready when you are."

Clement took several steps and then ran forward. His arms encircled Brad in a football tackle, picked him up, and flung them both through the portal.

It closed behind them with a loud *pop*.

The birds in the cedar forest were silent for a brief moment before resuming their high-pitched warbles.

*****

Virginia awoke in her bed at the student housing at the University of Regina with a sharp intake of breath. When her eyes shot open, there was a moment of confusion as memories warred with each other and threatened to overwhelm her. *Was this real?* She groaned and pulled the pillow over her head, then screamed.

The events would be unbelievable if she didn't go through it herself. One day, everything was ordinary with work and her research. Suddenly, Virginia was escorted through time by an FBI agent *and* a farmer from the 1700s, which blew her mind. At any moment, she expected to wake up in a psychiatric hospital with a series of doctors asking her questions as they fitted her for a straitjacket. She was twenty-three years into her past, in her old bed. It even *smelled* like her old bed.

How does this make sense?

She was excited to work on quantum mechanics, prove or disprove theories, and push scientific boundaries. However, when asked to help stop an actual black hole from destroying everything, she appeared to have issues. The main problem with black holes was that everything was theoretical. Some of the smartest people in history have pushed the boundaries of science, but in the end, most of it was just ideas. *Great* and educated ideas all the same.

"Brad? Clement?" she called out, despite the sense of being alone.

Everything was as she remembered, down to her first-year class schedule taped to the wall above the desk piled high with textbooks. The straps from her green backpack lay over the chair, and a few course books were still inside. Taking off her glasses, Virginia closed her eyes and breathed deeply. She could smell the faint aroma of incense that her roommate always lit after smoking out her bedroom window.

The Kīsik Towers had two or four-bedroom apartments, and Virginia had known someone from her high school looking for a roommate. Virginia debated moving into a student residence or living at home with her parents less than a twenty-minute drive away. However, with her course load and the late hours anticipated, she thought it would be best. The views from the fourteenth floor of downtown Regina were excellent, nothing like she had at home.

Virginia knew she couldn't stay in bed forever and slowly examined the apartment. Everything appeared to be the same, down to the smallest detail. From the kitchen window, Virginia thought the views were still lovely, but she was used to seeing the Rocky Mountains of British Columbia.

There was one significant difference between her current situation and her memories of the past. She appeared to be the only human alive in this strange pseudo-world. She could see Wascana Lake and the Trans-Canada Highway to the east and the Parkway to the west from the living room window. For the first time in the history of the world, there was no traffic. In fact, there were no cars or people. A glance at the clear blue sky confirmed the lack of aircraft. There was traffic on any given day, especially at nine o'clock in the morning. That was a fact of life.

Frustrated, she pounded her fist on the window, which vibrated like a drum throughout the apartment. Virginia sat on the futon and tried to calm down and think.

"First order of business. Where am I?"

That question wasn't as simple to answer as she thought. After patting the futon and studying the apartment, Virginia rephrased the question. "I should be saying, *when* am I?"

Brad had shown her Clement's farm and cabin, and she knew they were not visiting the actual property back in time but an alternate reality. One that they somehow had created.

"So," she concluded. "What I see isn't real."

While drinking with her roommate one night, Virginia used the coffee table's edge to open her beer instead of a bottle opener. Running her finger over the crescent mark left on the table, Virginia was amazed it was there. The details of this alternate reality or universe were perfect. Everything seemed so real that she couldn't help but call out.

"Hello? I'm ready to be saved now!"

Not surprisingly, there was no reply.

Virginia decided to make the best of it, unsure if it were an alternate universe, her world (but devoid of people) trapped within her mind, or something else she was unaware of. She would have to deal with it later. "Okay, time to stop talking to myself and go out and explore."

Smiling at her last statement, she left the apartment and knocked on several doors up and down her hallway. Two flats were locked, but most were open. It felt strange to look inside the other units. Regardless, no one was home. The elevators also didn't work. Virginia wasn't surprised when the button failed to light up. They had always broken down when she was a student.

Why should now be any different?

Once downstairs, Virginia stepped outside and enjoyed the moment. The sun felt good on her face, and the light breeze blew her blond hair across her eyes. She thought that she was alone, but on closer examination, she wasn't.

Out front of the apartment building, trees grew along the sidewalk in large square boxes. Darting in and around the branches were flocks of sparrows. The chirps and songs lifted the dark cloud on Virginia's heart as she watched their antics.

"Good morning, little birds."

Smiling, Virginia took her time and explored the little shops and cafés scattered over the campus. It looked like everyone had just stepped out and would be back momentarily. A sampling of the food in the coolers took the edge off her growling stomach. It was fresh and hadn't spoiled.

A newspaper in the Charlies convenience store confirmed the date—end of her first year of university, on 22 May 2003. Virginia knew the time period and remembered it well. Her exams were about to begin, and she had aced them. The novelty soon wore off. Exploring the empty shops creeped her out, and she found herself in front of the campus library.

Decades of her life were spent researching. That was one of her strong suits. There had to be an explanation and a way to deal with the black hole. She had all the time in the world and the whole library to herself. With the sun on her face and the birds singing, she knew Brad and Clement would find her. She was full of hope. If time travel was possible, then so was her rescue.

It was just a matter of how *long* it would take.

Chapter 34

Clement's knee landed on his kidney, and the air whooshed out of his lungs as Brad's face skidded across the cellar dirt floor. Clement's head collided with the wall with a hollow *thunk*. Despite the rough landing and pain, Brad was all smiles. "That's a relief."

Clement held out a hand and helped Brad to his feet. "Sorry about that."

"The alternative was worse." Brad wiped the dust off his face and clothing.

"I'll look for Virginia. Back in a second."

Clement stepped into the quantum realm while Brad went to the kitchen. The pitcher was full, and the water was still cold and refreshing. As Brad sat at the table, Clement appeared and shook his head.

"Nothing. I checked all along the timeline."

Brad wasn't too surprised and drummed his fingers on the tabletop while thinking about the possibilities. A feeling of dread settled in his stomach, and he tried to remain positive.

"What do you figure that temporary prison was?" Clement joined him at the table and poured water into his tin cup.

"I have no idea. It was like being stuck in a moment. There was no beginning or end. The place just *was*." Brad had a hunch of what that place could have been, but he didn't know how to describe it adequately. It reminded him of a scratch on a record that would loop the same music repeatedly. The glitch in time would have trapped them forever.

"How do we find Virginia?" Clement stared into his water.

"Could we grab her before she was knocked back with us?" Brad was throwing out ideas while he thought through the problem.

"I'm fairly sure it would be impossible to find her within the timestream. We've traveled back and forth through the area countless times, yet we have never passed ourselves. That's what we would have to do. Talk with ourselves and Virginia, and convince them we are right. Since that didn't happen, I doubt we could do it." Clement slumped in the chair and ran a hand through his hair. They were both frustrated.

"Since we can't track her through the timestream, we have to find a way to track her when she came out." Brad gave voice to a thought that had been nagging him. "Why does the stone always appear in this cellar? Why can't we summon it elsewhere? When I tried to call it to us, a portal opened here."

Clement tapped his gold ring on the table and ran a finger over the gemstone. "I think it's anchored here in some way. When I moved it from the woods, I noticed strange things. At times, I couldn't lift or barely move it. I've moved bigger and heavier stones from my field. However, once I moved it back to the farm in my wheelbarrow, my first thoughts were to hide it. So, I placed the meteor in the cellar."

Clement pointed to the cellar door. "I managed to roll the stone here, but it became light as a feather when I moved it down the stairs. I picked it up with one hand and carried it."

Remembering the stone's size, Brad wasn't sure he could move it easily, let alone with one hand. "Something changed the properties of the meteor."

He felt like he was on to something. The familiar feeling he used to have when he worked a case came back. Excitement. When in doubt, follow the evidence.

After opening the hatch, Brad stood before the low table. After a minute, Clement joined him after placing the lantern on the nail. "What are you thinking?"

Instead of answering, Brad parted the energy curtain hiding the stone. The familiar gust of displaced air rocked the lantern back and forth. Clement stopped it from moving.

Deep in concentration, Brad laid both hands on the stone, and waited. The interior light flickered deep within the rock, intensifying into a strobe. The energy glowed where Brad's palms made contact, pulsing to an unknown beat.

Clement grunted at the results. "This is new."

Instead of the meteor disappearing, it shrank in size from two feet across to fourteen inches at the widest point. Brad readjusted his position and brought his hands up and underneath the stone. He quickly cradled it along a forearm. The meteor diminished further in size until it was twelve inches across. Brad held it out and grinned.

Clement watched in amazement. "How did you do that?"

Brad shrugged and tried to explain. "If the meteor were heavy and very light at other times, that would go against what we know about gravity. Gravity should always be equal on an object, that I know for sure."

Brad handed the stone over to Clement and continued. "So, all I did was push the middle of the stone into the quantum realm, but not the outside. That should have altered how much the stone weighed and its size. The entire stone is still there but is out of phase with us."

The farmer easily held the stone in one hand. It barely weighed ten pounds. "How can this help us?"

Brad smiled. "As to how, I'm not sure yet, but I know one thing. I don't believe this is an actual stone or *just* a meteor. I guess that part doesn't make any sense when it can get smaller than that or larger. Although, I don't know why we would need it to be bigger."

This discovery was significant. As Brad took the stone back, he patted it with one hand. "I do know that this is the key. We have to go find the right lock."

*****

Virginia checked every connection multiple times. Despite her efforts, the computers in the library did not work. She wasn't surprised. However, the second floor had a dedicated wing dealing with mathematics, astrophysics, astronomy, and cosmology. She reviewed all the titles on her first day and compiled a reading list. The next morning, Virginia began her research and studied everything she could about black holes, quantum mechanics, and related subjects. Some of the material was outdated, or she had read it previously, but it was added to the list. Virginia wanted to be thorough.

After a few weeks of walking back and forth from her apartment to the library, Virginia had enough. Since she was alone, no one could object. The reading nooks at the far end of the library were piled high with cushions on the bench seats under the bay windows. It would be perfect.

The next morning, she packed her blankets and pillow with a few changes of clothes and brought them to the library. It didn't take long to rearrange the pads on the bench. After covering it with her blankets and pillow, she found it would work nicely.

The weeks turned to months, and she grew lonely. The need for fresh air and exercise forced her to wander around the campus. Like a voyeur, Virginia would peek into the lives of the students and those that lived nearby. Feeding the squirrels and birds became a hobby, and she found they were great listeners. Those moments would give her mind a break and help her process the information.

How do I get out of here and back to the real world?

She put a lot of faith in Brad and Clement, basically two people she had just met. Even though she had memories of Brad stretching back to her first year of university, the handsome man who helped secure a fantastic co-op placement was never forgotten.

Virginia continued her research, remaining positive that the situation was only a setback. During the first two months, she kept track of the days. However, seeing the tallies was depressing, so she stopped. Counting did nothing to appease her sanity. Virginia lost track of time on purpose.

One article had a few answers or *possible* answers, so she added it to the growing pile of material she kept to the side. Slowly, she arranged the library's main floor into her research area. Three long tables held most of the study material. Items she thought were worth revisiting were kept on the right, and discarded books went to the left. Her handwritten notes grew into volumes several inches in height.

For the last few years, Virginia had kept her hair shoulder length. It was easier to maintain, and it almost took no effort. While she didn't keep track of the days, it was apparent that she had been here for quite a while. Her hair had grown a few inches. She tied it back into a ponytail, realizing it would act as her new calendar.

Virginia wasn't sure how long she could keep doing nothing but research while waiting for a rescue. Hopefully, Brad was trying to find her. She may have all the time in the world, but her sanity may not last long.

Chapter 35

When moving forward or back in time, Brad would see various abstract imagery that flew past, either black and gray or brilliant white, depending on their direction in the timestream. Since the stone imparted a charge and granted them abilities, neither had attempted to travel with it in their possession. There wasn't any need.

Brad balanced the meteor in his left hand. "I want to bring this with us and see how far we can go foretime with it while we remain in contact."

Brad had lit a fire in the cabin to take the chill off while they brainstormed, but that wasn't the only thing getting heated. Clement shook his head and pushed the chair away from the table. "I don't think that this is a good idea. If this is the key, as you mentioned, something may happen to it if we bring it with us. There is only one meteor. We should keep it safe."

"I'm *trying* to do things that have not been done before. We need a different approach since nothing seems to work." Brad tried to keep the frustration out of his voice, but he wasn't succeeding. They had banged heads many times, and both were stubborn.

Brad thought an argument was brewing, but Clement abruptly strode to the front door and stared across the field at the apple tree for almost three minutes. He took a deep breath and slowly let it out. Brad remained silent as Clement's shoulders slumped in resignation, and his fists relaxed.

"I have tried many things to make changes over the years. Not just with the black hole but with other things as well. Nothing has been successful." Clement sounded tired, and his voice barely carried across the cabin. He was staring at the apple tree.

Brad understood. "I won't be going near the particle accelerator. Right now, I want to avoid that. But I think we owe it to Virginia to use the resources to try and find her."

Clement pulled the gold ring off his finger. A few drops of blood dripped off the nail and onto the porch. They were quickly absorbed into the hard-packed soil.

"You're right. We do owe it to Virginia to use *all* the possible resources." Clement dropped his ring in Brad's palm, the twin to the one on his right hand. "Right now, two lamps are plugged into the same socket, both drawing from the source. I'm unplugging one of the lamps to let yours shine brighter."

Shocked, Brad held it in the palm of his hand. He wasn't sure what to do with it. "What do you mean?"

"Relax, I'm not going to kill myself. However, without the prospect of death, life has little meaning. I've lived a long time and am just letting nature resume her course."

Brad was relieved Clement wouldn't end everything but didn't know what to say.

"You'll be fine without me second-guessing you. Before you start, I would ask one thing."

Concerned, Brad readily agreed. "Of course. How can I help?"

"Can you drop me off in Boston? I already have a place that I would like to use. Don't worry about me. We have a lot of money, but I can't stay here any longer."

Still in shock, Brad took a moment to realize that he would be working alone. After operating with Clement for a long time, he wasn't sure how to deal with this news.

"You're giving up?" Brad tried to wrap his mind around Clement's throwing in the towel after centuries.

Shrugging, Clement took a deep breath and let it out slowly. "Not giving up, but do know when I hold someone back."

"You're *not* holding me back." Brad ran a hand through his hair. "I don't fully understand your choices, but I respect them. Can we call it a break, and if I need help, I can count on you?"

"Deal."Clement shook his hand, then studied the property and the cabin a final time before nodding. "I'm ready."

~

It didn't take long to get Clement settled in Boston, and despite Brad's objections, he only wanted a ten-year window before the event. Money wasn't an issue long as they were not buying islands. Brad traveled forward in time with the meteor cradled in his right arm. He wanted to go ahead with his original plan and try an interception.

While moving forward in the quantum time-stream, Brad nearly ran into a thin, ragged line in mid-air. It resembled a long pressure crack on a frozen lake.

Then it happened yet again.

This doesn't look good. Oh my, God!

Brad was about to pass another line. He slowed his journey and came to a complete stop, neither moving forward nor back through time. Brad had paused at an in-between moment.

The fissure was random and came into existence and faded from nowhere. When Brad traveled farther uptime, more cracks appeared, increasing in size. Brad wasn't surprised when his hand phased through when he reached out to touch it. He was in a quantum realm or state, but the fissures seemed to go beyond. Unable to do anything about it, Brad tried to put it from his mind. However, it would be something he would ask Virginia, but he had to find her first.

At the TRIUMF building, Brad stayed in the quantum realm and moved about in real-time four days from the event. At this point, Brad tried something different. Instead of jumping around and creating a different timeline, he stayed along the prime pathway, watching from behind the curtain.

Technicians moved about in the control room, preparing for the experiment. Clement worked with the others in his lab coat, but he didn't perceive him. There had to be a reason, but it was beyond an FBI agent's reasoning. Nothing prepared him for this reality, and he had to trust what got him through his career.

Intuition.

Brad was reasonably sure Virginia would have been present if he hadn't taken her from the timeline. His mind tried to make sense of the situation. Virginia *did* conduct the experiment in a few days, which created the black hole, but she wasn't in the timeline yet. So, that would mean she *would* be found and continue her work.

"I can't second or third guess myself."

Now wasn't the time to dwell on the mind-twister, and Brad moved slowly forward in time to the twenty-four hours mark. The invisible wall prevented any travel ahead still existed, but Brad noticed the quantum realm's fissures were more extensive and frequent the closer to the event. Time was being fractured on all levels.

"I could really use your help, Virginia. I have no idea what is happening to the universe!" There was too much he didn't know, and he ground his teeth in frustration. Still holding the meteor, like a football cradled in his right arm, Brad concentrated and allowed time to resume forward at its regular pace.

He remained an observer in the quantum realm and watched three people appear in the hallway by the control room. It felt strange to watch himself interact with Clement and Virginia, and he was tempted to step forward and stop them from proceeding. However, Brad knew certain events had to happen, and he wasn't sure what effects would ripple outward from his attempts. He was currently *here* because of those events. If they were halted, *this* Brad might vanish. The Grandfather Paradox wasn't something he needed to test, and he was happy to leave it as a theory, and Brad remained an observer.

Staying in the quantum realm, Brad followed them through the doorway as Virginia worked the magnetic control unit. Brad noticed his past self habitually rocked back and forth while waiting, and Clement continually glanced over his shoulder as if he was expecting company.

It didn't take them long to finish their preparations and slide into the quantum realm. Brad had no idea if they could see him, but he didn't remember seeing anyone, so he felt safe for the moment. When they appeared before him, Brad gasped and opened his eyes wide, trying to understand.

Everyone was a translucent ghost, and Brad could see right through them a holographically projected image. He was reminded of ghost sightings or the horses at the farm. *Maybe they weren't ghosts, but people out of phase with their reality? Other time-travelers?* That theory made more sense than returning from the grave to haunt the living.

While moving forward through time, Brad kept pace. And just before the explosion happened, his game plan changed. If he could grab Virginia *now*, the timeline would remain intact instead of following her. Brad tried to hold Virginia's hand with the stone in his right.

Whatever internal instinct or guidance prompted him to change the plans was wrong. Dead wrong.

A bolt of blue electricity arced out of the meteorite with a thunderclap, and it chained into all four of them faster than thought. Strangely, Brad felt no pain but certainly remembered when it happened. Everyone else contorted with agony, but he couldn't hear the screams. Brad was currently out of phase with his past self.

The lightning coated him in a blue nimbus from head to toe. Flickers of energy appeared in a ring around his feet and rose about his torso. Once the power reached his head, it crackled like a Tesla lightning coil grounding, and it was redirected.

The energy was absorbed and consumed through his ring and into the cradled meteor. When the rock reached a maximum threshold, quantum energy exploded like a nuclear bomb of light and force. Brad was not affected at the center of the explosion, but the others were.

As his past-self was hurtled through time and space, Brad quickly followed. They still held Virginia tightly, and Brad darted forward, and he was about to join them when past Brad and Clement lost their grips. Virginia dropped out of the quantum realm instantly. For the second time, it happened too fast for him to react. Twice he failed to save her.

"No!" Brad screamed while it dawned on him that *he* was the cause of the explosion that sent them back in time. He was the reason Virginia was lost. "Fuck!"

Brad watched his past self and Clement fly head over heels before being ejected from the quantum realm. Their screams echoed in his ears and tore at his heart. Brad examined the exact place where Virginia was removed from the quantum realm. He hoped Clement was correct with the analogy of time being a river because he was about to check along the length where Virginia fell in.

Chapter 36

Virginia absently twirled her hair around a finger and tossed the worn paperback to the side. Her makeshift nest of pillows and blankets had grown in the window nook. After working her way through the library and all the reference books she could stand, she gave up and worked her way through romance, science fiction, fantasy, and various thriller novels. She had reached her limit in studying, for all the theory books in the world were just that.

Theory.

Her handwritten notes were extensive and filled a table in piles. There wasn't a need to pour over the material. She had long since memorized anything that would remotely help. Virginia coped with her favorite pastime as the months stretched past the two-year mark. She escaped into stories, helping take her mind off the situation and making her prison bearable. Virginia read stories with dragons and elves and laughed and cried with Frodo. Even murder mystery novels were considered fair game. If they had an attractive cover, she would read it. It took ten days to devour the entire Agatha Christie collection. A genre that she had typically avoided gave her refuge.

Virginia was smart enough to know she wouldn't last too long and keep her sanity. Humans, for the most part, needed company. It still felt like a jail for all the space she had available and an almost never-ending source of books.

She was reasonably sure there were a few times when she talked to herself and mumbled. Despite the birds and squirrels being good listeners, they didn't respond. Virginia figured she would be fine if she didn't answer or reply to her ramblings.

Virginia had told herself that more exercise would help take her mind off some problems. She ran and went to the campus gym every morning for twelve months. A light workout, followed by a hot shower and breakfast, helped pass the time. She was in the best shape of her life but was hard-pressed to answer what kind of life that was.

Recently, Virginia started to have problems falling asleep. She would stay up most of the night, then go for a run in the morning before collapsing in bed, totally exhausted. Other times she would stay up for two days straight before sleep finally overtook her. Her sleeping pattern wrapped around the clock so many times that she lost track.

Groaning, she tossed an old Tom Clancy novel on the nearby pile and pulled the blankets to her chin—Jack Ryan could wait. After being up for two and a half days, she could only look at the ceiling and wait for sleep. However, despite being exhausted, she was wide awake.

Initially, it had taken a few weeks to be comfortable enough to sleep in the library, but now, it was considered home. Giving up, Virginia groaned, threw back the covers, and made herself something to drink. She had always found something soothing about hot chocolate, which never failed to help her relax.

Virginia searched in a shoe box of supplies before finding an elastic. Her shoulder-length hair had grown, and it would get everywhere if she didn't tie it back. Her hair was almost twelve inches longer than when she arrived, hanging to the middle of her back.

Virginia had set up a makeshift kitchen with pilfered food and other items from the student rooms at one of the tables in the study area. Hot plates, a dormitory mini-fridge, and dishes were quickly found and relocated to the library. The university grounds hadn't changed since she arrived, as if everyone had just stepped out, and there was no lack of food or clothing. It was everywhere. One benefit of the new world—food didn't spoil. Otherwise, she would be down to eating canned foods or hunting. In a world without people, Virginia had no idea why electricity was running, or even *how*. The rules of this reality were confusing.

A Jack Daniels liquor bottle sat on the table, but the layer of dust on the glass was proof she didn't drink her worries away. Although, around her forty-fourth birthday, an impromptu party left a hangover that lasted for days. Virginia never really enjoyed alcohol, just the occasional glass of red wine throughout university and her adult life. On a few occasions, she had too much, but they were rare and only reaffirmed her decision to stick with water.

After filling the electric kettle from the water jug, Virginia opened a pouch of hot chocolate mix and poured it into her cup.

"If you have an extra mug, I wouldn't mind one as well."

Virginia's heart leaped in her chest. The mug shattered across the polished stone. The powder flew across her bare feet as she screamed.

Brad stood, grinning from ear to ear, with hands on his hip. He wore a short beard, blue jeans, and a dress shirt.

Virginia couldn't believe her eyes.

Have I finally lost my mind? Is this an illusion?

A delusion couldn't fake the smell of his soap and the sparkle in his eyes. Virginia threw herself into his arms and held Brad tight. The damn holding back her emotions shattered. Tears rolled down her cheeks while sobbing into his shoulder. His shirt was becoming wet, but he didn't complain.

It took several minutes before she wiped her eyes. "Oh great, you finally show up, and I'm a complete mess."

Virginia had found one of her old nightgowns in her dorm room, and for the most part, that had turned into her loungewear when she wasn't working out.

Brad grinned even wider and chuckled after a quick wink. "You look amazing, don't worry."

"Yeah, right. Can we go now? As nice as this place is …."

"I'm sorry that it took me so long to find you. I had to search in hundreds and hundreds of alternate realities."

"Thank you for not giving up on me." Virginia tried to fix her hair before giving up on the fruitless gesture.

"You're prepared to give up all this?" Brad grinned while he gestured toward the kitchen and her bed. "Are you sure?"

Virginia slowly looked around the library, her home for the last few years, and nodded. She couldn't control the tears as they started again, but they were tears of hope and joy. Brad held her tight before entering the quantum timestream. The library faded away in an alternate reality, like a distant dream.

*****

"Are you ready?" Brad handed Virginia the sheaf of papers and gave her an encouraging smile.

Virginia smoothed down her lab coat and studied the paperwork for the third time. It was the funding grant from the off-shore company her father had created—that *she* had made with Brad's money.

Virginia couldn't be alone for the first week, and she kept near him within arm's length whenever possible. Virginia quickly readjusted and adapted as she became immersed in everyday living. A trip to a salon took care of her lengthy hair, and after some "therapy" shopping, she was ready to carry on. Virginia agreed with Brad that maintaining the timeline was a priority.

The alternative would be to return to a new starting point and try everything again, with no guaranteed success. If possible, that was something Brad wanted to avoid. Virginia had mixed feelings once he told her about Clement. She could only move on and do what she could in the end.

"And besides," she had told him. "You aren't alone. You have me."

Once again, Brad was at the TRIUMF building in Vancouver to maintain the timeline. She took a small cloth, cleaned her glasses quickly, and took a deep breath. "Okay, I think I'm ready. Here we go."

Brad followed her down the hall and let her move ahead. Without looking back, Virginia briskly turned into the staff lunchroom.

"We got it! The funding has been approved!" A few cheers followed Virginia's statement. Based on her research, Virginia had more than a few ideas about eliminating the black hole, but Brad was tentative. If they were wrong, they would be dead, and there wouldn't be a second chance. However, Virginia seemed confident.

Brad waited outside and went over their next few steps in his mind. At this point, they both agreed to keep the timeline intact as much as possible. Creating a variant or alternate timeline could have consequences that would spiral out of their control.

Virginia had identified the cracks in the timestream as *quantum fractures*. A black hole exerts so much gravity that it could move a star many times its size and put it in orbit. Once a black hole is formed, it starts bending time and space to distort everything down to the quantum level—the effects are witnessed before the actual event, at least at the quantum level.

"All done."

Virginia walked out of the building's front door, wearing a short blue skirt and a white blouse.

"Did you want to change before any attempts?" Brad did his best not to look at her legs and remain professional. However, by the sparkle in her eye, he was caught.

Looking down at her outfit, Virginia shrugged. "You don't like it?"

Holding out his hand, Brad smiled. "It's going to be cold, but your call."

"I'll just wear your jacket if needed." Virginia smiled and squeezed his hand. Brad grinned and pulled them into the timestream.

The timestream's black and gray twisting nether hurtled by, and Brad halted them after a few moments. Instead of releasing the energy, he left them suspended for a moment.

"This is what enabled me to find you."

From his jacket pocket, he pulled out a small object and concentrated. In seconds it grew to the size of a football.

It was the meteor.

"I can travel through time, but that shocks me." She laughed.

"When I tried to call the stone to me through an alternate reality that Clement and I were in, it created a portal. I'm not sure if it's an alternate reality or universe or something else." Brad shrugged. "With the stone, I can open portals to alternate realities. I had to check many before finding the correct one. I wanted to show you in case something happens. I shouldn't be the only one to have this knowledge."

Brad concentrated, and from within the quantum realm, a doorway opened, and he stepped through. He held her hand as she stepped onto the grass and looked around.

It was a cold autumn day, with the sun at high noon. Birds chirped loudly from the woods, but Brad saw no turkeys across the field. The weather had turned toward winter, and the smell of frost lingered in the air. Most of the leaves had fallen off the trees. It was usually colder at night on the farm. Brad was sure the temperature would drop below freezing tonight.

"After you were knocked out of the quantum realm, I knew *when* but had difficulty finding *where*."

Realizing that he still held her hand, Brad let go. "This place is similar to where Clement and I met up. We thought it was a timeline or loop variation, but it may be an alternate reality. I seem to be able to search them rapidly now. Practice, I guess."

Brad focused on the meteor, which was soon tucked away in his jacket pocket. Walking down the rutted path, they passed the barn on their left and the woodpile. Brad noticed the ax resting against the side of the cabin. They both halted when the cabin door slammed open.

Wearing his old brown pants and a white cotton shirt, Clement Wallace scowled and looked them up and down. "Who the hell are you?"

Chapter 37

 "I'm Brad Holman, and this is Virginia Kincaid. Can we have a moment of your time?"

Now that Brad had sole control of the meteor, Virginia had a theory to deal with the black hole. The only one that could help them was Clement's past self.

Clement examined them further and blushed when he checked out Virginia's skirt, but his eyes didn't linger. After deliberation, he nodded and walked into the cabin without saying anything. The door slammed behind him.

Inside, Clement sat at the kitchen table and waited. "If you can find me in this place, you can have a moment of my time."

Brad nodded to Virginia and had a glance around the cabin. It was the same, except for the layer of dust giving it a musty odor. They sat at the kitchen table, and Brad began. "I'm not so sure how much you know, but there is a problem that will threaten the world at a much later date."

"How does that become *my* problem?"

"Please, just hear us out." Virginia couldn't believe the difference. Clement's old self was rough around the edges, and he had already had enough of their intrusion.

"I'm not too sure what costumes you are wearing. It looks like you wouldn't last a day of real work."

"Mr. Wallace, we're here because we know about the meteor. The stone you found in the woods, just off your north field."

Clement pushed his chair back, his hands gripping the table's edge. The knuckles turned white and cracked. "The meteor fell on my property, and it's mine. I think you've been here long enough. If you don't leave, I'll remove you."

The last thing Brad wanted was to pit the stone's abilities against itself. For all he knew, the results would destroy the world long before the black hole could.

"We'll leave, but I want you to read something before we do." Brad pulled two folded sheets of paper from his jacket and handed them to Clement.

"We don't know what is written down on there." Brad smiled as he passed them over. "That's for you to read. We'll wait outside if that is okay."

Papers in one hand, Clement barely nodded his permission while he stared them in the eyes. Flashing him a quick smile, Brad and Virginia went outside to wait.

Brad took off the suit jacket and picked up the ax. He shrugged a few times to loosen up before turning to the woodpile.

Virginia leaned against the side of the cabin, crossed her arms, and watched.

Flicking the ax down, he embedded the blade into the top of a round and brought it to rest on the chopping block before pulling the ax head free. The ax exploded through the cedar log with a sharp crack. The two split halves fell to the side with a *clunk*.

"Oh, you're so manly." Virginia smiled and continued to watch.

Brad held out the ax and asked, "Would you like to try?"

"With these hands? Not a chance. I just had my nails done. I'm teasing you. Now back to work!"

Laughing along, Brad continued to split wood. The exercise and familiarity felt good and reminded him how much he grew to enjoy the chore.

After thirty minutes, Brad's shirt clung tight to his back. Virginia sat in the sun and watched, tanning. The ax blade missed and skipped to the side when her legs crossed. Brad wasn't completely sure, but she would adjust her position to see if he'd miss. If he weren't careful, he would lose a foot.

When Clement joined them, he stood silently and stared across the fields. His gaze then rose to the sky, and he rubbed a hand across his face. Clement turned to Brad and lifted the pages. They had been crumpled at one point, then flattened. Clement was upset, and his eyes were still red.

"You said you haven't read any of this?" Clement held the papers up.

Brad shook his head. "No. We've both given our word. We haven't opened it."

"I don't understand most of what has happened to me, but I know one thing." Clement coughed a little, clearing his throat. "There's absolutely no way for you to fake what was written down. Only I could have written that."

Brad was tempted to ask but didn't want to intrude on the private moment.

"So, I am left with no choice but to believe that I wrote that note for myself. I was told to trust you both, and you *must* bring the stone back to me here in a few minutes to *keep the timeline intact.* Does that make sense to you?"

Brad nodded. "Yes, and I will do so. If I am not back here by then, that will mean everything failed, and I'm dead."

Clement jerked his thumb toward the cabin. "Don't screw me over on this. It's in the cellar, but you already know that. Get to it."

Curious about the letter, Brad tried to put it out of his mind. He found the trap door already open in the kitchen and made his way to the table below.

Brad was unsure how it was possible to have two of the stones when there was only one. Virginia had lectured him for over half an hour on how and why it could work. He was lost after a few seconds with her lectures on time travel theory. The end result—her idea should work.

The meteor sat on the wooden table. For some reason, Brad expected it to be different than the one he carried, but it was the same. Brad removed the stone from his jacket pocket and placed it on the ground. He pulled out a pocket knife, and after a flick, he buried the point in the palm of his right hand.

"Jesus. That never gets easier." As the blood pooled in his palm, he placed his hand flat on the original meteor.

Brad compared first bonding as if someone kicked open a new door in his mind, so he could feel the quantum realm and navigate the rivers of time, the very fabric of the universe. Now he felt that same rush, but this time everything was amplified. By how much, he couldn't gauge, but it was quite significant. It felt like someone had turned the volume eleven. The initial surge of power crackled between the stones before settling.

Brad pushed both meteors into the quantum realm, reducing their size to walnuts without difficulty before slipping them into separate pockets. Brad wrapped Virginia in the quantum field, and he joined her. All this was done from the cellar.

"That's new." Virginia appeared beside him in the timestream, all smiles. "How did you do that? You didn't even hold my hand."

"Things have been kicked up a notch." Brad gave her a wink. "Ready? We have a few things to do."

Leaving the alternate reality behind, Brad shot them forward into the future. Previously, when traveling, they had been transported through a white brilliance. Now everything had a golden hue. Despite not needing to hold her physically, Virginia's hand found its way into his as they gazed in wonder at the scenery.

Soon they passed another quantum fracture, but this one was different. Instead of a crack in the ice, it resembled a forked lightning strike frozen while branching into the infinite. A glowing surge pulsed up and down its length like a heartbeat.

"Subjective time does not work in the quantum realm. This results from the black hole distorting time—fore and back from the event horizon. The larger it gets, the more it will warp space, affecting the quantum level. Soon navigation will be impossible." Virginia seemed confident.

"Is there any way to patch the fractures?"

Shaking her head, Virginia was adamant. "Not a chance. The only way to fix it is to stop the black hole."

Continuing, Brad brought them back to the TRIUMF building in Vancouver. They passed many quantum fractures along the way. Currently, they are six days away from the event.

"Okay, I'm back in my subjective time. I have some work to do if the experiment continues. I have to pay the bills and allocate the funding."

"I'm returning to Washington and wrapping things up with the FBI. If things all go well, I can't see myself returning to work for them, now that I know how they will react should push come to shove."

Brad filled her in on the assassination team during one of their long talks. If the government wanted to kill Brad and Clement that badly, he wanted nothing to do with them. For Brad saying goodbye to the FBI would be challenging, but he knew it was the correct decision. In subjective time, Brad hadn't reported for work in many years.

The former FBI agent looked forward to resolving the black hole with a vested interest in living beyond the event.

"I'm fairly sure you don't need to work for money now." Virginia chuckled at Brad's expression. "If you need money, you just have to go back in time and invest in computer stocks in the mid-nineteen-seventies. Or you could invest in a certain search engine company."

Brad hadn't thought of this, and his eyes opened wide when the realization hit him. Virginia laughed harder at his reaction. "Okay, fine. I hadn't thought of that, and it sounds easier than working around a lottery. I'll be in touch soon."

Virginia brought her arms out to hug Brad, but before she made contact, he slid into the quantum realm. Virginia missed her mark and stumbled through the empty air.

"Seriously?"

Sighing, Virginia shook her head and walked into the building. From the quantum realm, Brad chuckled. *First things first, we have to save the world.*

Chapter 38

 Having both meteors in his possession gave him the potential to change many things, but Brad wanted to ensure success—a few tasks he needed to complete for a level playing field. A look up-time showed that the invisible wall that previously held them back was gone. But it was clear that the black hole still would detonate. Reality warped from within the timestream the closer he got. Beyond a certain point, the future did not exist.

Brad relocated to the Cheyenne mountain complex, not wanting to push his luck. Although his credentials would grant him access, he did not want to alert the air force base to his presence. In subjective time, the fragment was already taken by Clement.

Staying in the quantum realm, Brad slowly moved backward through the timestream. The complex's seed catalog area was empty, except for a few technicians who checked the freezer controls and display readings.

The flash of light halted his journey. It was the sign Brad had sought. He stayed in the golden-hued realm to observe.

When Clement stepped out of the undertime, he read the serial numbers on the containers' sides. Brad was above Clement's abilities, and he remained hidden. Although, before Clement opened the freezer bin, he quickly looked along the length of the hall.

Clement shrugged, wiped his hands across his blue T-shirt, and opened the freezer compartment. After he read the note and crumpled it into a ball, Clement whipped it into the bin. The farmer quickly disappeared into the timestream, and Brad knew Clement was about to meet him on a rooftop patio in Boston.

Brad moved farther into the past until the air force captain switched the meteor fragment and left the note behind. The soldier had followed Brad's instructions correctly.

Virginia had mentioned that they did not want to create an alternate timeline. To avoid that possibility, Brad traveled farther backward before the captain arrived. He wanted to ensure a gap where the fragment could be replaced before the captain removed it to prevent any changes.

Brad retrieved the stone fragment and relocated to Washington, DC, before removing the small meteor from his jacket, and it promptly enlarged to its original size. Brad held the recently retrieved fragment above the depression and waited.

Nothing happened.

It fits inside the appropriate place, but it wouldn't stay. Brad caught it as the fragment fell. There was one further step he hadn't taken yet. Brad hadn't bonded to the piece of stone. Finding the steak knives, Clement had bought still in the packaging didn't take long.

"Hopefully, these are clean."

He held the knife tip in his left palm and buried the point deep. The sting disappeared once he had the fragment in his left hand, and despite the painful sting, he smiled. The difference was more subtle than what he had previously gone through, but Brad was now attuned to the small fragment.

The two pieces of stone were rejoined with a click, and the cut had healed. Brad was getting a collection of thin white scars on his hands. After bringing out the original meteor, Brad enlarged it and placed it beside its doppelgänger to compare. Except for the one missing fragment, they were identical. Laying his hands on both, Brad closed his eyes and opened his mind.

Listening. Feeling.

It didn't take long before a thrumming sensation made the ring on his right hand vibrate, but the notes were out of tune.

When Brad turned thirteen, he wanted to play an electric guitar, so his parents gave him an acoustic and signed him up for a few lessons. They would get an electric if he did well and was interested. The first lesson was how to tune the guitar and hold it properly. Besides using a tuner, he was taught an alternate way to check the strings.

Harmonics.

Instead of pressing down on the strings between the frets, you lightly touched one and plucked it. You would get a harmonic note if your fingers were in the right position. When you compare that sound with another placement on a different string, it should be the same if the guitar is in tune. Brad sensed the same resonating frequency from both stones. However, one was slightly out of tune with the other.

I need both fragments, just like Virginia had predicted.

Brad once again headed back to the place where it started. Kentucky. It would also give him time to check into something that bothered him. Arriving at Fort Knox, Brad stayed in the quantum realm and walked to the depository. When a guard on patrol opened the door, he slipped inside.

He worked his way through the building to the vault in this manner. The gold on the pallets and shelving still gave him a sense of awe. Each bar weighed twenty-seven and a half pounds, and with the current prices, each one was valued at over seven-hundred and fifty-thousand dollars. Brad couldn't help but chuckle. A room full of gold still impressed him, even though he was used to time-traveling.

The pallets of drugs inside the alcove and the metal box which had stored the meteor fragment remained untouched. Concentrating, Brad slowly moved back in time. He searched for the instance when Clement took the stone, but the moment never happened. Brad passed the moment when the guards frantically checked the vault for clues after the gold was discovered outside.

Continuing, Brad went backward, over sixty years, to resume his hunt. However, there still was no sign of Clement. In 1950 Brad felt safe to step outside the timestream and into the vault. The technology didn't exist to detect his presence in the secure area, and he ensured it was the middle of the night. Not that he worried about security, but it was better not to meet anyone. The shelving units have not changed, and the same amount of gold bars were present.

The skids of narcotics were absent, as well as several wooden crates along the wall. The same steel shelf held the metal case for the meteor. Brad was amazed that no one had moved it for almost eighty-five years. Ignoring the engraved words, Brad flipped the hasps and raised the lid.

The metal box was empty.

"What the hell?"

Confused, Brad closed it and looked around the small room. There wasn't another bin. He returned to the quantum realm with no other choice and went farther into the past. He continued to search for the moment Clement took the stone fragment.

Brad soon arrived when the metal chest was brought into the vault, but Clement never appeared. At Roosevelt's orders, two rather large men in dark suits and fedoras carried the trunk into the vault. Brad waited until they had left, and the area was clear.

The metal box looked the same inside.

Empty.

This might be a problem.

Chapter 39

After knocking on the door, Brad waited. He was outside a residential area in a suburb of Boston, in Brookline. Clement's large property backed onto a country club with a beautiful two-story home and wrap-around gardens with an attached double garage.

Brad was shocked when Clement opened the door, but he quickly recovered. Clement had aged and would be fifty years old. His hair looked like it was playing catch-up and had turned gray. He looked physically strong and in good shape, just a little older. Clement was naturally on his way to resembling an older adult. After being caught in the time trap, Brad knew how he would look in a few decades.

Five years have passed for Clement since he last saw Brad, and he looked comfortable in his khaki pants and dress shirt with a white golf sweater draped over his shoulders. The sleeves were crossed on his chest like a county club magazine model. Brad couldn't help but grin at the change.

He's settling in well.

"Looks like a nice place."

"Thank you. Come in." Clement gestured for Brad to enter. Immediately off the foyer was a formal living room. Despite the appearance, the couch was comfortable.

"Since you're here, I guess things are not going well. I have what … five more years until the black hole goes off?"

"Five years, correct. Things are going well, and I've found Virginia. She was stuck in an alternate reality and is currently working uptime."

He pulled the two meteors from his pocket and showed them to Clement. "Whatever it was you wrote out to help your past-self worked. We were allowed to borrow it, and hopefully, I'll be returning it soon."

"Something went wrong? Unless this is purely a social call?"

Brad shook his head. "I wish, sorry. I need to know when you got the fragment from Fort Knox. I checked the full timeline, and it isn't there at any time period."

Clement leaned forward, hands on his knees. "It should be there. From what I gather, I was there just before you were assigned the case."

"It isn't there now. Not sure what's happened."

Clement closed his eyes for a few moments to think before he opened them again. "Somehow, things have changed. We must have done something to change the timeline during our travels. Just enough to change one variable. Maybe more will be discovered."

"That makes sense." When Brad thought about everything they had done and all the possible places, a small change *must* have happened. It would be almost impossible to find their mistake and fix it. It would be like finding a needle in a haystack. Brad rubbed a hand over his short beard. "The two stones are out of alignment with each other. With what we have in mind, they must be the same. We need that one missing piece of stone at Fort Knox, but it doesn't seem to exist now."

"What did the journal say?"

"I never checked it. As far as I know, it was returned to the president."

"Go and check the journal. Everything each president had done was written down. Those were the clues that I had followed."

Clement then gave Brad detailed instructions on where the journal was hidden and how to access it on the Resolute desk.

They caught up on what Clement had been doing in the last five years. Despite being horrible at it, he had taken an interest in golfing and went out a few times a week. He hadn't spent much of his savings, just enough to get by. However, his house had all the latest computer gadgets and technology. He could afford it many times over.

After a quick tour where Clement proudly showed off his modern home, they returned to the foyer.

"Let me know how it goes. Good luck."

"Will do. If things go bad …."

Clement shrugged. "I'll never know. It will end quickly, I'm sure. You got this."

Brad silently agreed before stepping into the quantum realm. His mind was already turning to the task ahead.

Brad had some trepidations about entering the White House. Still, he was more worried about the blackhole destroying the planet and every living soul than opposed to being in the president's office without an invitation. He had to read the journal.

Brad arrived at the White House late afternoon, four days before the event. He wanted to ensure anything written prior would be captured. Any additional information could prove essential.

Despite it being the weekend, many still worked at the Oval Office. The hallways were crowded, and a flurry of activity was happening. Brad wasn't sure if this was normal or if they were preparing for a media event.

Having never been to the White House, Brad followed the stream of people safely from the quantum realm, and he eventually found the room in the West Wing. Brad couldn't appear with the security and officials present, let alone the president. After a quick jump back in time, he found the office empty at four o'clock in the morning.

Brad had heard tales of the security within the Oval Office throughout his career, so he didn't waste time when he popped out of the quantum realm. The bottom right drawer of the desk opened, and he saw the decorative trim Clement had mentioned. The small wooden section moved forward an inch until a *click* was felt, and it released a hidden latch. Brad closed the drawer quietly, returning everything as to how he found it. He found the panel that tilted outward from the side within the footwell. However, the journal was not there.

You've got to be kidding me.

After closing the compartment, Brad slipped into the quantum realm to review his choices. Only one option came to mind, so he allowed time to move forward slowly while waiting for the right moment.

Brad confirmed that President Kelly Bower arrived in his office early in the day, and he was alone with briefing notes. It was a short window of opportunity, but it should work.

He waited until the president was distracted with reports in one hand and a mug of coffee in another. He stood near the window for the natural light. Brad stepped out of the quantum realm and waited inside the office door.

There isn't a good way to do this.

Brad cleared his throat. "Mr. President."

Bower jumped and skillfully avoided spilling coffee on the reports. "Jesus Christ! Who let you in here?"

"Sorry to disturb you, Mr. President. I need to see the journal one more time, but I can't find it."

Bower took a moment to regain his composure, and he quickly sipped his coffee before placing the mug on the desk. He neatly stacked the paperwork beside it before staring at Brad. "What are you talking about, and who exactly are you? My schedule is cleared for the next thirty minutes."

Wondering if this was a joke, Brad wasn't sure how to respond. "Special Agent Bradley Holman, FBI. I'm still working on the case you assigned me, Mr. President."

Bower cleared his throat again and leaned forward on the desk. Both hands were in a fist, and his knuckles cracked when he shifted his weight. "I have *absolutely* no idea what you're talking about or who you are. I'm going to let the secret service deal with this."

The president broke eye contact with Brad as he pressed a large button on the side of the phone. Brad didn't know what else to do besides leave. Stepping into the timestream brought an immediate sense of relief, but he had to see this through.

He still couldn't tell if the president was acting to protect himself or not. However, four secret service agents entered the room when the president pressed the panic button. Bower yelled at the agents while pointing out where Brad had stood by the door five seconds ago. Quickly, the secret service locked down the entire building and began a full search while the president was hustled to the bunker for safety.

Brad thought about going earlier for another attempt, but the president either had no idea what was happening or had an ulterior motive. Regardless, he knew who would be able to help. He allowed time currents to carry him away.

Chapter 40

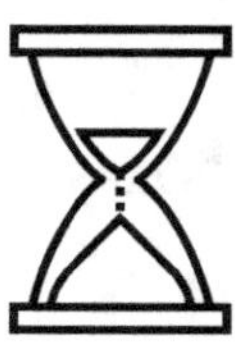 Brad leaned on the railing outside the TRIUMF building and loosened his tie. He was hard-pressed to develop a reason to wear the suit besides habit, and he vowed never to wear one again. If the world ended, it would be an easy promise to keep.

He had taken a short stop along the timeline to verify that there were no other changes he could easily spot. The *one* change he desired was eminent. The black hole was still created, and the planet would be destroyed. When the door opened, Brad temporarily forgot about the possibility of death and was tempted to let out a wolf whistle.

Virginia sported a new look with jean shorts and a yellow tank top with her hair held back and a red headband. His pulse raced, and Brad was sure that he liked that look.

"Do you have a few minutes? I've run into a problem or two."

When she saw Brad, Virginia smiled. "Dinner? I'm starving."

They walked into the University Golf Club Restaurant. Brad offered to bring them directly, but Virginia didn't mind and drove them over in her older Honda Accord. It wasn't too far from the TRIUMF building.

The restaurant was within the clubhouse at a golf course, and Virginia had been coming there for years. No one had asked if she was a member, and she explained she was now considered a regular.

They sat at a table near the fieldstone fireplace with a great view of the green for the ninth hole, surrounded by the trees and the manicured landscape.

"Thanks for coming. I've been craving a burger and fries all day." Virginia didn't bother to look at the menu.

"Sounds good to me."

Virginia ordered at the counter and sat back down. "Okay, what's going on?"

Brad quickly filled her in on the details and apparent timeline changes. Virginia shrugged. "I've read a great deal about theoretical physics, but there isn't too much information on fixing altered timelines."

"The timeline hasn't altered for you or me. Clement seems to remember everything properly, so I guess he's fine."

Their food arrived, and Virginia dug in. "Sorry, I haven't eaten all day."

After the first bite, Brad realized he wasn't sure when he had last eaten. It could very well have been years. *That* didn't make any sense, and he was obviously forgetting. However, the food was delicious, and Brad barely kept up with Virginia as she devoured her meal.

Brad wiped his face with a napkin and sipped his water. While eating, a solution leaped to mind, and he wasn't sure it was the right answer. "There's only one way to discover what happened to the fragments. I need to go back and follow it through the centuries and track it to a current location. Possibly in real-time."

Virginia's eyes opened wide, and then she chuckled. "You'll be a few centuries older than me when you are done."

Brad gave a wry smile. "It's just a number. I don't know what else to try."

"Try not to forget me in your senior years."

Brad couldn't help but grin. "Thanks for lunch."

Virginia was about to reach for his hand as he slipped into the timestream. Brad moved through the centuries until he was back in Boston, Massachusetts.

If I am going to follow the fragment, I may as well start at the beginning.

As Brad looked around the woods, he wondered how this property was tied to the event. The trees were nearly bare of leaves, and he had a good view of the landing zone. Despite being in the quantum realm, he didn't want to be too close to the impact crater. Fifty feet away, Brad stood beside a massive white pine and waited. Even with the elevated view, he couldn't see the cabin.

It was cold in the woods without the direct sunlight, and his breath plumed before him. The suit jacket did little to keep him warm, but thoughts of a hot coffee were forgotten as the world cracked.

It sounded like a tree was ripped in half, and the noise echoed across the farm and fields. Brad turned his head too late, and the intensity almost blinded him. The brilliant flash of white light danced across his vision.

The meteor streaked across the sky and headed straight toward him. An adrenaline surge sent his heart into overdrive, but he couldn't move his legs. There wasn't time to save himself and seek shelter. His only hope was that history repeated and the meteor landed in the same place.

Brad wasn't prepared for the concussive wave of energy that exploded outward at impact. The force picked him up like a leaf and threw him into a tree trunk ten feet away. The air blasted out of his lungs as his head slammed into the bark. Brad struggled to remain conscious as a black circle shrunk his vision.

He realized he would survive when he fell to his hands and knees and gasped for breath. Barely. It felt like he was in a car accident with another goose egg on his head.

"Jesus …" A quick check showed no blood, just a growing bump. Brad used a tree to help him regain his feet. "Not one of my smarter moves."

Edging behind the large tree, Brad didn't have long to wait. Clement approached, dry branches cracking underfoot. Clement held a long limb and poked the meteor. After a minute, the farmer walked back to the cabin.

Once the area was clear, Brad headed downhill toward the impact area. A sharp pain ripped through his head when he was within ten feet. It felt like a twelve-inch spike was being driven deep with a sledgehammer. As his eyes watered, Brad felt both meteors in his pocket as they vibrated, and his vision doubled. Then tripled.

The stone in the ground emitted a high-pitched squeal, like feedback through a sound system. Brad could hear and feel it on many levels, mostly through the quantum realm. As Brad stepped forward, the pain increased, and the noise escalated. After three steps back, the intensity lessened. Having gone through enough, Brad slipped into the quantum realm and retreated uphill with both hands pressed against his head in a feeble attempt to stop it from splitting. For a moment, he had double-vision, but it stabilized.

The proximity of three meteors at once was overwhelming. Brad didn't want to know what would happen should he remain. When he stepped out of the timestream, he felt immediately better.

A tear in time? An explosion? Not an experiment he wished to try again.

As he got his breathing under control, movement below caught his eye. Clement had returned. Once again, picking up the long stick and poking at the meteor. Brad had the feeling of déjà vu as Clement performed the *exact* same movements. He threw the branch on the ground and turned away as a *second* man stepped out from behind a tree with a shovel.

Both men stared at each other for an awkward minute.

They were precisely the same, an exact copy, down to their dress and mannerisms. *Clement had met himself for the first time.*

Brad remained behind the tree and stifled a groan. *I wish the meteor came with an instruction manual.* When he went over to the stone and jumped back into the timestream, he caused a loop-effect in the area—an unfortunate consequence of having the three stones close to each other. Brad wasn't sure.

Both men spoke in hushed tones, and Brad couldn't hear what they discussed. After they shook hands, one man returned with a wheelbarrow, and they turned their attention to the meteor. While one Clement was in the crater with a long stick to dig, the other worked with the shovel above to pry the meteor loose. Brad lost track of which man was the original and which was a copy. Then again, he was never positive, to begin with.

It wasn't long before the shovel slipped. The edge grazed the other's arm, and one cried in pain. They were about to continue their efforts until the man with the wound leaned against the stone. Brad knew the blood unlocked the stone's abilities as Clement first bonded with the meteor.

Brad watched in wonder as everything changed. Clement sat on the edge of the hole and stared at his forearm. It had fully healed.

When the man in the hole disappeared, the one that remained staggered backward. The shovel was across his chest like a shield. Brad tried to track Clement through the quantum realm, but he disappeared. The man waved the shovel through the vacant space but didn't connect with anything. As he peered around the woods, Brad realized his mistake. It was too late to move. He was spotted.

Clement had a stern look, and he stomped uphill. Many options ran through his mind, but Brad had an idea of what would happen and remained firm.

"What's going on here? What the hell are you wearing?" Clement gripped the end of the shovel tight, and Brad could see the corded muscles in his arms ripple with the effort.

Brad held his hands in the air to show he had no weapons. He thought of saying something to throw him off, but Brad answered him truthfully. "The meteor has a way of controlling time, allowing a person to travel to the past and future. Your other self bonded to the stone, and I believe he slipped into an alternate reality."

Clement's brows furrowed as he tried to understand. "Who are you? Why are you on my property?"

"I'm here to understand what's happened and solve a mystery." Brad slowly lowered his hands.

Clement blinked rapidly and shook his head. He dug the shovel into the ground with one hand and used it to steady himself. "What's happening to me?"

The farmer dropped to one knee, and Brad tried to calm him down. "Clement, it's okay. I think this time loop is coming to an end. You will merge with yourself. I think."

"I *am* myself! How do you know my name?"

Brad dropped to one knee, looked him in the eye, and warmly smiled. "You're correct. I have known you for a *long* time and know you are also a very good man."

"So, this is it for me? I'm dying?" Clement used two hands on the shovel for support. Brad could see *through* Clement. He had started to fade, and his voice was barely above a whisper.

"No, you will continue to live. You're a good man."

Brad saw a brief flare of light in Clement's eyes before he disappeared completely. Nothing remained but the shovel as the time loop finished its course and subjective time resumed. The remnant had dissolved as the new timeline took effect.

After brushing the dirt from his knees, Brad tried not to worry about Clement, that disappeared. *Was he real or just a copy?* The thought nagged at him as he walked down to the meteor crater, but he didn't have an answer. It took a few minutes to locate the fragment near a large rock. Not wanting to disturb the timeline, Brad left it alone.

Okay, so far, so good.

As he stood back and thought about the encounter, Brad realized that he was the reason for Clement meeting himself.

"What have I done?" He closed his eyes and groaned.

His bumbling with the powers of time caused nothing but problems. Brad's interference had changed many things, and he couldn't help but wonder if history would have turned out the same had he not interfered.

I must be more careful.

Brad stepped into the quantum realm pondering the chicken and the egg riddle. "Are events happening because I caused them, or is everything happening as it was supposed to? Because I've already done so, and there are no choices?"

Unsure, Brad had to put it out of his mind and finish what he had started. Too much was at stake.

Eighty feet away, the only witness shook high in the treetops, frozen in fear from the noise and activity. Quickly, the black squirrel burrowed back into its nest when Brad disappeared.

Chapter 41

Brad followed the meteor's fragment from decade to decade, occasionally stepping out of the timestream to confirm its location before continuing. Each president allowed the piece of stone to be examined and tested by scientists. It always returned to the White House, as the secret was maintained.

During President Roosevelt's years, Brad followed the fragment to a small laboratory run by a scientist named Rollin Chamberlain at the University of Chicago. The segment was clamped into a vice and subjected to several tests.

The geological expert was also quite muscular after decades of moving large amounts of rock. While attempting to retrieve an inner-core sample with a machine the size of a VW Beetle, the fragment broke in twain. Chamberlain continued to study both pieces, but after two months, his efforts were in vain. The samples were examined individually before being returned to the president.

Finally, the day arrived when President Roosevelt went to Kentucky to officiate at the Fort Knox opening. He had two agents carry the metal box into the vault. Far as Brad could tell, it stayed there undisturbed and empty.

Once again, Brad watched himself enter the vault and inspect the metal chest with the police chief.

I'm missing something. If Clement never showed up to get the fragment, a critical step hasn't happened yet.

The longer he mentally untangled the situation, the more apparent the answer. It was the *only* answer. Brad knew what had happened because it already *did* happen. It was history. So, Brad had no choice but to make sure history occurred the way he remembered it, to keep a timeline intact.

Brad started back in Chicago and viewed the actions of the geologist once again. It was a simple matter to follow the man to the White House, where he submitted a report to Roosevelt in person and left the meteor fragments. Roosevelt read the papers and hid the stones with the journal inside the Resolute desk.

The commissioned metal box arrived four weeks later and was left in the Oval Office. The president arrived early the next morning using a cane but still moved without help. Brad wasn't sure what had happened, but he needed help to walk. Roosevelt placed his cane on the desk chair, opened the hidden panel, and pulled out one piece of the meteor fragment. The thirty-second president of the United States adjusted his suit and gave the stone a final examination.

With a final polish on his tie, he shrugged and placed it on the wooden supports inside the box.

Before the president removed his hand from the meteor fragment, Brad froze subjective time in a bubble around the Oval Office.

If there was ever going to be a moment, this was it.

Soon as he stepped out of the quantum realm, Brad gently grabbed the president's wrist. As he looked up at the taller man, time resumed. "I'm sorry, Mr. President, but I need that stone fragment."

Roosevelt stumbled back and nearly lost his footing after bumping into a wall. A vase on a display table threatened to tip over when his hip gave it a glancing blow. He looked at the fragment in his hands and then back up at Brad.

His eyes were wide, and he had trouble breathing while clutching his chest. "What is this? Oh, my God!"

"I can't tell you anything, Mr. President. There can be dire consequences, but I *do* need that stone."

This was the first time Brad was glad to wear a dark suit. Despite the cut and tailoring differences, it was close to the president's style. He didn't want to meet such a prominent figure under-dressed.

Clearing his throat, the president seemed to calm down. "You appeared out of nowhere. Are you a ghost?"

"Mr. President, I can't tell you anything. You're going to have to trust me. I need that fragment. You're also going to have to carry on with your plan. You must place the box in Fort Knox as if the fragment were still inside."

"How did you know about that? I have told no one those details!"

With a little grin, Brad shrugged and held out his left hand.

"Does this have anything to do with *time*?"

Brad just stood there with his hand extended.

It didn't take long for Roosevelt to make up his mind, and he shuffled forward to drop the fragment into Brad's left hand.

"Thank you, Mr. President. It's been an honor meeting you. You also can't tell anyone about our meeting. Not that anyone is going to believe you."

Brad shook President Roosevelt's calloused hand. Once he let go, the timestream folded around him. The president waved his arm back and forth in the empty spot. He removed his glasses and polished them with the cloth from his breast pocket as he shook his head.

President Franklin D. Roosevelt closed the metal box. When the latch clicked, he chuckled. Brad was right. No one would believe him.

~

Brad appeared at his condominium in Washington, DC, and rifled through the paperwork Clement left on the kitchen table. He had some work to do if history had to happen in his future.

It didn't take long to find a pen and blank paper. Brad also found the legal documents for the property in Wyoming. In another folder were the offshore accounts with his share of the money. He couldn't help but whistle at the amount Clement had deposited.

If everything went well, the last place Brad wanted to live was in a condo in the heart of Washington. His plans to leave the FBI seemed inevitable regardless of the outcome. He still believed they ordered the hit on him and Clement. If they turned on him once, they could certainly do so again when it suited them.

After finding a pen and blank paper, he quickly wrote a note and purposely did not sign it. The timeline was messed up enough. He didn't want to contaminate it further.

Taking all the paperwork, Brad stacked it neatly inside a large accordion folder and placed his new identification into his pants pocket. As he looked around, Brad realized no other personal items were in the condo. They had met and eaten here a few times, but that was it. It was just a place.

A place he wouldn't be coming back to ever again.

Casper, Wyoming, was the second-largest city in the state, with just over fifty-five-thousand. Brad guessed that number of people would fit into a small Washington square block with lots of room left over. While Arrow Point was rapidly growing, he passed on the quaint city.

Sliding back in time to six years previous, he walked up E 12th Street and stopped in front of a store with a bright red awning. The sign said Macintyre Real-estate and Associates. Inside, he found a small waiting room with several dozen listings on the wall and a receptionist behind a low counter.

"Hello, how can I help you?"

"I would like to see an agent about a few business matters."

Brad pulled out some of his paperwork when a young lady walked around the corner and held out her hand. "Hi there, I'm Kathie Macintyre. How can I help you?"

She was smartly dressed in matching pants and a jacket. The oval, wired glasses suited her, and Brad's first impressions were that of a librarian.

"I have a few thousand acres just west of here, and I'd like to buy up some of the property around me. I also have a condo in Washington, DC, that you can have the listing. I need it gone."

Kathie smiled and invited him into her office. After a few pleasantries, she printed out the forms, and they filled out the paperwork. The agent seemed rather happy to have this work fall into her lap.

After locating Brad's property, she noted the surrounding tracts of land. "I'm not sure if they are willing to sell or not, Mr. Sheppard."

"I'm authorizing you to buy them out. I'm sure the owners have a price they would be willing to settle on. I'll send you fifty million plus the money you receive from the condo. Whatever you can buy them out for, deduct it, and you can keep the remainder. Deal?"

The young woman was in shock and nodded slowly. "What if it costs more? I can't promise they will budge."

"I value my privacy, and money isn't an object. I'll make a note on my account. You are authorized to do so if you need to draw more to make this happen." Brad was about to stand when he thought of something else. "Do you know anyone that can clear land and build a timber cabin?"

Kathie nodded and flipped through her phone for the information. "Yes, Precision Builders. They specialize in cabins like that."

"If I gave you another five million, do you mind clearing the best spot on my property and hiring them to build me a cabin? You can keep the change."

Times must have been challenging selling property in Casper. After fifteen minutes in her office, she had won the lottery and was all smiles.

"I can certainly help, Mr. Sheppard. I would be glad to!"

Brad quickly sketched a huge cabin he wished to have built. "Something like this will do, and I want solar power and running water near one of the lakes on the property. Use your judgment, please. I don't need to live by candlelight."

Brad tried to hold back the bark of laughter, but it was too late when he saw the look in her eyes.

She thinks I have a screw loose. I don't blame her. How often does this happen?

"How about I transfer the money now and give you signing authority to make all this happen? I won't be in touch for five years or so."

Relieved, she nodded. "That may help."

They switched seats, and Brad stood after punching in the information and transferring the money.

"Thank you, Mrs. Macintyre." After they shook hands, Brad left the agency and headed east. He ducked into an alley, then the quantum realm, with a quick look over his shoulder. His personal future seemed secure, and now he just had to save the world to enjoy it. Easy peasy.

Chapter 42

Virginia sat at her desk in the small office assigned to her while working at the university. With three and a half days until the black hole formed, she planned to go ahead with the experiment and trust in the research. She also had to trust Brad and his abilities.

Clement and Brad mentioned the event still happened regardless of whether Virginia was involved. By ensuring her team was going ahead with the experiment, she could do everything to ensure it went as planned and minimize potential mistakes.

Hopefully, the few years she spent trapped at the university library were not in vain. While informative, the sheer amount of information Virginia had read was based on theory. From the greatest minds over the last one-hundred and fifty years, good views, but ideas, nonetheless.

There comes a time to put a theory to the test.

Virginia sighed and sipped her cold tea. That is why she had researched to prove such theories, specifically Hawking's Radiation. The electromagnetic radiation emitted by a black hole had been mathematically proven, but not physically. If that theory proved correct and the technology advanced enough, an unlimited power source could be harnessed. A stable event horizon should be possible, even with a black hole's decaying rate subjected to the earth's gravity.

One of her technicians called on the intercom, telling her they were ready for the instrument calibrations test.

"I'll be there in a minute."

After logging out of the computer system, Virginia turned to find Brad in the doorway. He watched her work in silence with a gentle smile.

Blushing, Virginia asked, "How long have you been there?"

"About five years?" Brad winked.

"You owe me for lunch! That was the most unusual way to get out of paying that I have seen."

Brad tried to look apologetic. "Sorry about that."

"No problem. Everything okay now?"

"On track for … whatever may happen, I guess."

"Did you find the last piece?" Virginia wanted a cell phone that would work through time to stay connected. No chance of that.

Patting his jacket pocket, Brad nodded. "I just got back. A few complications, but I have it."

"Did you get it from Fort Knox?"

"No. It wasn't there. I got it from the White House directly."

Virginia shook her head. "You have to keep the timeline intact as much as you can. The little changes in the past can change the future."

Brad agreed. "I have something in mind to help keep everything on track."

*****

Clement dragged the wooden chair out to the porch from the kitchen and waited. He carried the handwritten note and repeatedly ran the contents over in his mind. Across the field, the apple tree held his attention, and he wondered how it would ever get better.

Brad and Virginia departed less than five minutes ago, but he never saw them leave. Without the meteor, he was stuck here until they returned.

Not that I had any plans of going anywhere.

He wasn't sure what this place was, but he knew it wasn't his real farm and property. It was close, but there were some differences. The seasons were slow to change, and as much as he tried, he couldn't get his crops to grow fully. The lack of visitors didn't bother him at all. People used to regularly turn up, asking for jobs or a meal for a day's work. His wife used to welcome strangers and found things for them all to do and help out. Right now, he enjoyed the solitude.

After reading the note for the fifth time, Clement's eye caught a folded piece of paper on the grass at his feet. He was sure that it wasn't there when he sat down.

Very sure.

313

Scowling at the paper didn't accomplish anything, so he picked it up. The handwriting wasn't hard to read, but it didn't make sense.

You will collect the meteor fragment from Fort Knox at 4 PM on August 23, 2019. Exactly. Read the President's Journal.

Clement read it several times, but he had no idea what 'Fort Knox' was or what the 'President's Journal' could be. However, it was the date that threw him off the most.

That is two hundred and thirty-six years from now!

The note had to be a joke, but Clement realized he was the only one there. Folding the paper, he placed it with the other note into his pocket. Too many strange things were happening, and he just wanted to be left alone.

*****

Again, Brad found himself at the gold depository in Fort Knox. He exited the quantum realm inside the antechamber and opened the metal box. With a final look around the sealed room, he laid the fragment inside the wooden stand.

From a fold in reality, he waited.

As requested and on time, Clement stepped out of the quantum realm and looked around at the vault. He wore a light blue T-shirt and jeans with running shoes. The same outfit that Brad had seen him in on the rooftop. It had taken a note, delivered centuries ago, to place events back on track.

Not how I thought it would go, but it's happening.

The nearest shelf unit had over eight dozen gold bars stacked next to the pallets of the government's stash of drugs. Clement picked a bar at random and hefted it a few times. Despite the wealth, Clement returned the bar to the shelf and approached the metal box on the shelf unit.

Before opening it, Clement ran his finger over the engraving as Brad had done. With the fragment in hand, Clement paused. He looked over his shoulder and around the vault slowly and deliberately before disappearing. Brad wasn't sure why Clement couldn't see him, but both stones' abilities kept him cloaked in the quantum realm.

There was another item he had to accomplish to make sure the timeline remained intact. Brad stepped out of the timestream and took off his suit jacket. Careful that his fingers never touched anything, he picked up the gold bar Clement handled and slipped back into the timestream.

Two minutes after four o'clock in the afternoon, Brad moved within the quantum realm, outside the employee parking area, and looked around. He could see the security gate from his position, realizing he was in the wrong spot.

Brad walked thirty feet down the road as the gate opened and waited. He was ready when a dark blue Crown Vic government car slowly drove out. Brad knelt in the under-time and placed the gold bar on the ground. Brad waited until the police chief glanced below the dashboard as the vehicle approached.

Once the bar was lined up properly, he pushed it out of the quantum realm and grinned. The front tire hit the gold and rocked the driver to the side. Once the rear tire ran over the bar, the vehicle stopped. The world's most expensive speed bump worked.

Brad was glad that things seemed on course for what occurred in *his* history. The timeline, so far, would be preserved.

If Clement didn't move the gold bar onto the road, someone certainly had to. Brad wouldn't have been called on the case if the bar were never run over. If the president didn't call Brad, none of the previous events would have happened.

But since the events *had* happened, he had to ensure that they *did* happen. Since Clement believed there was no such thing as a paradox, Brad worked hard to ensure that all bases were covered.

Maybe paradoxes would happen if someone didn't go around fixing things.

Brad couldn't help but chuckle at that line of thought. Thinking back, he ran through the checklist in his mind. He believed everything was covered. Now that the timeline was secured for the one fragment, his plan may actually work—time to find out.

Chapter 43

 Looking around at the farm property, Brad had trouble accepting the chain of events that led him here, but Virginia thought on a level above him. *Who am I kidding? She thought several stages above me.*

Since he was not acquiring the fragments to complete the second meteor from *actual* time but from an alternate timeline, they should not affect the historical timeline as long as the pieces were returned to the alternate timeline to resume their place within history. When Brad asked about its reasoning, Virginia lectured him for over thirty minutes about dualities and specific wavelengths that could cancel each other out. In the end, he just agreed. It was just easier.

Her ideas finally led him to the cabin, in the alternate reality or time-loop that Clement had created. The night air had a crisp cold smell to it. Brad knew frost would be on the ground soon.

He wasn't sure if he should knock or walk in, so he just stood outside the cabin door.

"Don't just stand there. Come on in."

Surprised that Clement knew he was there, Brad opened the door and entered the cabin. Clement lit the lantern on the table and a small fire in the kitchen hearth. The warmth felt good after the night air.

Laying on the bed just inside the door was himself. Past Brad was sprawled unconscious, with a kitchen chair as a nightstand. Brad's wallet, knife, and a bottle of pills were next to the tin cup of water. Everything was just as he recalled. Moments ago, that Brad had accidentally stabbed himself with the knife while examining the fragment in subjective time. Clement brought his past self back to the cabin to explain.

He was not prepared for the draw that the drugs still had on him. After seeing the bottle, Brad resisted the urge to pocket them. From everything he knew, long as he didn't succumb to the desire, the longing for the drugs would fade over time. Fade, but not completely disappear like a former smoker still desiring a cigarette even though it's been over twenty years since the last.

"I'm guessing something has gone wrong."

Clement pushed a wooden chair away from the table and gestured for Brad to sit.

"I don't know if you could say it's horrible, but certain events *must* happen, or it could turn the timeline upside-down." Brad was reasonably impressed with how Clement was reacting. The doppelgänger to the unconscious FBI agent just walked into his cabin, and the first thing he does is offer him a chair. "My current opportunity to get the fragment is now before the *other* me wakes up tomorrow, and you both insert it into the stone."

Clement frowned. "Why do you need the fragment from now?"

"I'm attempting to keep the timeline intact to avoid problems. I'll bring the fragment back soon. Well, soon for you. Far as I remember, I don't wake up until noon the next day." With a jerk of his thumb, Brad gestured toward the bed.

"With the fragment, will you be able to stop the black hole from happening?"

"Virginia seems to think so."

Clement frowned. "Do I know her yet?"

Brad couldn't help it, and he winced. "I'm not good at keeping timelines intact. No, you don't know her yet."

"It takes a while to get used to it. Now, I must be careful not to reveal anything that will change *your* events." Clement stood and paused in front of the cupboard door. He removed the fragment stored next to the plates and handed it to Brad. "I'll see you soon when you return that?"

"I hope to return it for sure. If you don't see me, all this planning and actions may not work." Brad paused, then added, "But, since I have already done so, that means that I will return it."

"Stop. Just deal with the present. *Your* present. You'll just confuse yourself. Let the future take care of itself."

That makes sense.

Brad removed one meteor from his jacket pocket. When the stone hit the plank floor, it increased to its full size.

"That's new." Clement stared, eyes wide.

Brad took the fragment and aligned it with the depression on the stone. With a light *click*, it merged. Brad knew his past-self had bonded with the stone. Apparently, it was good enough for his future self.

Immediately, the cabin vibrated with a high-pitched tone, resonating deep in their bones. Clement glanced at the cupboards as the dishes shifted. A third note sounded as the two meteors rang like a tuning fork. The resonance grew, and Brad felt a pain building behind his eyes.

Brad shook Clement's hand. "I have to go. Having three stones in the same location sets this off. Don't mention any of this to myself."

"Not a problem. Go. I'll see you soon."

Brad picked up the meteor, which shrank in size to fit into his pocket again. Giving Clement a quick nod, he stepped into the timestream. It was time to join Virginia, three days before the black hole formed and the world ended.

Time to save the planet.

No big deal.

Chapter 44

The last two days were a blur, and they made the best of it. Brad had wanted to go out for a movie and dinner, but Virginia spent all her time at the TRIUMF building, preparing.

"The world may end. Shouldn't we enjoy what time we have left?"

She winked and passed him a novel on the theory of time. "You never know. Some of the material could make a difference."

Giving up, Brad had read the novel and some of her handwritten notes on why it would work. *Should work.* Brad seemed fine to all external appearances, but his stomach and nerves told a different story. Virginia had left him alone in the office to check the alignment of the magnetic coils. To temporarily take his mind off things, he quickly called to confirm the property's status in

Wyoming. His two-thousand acres had doubled, and the cabin was completed and furnished.

As a surprise, the real estate agent had stocked the small lake a few years ago with several species of trout. The thought of fishing and not worrying about the future almost made him feel better.

Almost.

After making arrangements to pick up the keys in a few days, Brad hung up.

Hopefully, he'll be alive to see it.

Twenty-four hours before the event, Virginia wanted to ensure everything was perfect. She was meticulous over every detail and checked the data and calibrations several times. Brad read the paperwork and wondered if they were risking everything on a theory or if the science actually backed it up.

"Quit fretting. I'm positive it will work."

Brad jumped as Virginia snuck up behind him.

She returned to wearing her white lab coat and tapped a pencil against a clipboard.

"Hope so. Pretty much everything rides on this."

"We're going to start the test run. If that is good, we're on schedule for tomorrow morning."

"So, this could be our last night. Do you want to go out for dinner?" Brad watched Virginia think about the offer.

"I'm driving everyone crazy, and they basically told me to leave. If we go out for dinner, will you run out on paying the bill again?"

Brad apologized, "Sorry about that. Off to save the world and all that."

"If you're buying, I'm up for it. You can pick me up at seven o'clock if that's good? I need a shower."

"I think my schedule is free. Maybe we can—"

A technician yelled from the control room. "Dr. Kincaid, we have a problem."

The woman screamed before she was abruptly silenced. Virginia gasped, her eyes wide in fear, and stepped inside the office.

Brad made a "quiet" gesture with one finger to his lips. Before Virginia could blink, he slipped into the quantum realm and froze time. Brad swore and clenched his fists. Police officers in full tactical gear and assault rifles had charged into the building. Virginia's co-workers lay on the floor with plastic straps binding their wrists behind their backs and duct tape across their mouths. The control room had turned into a prisoner corral. They were being kept under guard, with weapons pointed at the back of their heads. They were not going anywhere.

RCMP in bright white letters was stitched across the front of the bulletproof vest and on the back, Police. The green laser from their assault rifles highlighted their targets as they swept through the building.

"Director Adam's work, I believe," Brad growled through clenched teeth.

Brad hadn't counted on the government and their long-reaching network to continue. Outside the building's entrance, three men waited dressed in suits, and the short man in the middle carried a set of papers. The cruisers lined up outside the building must have approached with their sirens and lights off. Brad and everyone else would have heard them otherwise.

Stepping around the frozen police officers, Brad approached the three men to examine the papers. The top page had the warrant to enter the property; the second had Brad's name. A federal warrant for his arrest was issued and executed by the Canadian police force.

Brad had worked with the RCMP a few times during his career, and they were reasonably competent but were light on funding and resources. The Canadian government couldn't throw money around as much as the FBI received. However, the Colt M4 carbines were new and very effective. With the laser sighting, it was deadly in the right hands.

"Fuck!" Now wasn't the time for a wrench to be thrown into the plan. It wasn't like the world needed saving.

Brad pounded his fist in frustration. He didn't see a way out and wanted to avoid hurting or killing anyone. They were after him, and he didn't want to alter the experiment. Too much effort had gone in for tomorrow morning to be successful. He could easily return here in time, leaving him only one option.

Once past the cruisers, he stepped out of the timestream. "Hey! What is going on here?" Brad tried to use his command voice, ensuring he had their attention.

The three men in suits immediately turned, and once they saw Brad, one man lifted a radio and yelled instructions to the assault team. Brad lifted his hands in the air to show he was unarmed.

Three seconds later, the police officers burst out of the building and began their verbal assault.

"Get on the ground! Get down!"

It was designed to subdue a suspect, to prevent them from rashly acting out. It was the same tactic the FBI used, and Brad knew how effective it could be.

"Not happening, guys. Get the suit over here and show me the paperwork first."

Shortly, there was a ring of six police officers with weapons trained on him, and they began to work their way closer, tightening the circle. Brad knew one would charge and force his hands behind his back to immobilize him. It would be the large officer that slowly made his way to stand behind him.

"Get on the ground, now!" One man kept the butt of the rifle in his shoulder and stepped forward.

He would be the main distraction while the other man moved on to my six.

"I'm cooperating. Show me the paperwork first. Also, you have yet to identify yourself, or any arrest at this point will result in it being invalid." Brad remained calm, and his last remarks were addressed to the man in the brown suit who held the paperwork in his left hand.

"Bradley Holman, you are under arrest. A warrant has been issued. You will be extradited to the United States."

Brad grinned. "See? That wasn't too hard. Now identify yourself."

Instead of meeting Brad's eye, the man slightly nodded to the officer closing behind him. Brad knew what was coming, so he halted time and looked over his shoulder. The officer let the carbine hang down from the combat sling and spread his arms wide. The large man was about to tackle Brad and take him down.

Brad tried to keep the grin off his face but failed. He stepped to his left and allowed time to resume. The police officer charged him for the takedown when Brad leaned to the side. He ducked under one arm and stuck out his right foot. As the officer fell on his face, Brad reached with his right hand and grabbed his opponent's wrist. Before he could bounce, Brad torqued his arm behind and up his back. The officer was pinned to the ground in a sudden reversal.

Brad saw the disbelief on their faces as they watched him move. The man on the ground struggled, but he was held tight. For good measure, Brad dropped a knee on his back.

"Last time, guys. Identify yourself. Hand over the warrants. I'll even give them back when I'm done reading them."

Black Suit man didn't look impressed and just said, "Get him."

The man on the ground tried to gain his feet when the others began their charge. Brad allowed him to kneel before shoving him into the next man's path. Slipping back into the timestream, Brad assessed the situation while everyone remained frozen. The last thing he needed was a report of him being able to disappear or turn into a superhero and disabling six trained tactical officers. The event wasn't due to happen for almost a full day. Twenty-four hours should be enough time to play this scenario out.

Three remaining officers moved together to take Brad while one stood guard, ready to fire.

To keep up appearances, I have to be captured. Shit.

Looking down at the man on the ground, he saw what he needed hanging from his utility belt. With a twist, it was quickly placed in his back pocket.

Once back into position, Brad allowed time to resume. The air was knocked from his lungs as he was pinned to the ground by three powerful men in full gear. He was flipped over and cuffed, and they weren't gentle. Brad was sure the kick to his ribs was from the guy he embarrassed.

"Get him into the cruiser. Quick." The man with the paperwork sounded excited that they finally had him.

"Let the others inside go. You have me."

Brad felt the hand at the back of his head guide him into the cruiser's backseat. A punch to the kidneys turned him sideways so he would sit. He ignored the pain as he looked out the passenger window. Virginia was being escorted down the steps with her hands flex-cuffed behind her.

"What the hell is going—" Brad felt the syringe prick the side of his neck and slide deep. He tried stepping into the quantum realm but couldn't focus.

His eyes rolled back in his head two seconds later, and Brad was unconscious.

Chapter 45

Brad drifted in and out of awareness as he tried to fight but had no chance. Strong hands held him tight as another syringe plunged into the side of his leg. Once again, the darkness wrapped him in its soft embrace.

With his mind and body being addled, he had no idea of the time, just a vague rocking sensation. When a bucket of cold water hit his face, it shocked him from a deep slumber. Gasping, he struggled to move and blinked the water out of his eyes. Brad tried to clean his face but was handcuffed to a chair. A quick attempt to kick his feet showed his legs were also bound. The metal cuffs rattled against the arm rails, and no amount of effort would break them.

As the adrenaline spiked, he opened his eyes fully. Brad was in a medical laboratory. His immediate area was sectioned with sheets of plastic hanging from the ceiling. Electrodes were connected to his chest, arms, and face. The wires ran to several machines on the nearby table. Five feet away, next to a hospital gurney with thick brown canvas straps to secure patients, was another bucket of water.

A movement to the side drew his attention. Someone dressed in an orange biohazard suit with a full mask and respirator placed the empty bucket down. His captor flicked a switch on the wall, and an overhead fan drew air out of the quarantined area. The plastic sheets bowed inward from the pressure change.

Brad couldn't see many details. The man stood five-foot-eight inches and appeared to be an older black man with dark brown eyes. When he moved, the bio-suit crackled, and the boots stomped through the small puddles of water on the steel floor.

An IV was taped on his hand, attached to a bag of fluid hanging from a stainless-steel pole beside the chair. Brad still wore the suit, and water had soaked through the material. Another area was sectioned off thirty feet away through the plastic curtains. It looked like the same set-up as his cell. However, Virginia was strapped to the hospital bed and wasn't moving.

Second by second, he shook off the effects of the drugs. A brief flash of warmth from his ring brought a quick smile. Brad croaked when the man in the suit turned to confirm he was awake. "How about a glass of water instead of a bucket?"

Brad's throat burned, and he sounded horrible. It reminded him of being *very* hungover. It wasn't a feeling he wished to repeat. Another thing he noticed was a gentle, rocking motion. At first, he thought it was an after-effect of the drugs, but he figured it out.

He was on a ship.

The man in the bio-suit ignored Brad, opened a laptop, and spun the wheeled table around to place it a few feet from him. Orange-gloved fingers pecked away at the keyboard before he stepped out of sight.

Before the video chat opened, Brad glanced at the clock in the bottom right corner—three o'clock in the morning. That left him just over six hours before the experiment was due to start. Relief flooded throughout his body, and his tense muscles relaxed.

Where there's time, there's a chance.

When the video flickered to life, Brad stared at a familiar face.

"I would like to say it's a pleasure to see you, but I would be lying." Despite the hoarseness, Brad's voice was cold and emotionless. All his suspicions were confirmed. An ember of anger flared to life inside his chest, and he fanned the flame.

"I need a few answers from you, Holman. We can't take any chances."

Brad looked over his left shoulder to see the man in the orange suit holding a syringe at the IV bag's medicine port, ready to inject.

"You're not inspiring any faith in me right now."

"Unfortunately, Virginia Kincaid will be next."

Brad flicked his eyes above the laptop screen to see Virginia. She appeared to be sleeping. "How about you explain why you have abducted me?"

The director slowly shook his head back and forth. "You were sent to investigate an impossible theft at Fort Knox involving a fragment of stone that has properties that distort time. You have been confirmed in many locations simultaneously, from Boston to Madagascar. Then finally, you were in the *damn* Oval Office talking to the president directly. Do you know how many cameras and recording devices were in there? He's burning his bridges."

Adams held the journal up to the camera. "Once this is gone, there will be no other record. I'm following lawful executive orders for the protection of our country."

Brad lifted his arms, and the cuffs rattled against the metal tubing. Every second that passed allowed him to recover and shake off the effects of the drugs.

"If I answer your questions, will you let the doctor go?"

Director Adams leaned forward and nodded. "Of course."

He didn't buy the act. It was way too easy. "Ask away."

"How did you do it?"

Brad took stock of his injuries. The pain in his kidney and ribs were gone, and the tightness in his head had begun to lift. "I didn't want to mention this, but I am one of a set of triplets. The other guys were my brothers."

Adams frowned, and Brad could almost picture steam rising from his ears. "How do you explain this?"

With a series of clicks, footage of Brad and Clement appeared on the screen. They were at the market in Madagascar, shopping for fruit and vegetables.

"This was taken several hours ago. At the same time, you were *already* in custody. Who's that man with you? Explain."

Brad shrugged and said nothing.

Adams sighed, and Brad watched him toss the journal on his desk. The split-screen disappeared. "You were a fine agent and could even have sat here one day. We can't risk having you free. Goodbye." The director nodded to the man behind him.

Out of the corner of his eye, Brad saw the plunger had depressed, and without watching the results, director Adams cut the feed.

A milky-white substance snaked through his IV tubing, about to enter his bloodstream. The moment had come for Brad to penetrate the quantum realm, and as time halted, he felt nothing but relief. While his abilities weren't disrupted, there was still some doubt.

Brad studied the handcuffs. They were the flat-black carbon Smith and Wesson models with two links. The handcuff key he took off the policeman's belt may work if it was still in his back pocket. Regardless, he couldn't reach it.

The cuffs were standard issue for law enforcement, but he doubted they were an RCMP tactical unit. It was more likely a wet team or mercenaries sent to work outside the States and authorized by the president.

Brad concentrated and used the quantum realm to relocate across the medical bay. He stood on the other side of the plastic barrier, and the man in the orange suit remained frozen behind the chair.

"That was close." Brad stripped the bandage and medical tape off his left hand. It wasn't over despite him being wet and the near-death experience. A quick check showed the meteors had remained in his jacket pocket. *Did they think they were rocks? Could they see them?*

Brad must have been searched for weapons unless they were incompetent. Virginia appeared to be okay, so he took the time to explore the passageway from the interrogation room.

The first opening led to a storeroom filled with shelves and medical supplies. The next room down the hall resembled a military barracks with bunk beds against the bulkhead next to a small galley. A long rectangular table filled the room, and the six 'police officers' sat drinking beers and cleaning weapons.

As Brad stepped out of the quantum realm, picking up a Glock 19 and loaded the magazine. The men reacted slowly, but one called out at his sudden appearance. Brad engaged the slide and chambered a round. Aiming, he squeezed the trigger at the close targets. The sound of each shot was amplified within the small room, and his ears rang. Two men had time to gain their feet and reach for their pistols before Brad dealt with them. The youngest man on the left managed to slide off his chair, screaming for help. Brad unloaded three rounds through the table. He didn't miss.

The rage faded as he walked back to the quarantined area. However, it flared to life as he saw the orange-suit man beside Virginia's IV. Brad automatically adopted the Weaver stance and fired through the plastic sheeting. Two well-placed 9mm rounds found their target and hurled the orange figure into the bulkhead.

"It's going to be okay. I'm here."

Brad checked her pulse and brushed the hair out of Virginia's eyes. Once the straps were unbuckled, he gently pulled the IV out of her arm. There were no visible wounds, and when he picked her up, Brad cradled her tight against his chest.

He stepped into the quantum realm with a final look around the ship. They both needed to recover and heal before Brad closed a chapter on his life. *It was time.*

Chapter 46

Unable to watch the execution, Director Adams turned off the video feed. He had sent his receptionist home hours ago as he monitored the deployed teams worldwide. The conflicting reports of targeted sightings threw him off, but he had no choice. The president's orders were delivered in person. Bowers had leaned forward and whispered in his ear for their brief meeting. Such decisions were never to be written or given on the phone. Despite his misgivings, he gave the green light to different teams worldwide.

Opening the journal, he looked at the signatures from George Washington to the current sitting president. It made this book invaluable if someone were to price it. It should be in a museum, but its information ensured it would never happen.

Taking all the recent paperwork and the personal file of Supervisory Special Agent Bradley Holman, he dropped the journal on top and bound everything with elastics. The items barely fit into the red and white striped burn bag.

The FBI had avoided using the burn bags for the last fifteen years, but Adams had to ensure nothing remained. Shredded documents could be reassembled, and there was only one way to make sure they never fell into the wrong hands. Cleansing fire.

Before turning off his computer, Adams sent the email to scrub the FBI personal file for employee #R-4523999. It would remove absolutely everything to do with Holman on the computer systems throughout the FBI servers. This has been done a few times previously, which usually signaled an intense undercover operation. Once the history had been deleted, it was up to the director to install the backup files and "recreate" an agent's life.

The next step was to ensure anyone who had worked with agent Holman would be scattered across the States. No two individuals would work again with each other. He was being erased from people's recollections as well.

The final email authorized the NSA to remove Brad from all systems thoroughly.

Everywhere.

When they were done, there would be no record of Holman attending public school, college, or Quantico. There would still be yearbooks and memories of people who knew him, but recollections would fade, especially with no one contacting or finding him anywhere online.

After he logged out of the system, Adam sighed and ran a hand over his face. *I need a drink.*

Ready to head home, he tried to stand.

A strong hand gripped his shoulder, pressing him back into his seat. The large desk was tight against the wall, with bookshelves on either side. There was no way for anyone to sneak around with the office layout and come up behind him.

It was impossible, but it still happened.

A scream escaped, and he came close to wetting himself. When he heard the voice, the bottom dropped out of his stomach, and he couldn't have stood if he wanted to.

"Now that I have your attention, Director, we should talk in person."

Without turning around, he whispered. "This isn't possible."

Former Special Agent Holman walked around, leaned forward, and planted both hands on the desktop. "It *is* possible. I'm right here."

Brad was dressed in a dark suit and tie, freshly shaven, and showered. Adams could smell the shampoo and soap. Contrary to the circumstances, Holman appeared somewhat energetic and in a good mood. One minute ago, Brad was handcuffed to a chair two hundred miles off the coast of Vancouver. Now, he leaned forward and grinned across his desk in Washington.

"I'm just following orders." Adams's mouth was suddenly dry.

"Unfortunately, you don't know the whole story, but you had choices to make. You have chosen wrongly."

A deep sinking feeling settled in the director's stomach, like plummeting down an elevator shaft. He thought he would be sick. One small hope leaped to mind. Years ago, he kept a small pistol in the bottom drawer of his desk, but he couldn't recall if it was even there, let alone loaded.

"I would like to say I'm sorry, but I'm not."

He was about to reach for the drawer when a sharp stab of pain flickered through his chest. Adams gasped. "What did you do?"

The agony grew as the sensation shot down his left arm, numbing his fingers. He leaned back in the chair, and Adams felt like a great weight was pressed on his chest. Each breath was agony, and he struggled to move.

"I did nothing. You only had a few years left, anyway. Your heart seems to have aged slightly. All perfectly natural."

One hand gripped his chest, and the other clutched to the armrest. As his last breath trickled out, he stared at Holman, not blinking. Adams didn't have time to think about what was possible or what wasn't. That didn't matter anymore.

Before the light left his eyes, he watched Brad pick the burn bag up from his desk and disappear. The last thing Adams saw was the impossible, and the confusion followed him to the grave.

*****

"Ten minutes until we start the run. Here, this should fit you."

Virginia held out a white lab coat for Brad, then clipped an identification tag onto the front pocket. After their last episode, they took a few days to recover and heal. Brad hadn't mentioned how he dealt with the FBI, and Virginia pointedly never asked. Both had a little sun, and Brad could still faintly smell Virginia's sun-tan lotion.

Coconuts and the surf aren't too bad.

"Try and stay out of the way for the first part. I'll be busy. Either it will work, or it won't. There are no more changes to make." She paused and looked him in the eye. "Why are you grinning?"

"Nothing in particular. I'll stay out of your way." Brad slipped into the coat and made some adjustments. It was tight across the shoulders, but it would be fine.

When she arrived early this morning for work, Virginia explained the police had a case of mistaken identity. Once Brad had been captured, the others were set free with apologies. A few were rattled, but everyone had arrived for the experiment. No one within the building had seen Brad being taken down, so their cover story was easily accepted.

Brad had mentioned they would have no further problems from the FBI or any other law enforcement agency from here on in. As far as the government was concerned, Brad Holman had ceased to exist. Bowman would hear about the FBI director's natural death with his morning briefing. If he didn't get *that* hint loud and clear, Brad would have no problems delivering a more personal message if required.

"If you need me, just shout." Virginia pushed her glasses back up her nose before scooping a clipboard off the desk and going down to the control room. She was all business, focused on the experiment and ensuring she did her best.

Brad passed the lunchroom and slipped behind the barrier for the VIP viewing area in the control room. A few others had gathered on the catwalk, and they silently looked on. The technicians finished a diagnostic test to verify their instruments were functional and reviewed the warm-up sequences. Virginia walked to each station and went through her checklist. So far, everything is on schedule, and no issues have been found.

She would sneak a peek at Brad and give him a quick smile before turning to another item that needed her attention. Extending his senses out through the quantum realm, Brad could feel the time for the event moving ever closer. The fact that the black hole was only a few minutes away from destroying the planet made him anxious and second-guessed everything. He rubbed his damp palms on the lab coat, breathing slowly and steadily.

The time for adjustments was long past, and even if the event was successfully contained, there was no guarantee he would survive.

Brad drafted up his will last night without any family alive and the only close friends he ever had worked at the bureau. He left everything to Clement and Virginia. However, if the black hole destroyed the planet, it wouldn't matter. The paperwork kept him occupied and his mind off the possibilities.

Lost in thought, Brad was surprised when Virginia made an announcement.

"Five minutes." Virginia visited each station once again to verify they were ready. Unable to sit, Brad stood against the back wall behind the VIP seating area. His foot tapped against the tiled floor with nervous energy.

"One minute. Begin the sequence."

All too soon, they counted down from ten in the same manner as the prior experiment.

It was showtime.

"Six, five, four …."

Brad spotted something he had forgotten on the control room's rear wall. A small black square box was mixed in with a few panels. With a sidestep, Brad detached it from the wall. He placed it into the pocket of the lab coat, making sure the front faced away from him.

Assuming events were occurring at the same time, the *past* Brad and Clement were in Madagascar and downloading the feed from the camera. If their past selves knew Brad was here attempting to stop the event, their actions might be influenced and changed. Brad didn't want anything altered, for it had all led to this event.

Brad stepped into the quantum realm and his worst nightmare at the count of three.

Chapter 47

 The timestream was filled with quantum fractures. Not just the one or two that Brad had seen previously, but an infinite number stretched along the time corridor. The fractures were more extensive and pulsed with a bright white light that seared into his mind.

With the utmost care, he moved forward half a second in time. The results were dramatic. All the quantum fractures bent toward a central point, and those farthest away began a rotational spin. As the golden light of the realm warped, Brad felt himself being pulled in the same direction as the fractures.

Almost there.

With another full-second jump forward, Brad finally saw through the quantum realm as it overlaid the real world.

Even though Brad halted time, light and energy swirled around two black holes that sprang into existence. The fractures had flattened out, and a disc started to expand. The singularities were gaining momentum as energy was absorbed.

This was the moment Virginia had discussed with Brad, and this *exact* moment was the most crucial.

The plan was to halt all matter from entering an event horizon. It should stop its exponential growth, and it would feed upon itself, causing it to shrink and evaporate. At a certain point, the matter and energy should release in an explosion of light, resulting in an outward pressure. Virginia called it a *quantum bounce*.

The process could take upward of billions of years, except they couldn't wait that long for the event horizons to settle.

Time to speed things along.

Brad pulled the two meteors from his pocket and returned them to full size. He had never done so while in the quantum realm before, and he was surprised to find they stabilized the area immediately around him. The stones were not subject to the graviton pull from the black holes, and the tugging sensation disappeared.

More confident, Brad reached out with the power of the meteors and wrapped a time-loop bubble around the two black holes. It should halt any energy and particles from passing through the quantum field. With a shift, he sent the black holes into an alternate universe with no power or matter to feed them to stop them from growing.

The field worked for a quarter of a second, but something unexpected happened. With the lack of external energy feeding the black holes, they rotated once, then turned on one another.

They pivoted in a slow spin, edging closer and closer. It happened too fast for Brad to follow, but the two spinning black holes merged into one.

The shield Brad had thrown around the black holes vanished. The new combined event horizon's doubled strength pulling more energy and light. The meteors were Brad's anchor in the quantum realm, but that would not last. He tried to place another shield around the black hole, but it had gained too much energy, and any attempts were fruitless. The gravitational pull brought him closer.

The black hole only answered its own natural law and couldn't be controlled.

The event horizon was the size of a quarter after being formed. Now it was the size of a football after merging with the other. There was no indication that it would stop or slow down.

Running out of choices, Brad glanced at the two stones and had an idea. Since the quantum realm did not affect the rocks, he hoped his plan would work.

It has to work!

Brad picked up one of the meteors. He was surprised that even at full size, it weighed nothing while in the quantum realm. Brad used that to his advantage, stepping toward the black hole. With a grunt of effort, he whipped the rock side-armed across the remaining distance toward the darkness. It would have fallen short if the black hole hadn't drawn it in. Brad allowed the inside of the meteor to grow, becoming larger than the original.

A painful tone echoed across the universe when the two forces connected, followed by a golden flash of light. Blinded, Brad turned his head. When the moment had passed, he lowered his arm. The meteor had grown larger than the opening and acted as a stopper.

For a split second, nothing happened, then a rolling thunder behind him. It sounded like a storm front moving in quickly, and the deep vibration made his chest vibrate.

When the universe sang a song in response, his breath caught. A steady harmonic note played counterpoint to the thunder. It was the most horrific and beautiful sound he could have imagined. Tears of joy and horror ran down his cheeks as he was overwhelmed by the display.

The vibrations increased, and his vision doubled, then doubled again. Despite the problems, he couldn't look away.

The meteor acted as a plug, but the black hole continued to change. It stopped increasing in size and bulged around the middle.

The harmonic note passed beyond his ability to sense, and the only sound was the beating of his heart. The singularity resembled a volcano, ready to expel the meteor as the pressure increased.

As Brad allowed time to resume, all the power of the black hole was released in an explosion of light and energy. He raised a hand in a futile gesture and waited for death. But he realized the power wasn't directed *outward*. The meteor acted as a reflective shield and channeled the energy *back* through the event horizon.

With a subtle pulse, the black hole changed polarities. Instead of absorbing light and matter into black nothingness, the singularity emitted a white light.

As time resumed its natural linear pace within the quantum realm and in the real world, the singularity increased in size, but Brad wasn't worried. The meteor shook and rotated in position, ever-increasing in speed.

Brad knew it wasn't over when the white light expanded and grew larger than the meteor. With a *crack,* the stone shot through the new portal.

The black hole had transformed into a *white hole,* acting as a doorway. Looking through the opening, Brad gasped. He could see the tree line above Clement's farm and fields as the stone turned into a blue-and-white energy streak. Like a cork from a bottle, it flew across the sky.

The meteor clipped a tall pine before continuing its journey over the barn and fields before crashing into the woods.

Everything was a circle of events, but I've broken the loop.

Soon as the meteor landed in the woods, the white hole shrank. Brad glanced at the remaining meteor. There were a few things to do before he could end this.

He was about to pick up the rock when he felt a hand on his shoulder and a voice whispered. "You did good, man. Don't worry about anything else. I have it from here, go and say goodbye."

The voice was sympathetic, warm, and very familiar.

Dread washed through him when all the facts came together. Instead of being reassured, it made him sick. He didn't have long to finish the circle of events. With what time remained, it had to be used wisely—every second counted.

"Thank you. Good luck."

With a deep breath, Brad Holman, former special agent for the Federal Bureau of Investigation, left the quantum realm for the final time.

Chapter 48

Dr. Virginia Kincaid looked up from the monitor and scanned the results. There was a spike in energy readings from the cyclotron. However, the black hole formation didn't happen.

A series of groans from the staff and technicians rolled across the control room as they studied the data. The test was a failure. Realizing that Brad had disappeared and no one in the control room noticed gave her mixed hope. The fact she was alive meant he was successful. Since Brad wasn't with her, it didn't look good. A lone tear rolled down her cheek, and Virginia held back her emotions. There would be a time and place to have a meltdown.

"Forward all your results through the server. I'll be in my office. Thank you, everyone. That's it for the day."

Many thought she was upset over the experiment, and Virginia didn't correct them as she hurried along the hallway to the office.

This isn't fair!

It was the only thought that ran through Virginia's mind as she wiped her face on the sleeve of her lab coat. Emotions warred against logic as she threw the clipboard across the office. Papers were scattered all over the floor.

"Is there something wrong that I should know about?"

Virginia turned and launched herself at Brad in a huge rib-cracking hug. "Oh, my God!"

"Sit down. I have some bad news."

Virginia's heart skipped a beat, and she was barely aware that Brad had guided her to the chair. "What's wrong? Are you okay?"

"Good news first." Brad knelt and smiled at her. He wiped away a lone tear that trickled down her cheek. "The black hole is gone, and the quantum realm is stabilized. I used one of the stones to change the black hole into a white hole, which opened a time portal."

Virginia's eyes opened wide at the possibilities.

"I sent the stone back in time to where it was found originally."

"So, that means that it was sent back to stop the black hole in its *own* future?"

"A horrible circle for sure, but now we have stepped outside the loop. It's closed off permanently, so don't worry. Which leads me to the bad news."

Scared, Virginia reached out and held his hand. She didn't realize she was holding her breath while waiting for the hammer to drop.

"I'm the remnant of a time-loop."

Virginia looked confused. "What's a time-loop remnant?"

Brad collapsed onto both knees as he blinked rapidly. Her grip remained firm and held him as he swayed. She didn't want to mention how pale he looked. "It means I don't exist within this timeline, and the timeline where I am from is now over."

Tears poured down her cheeks once again as what he said sunk in. The ramifications were a little clearer. Brad's image flickered, and Virginia realized she could see right through him.

Brad smiled and whispered, "Goodbye, kiddo. I'll miss you. I—"

Virginia kissed two fingers on her hand and laid them on his lips. Instead of connecting, her fingers passed right through him. He faded away like a ghost that never was.

Bringing both hands to her face, Virginia silently sobbed.

She didn't know where to begin. Her feelings were all over the map. Virginia knew something was starting, and she cared for Brad. Now she would never know what may have happened, which tore her apart. Hurt was too easy a word and didn't fully describe the pain.

The priority was to save the world, and she would still make the same decision every time. Personal feelings had to be put aside. That was the scientific side of her brain talking, and she tried to tune it out. Now that it was over, Virginia wasn't sure if she wanted to start throwing things around her office again or go for a drink.

Digging around her desk, she found some tissues and cleaned up as best she could. Virginia pulled out a small mirror from her purse and tried to fix herself. In the end, she just gave up.

One thing she did know was that she couldn't stay here. She cleaned up her notes, placed them all in a large folder, and locked them in the desk. Right now, she had problems caring about the research, especially when the consequences of quantum physics could mean the end of the planet and everything she knew. Further studies along those lines would not be happening by her.

Maybe I could find a job teaching physics.

With a brief stop in the lunchroom, she thanked everyone before saying goodbye for the weekend and headed to her car. Thoughts of a liquor store were quickly dashed from her mind as she stepped outside.

A large Winnebago motor home sat running at the bottom of the TRIUMF building steps. It was over forty feet long and looked brand new, with lots of chrome and decals running along the sides.

A figure behind the wheel honked and waved. The air horn made her jump, but Virginia couldn't tell who it was with the tinted windows until he opened the door and walked around to her side.

Brad wore a short dark beard, cargo shorts, and a light green Hawaiian shirt. "Sorry, I'm late. I got stuck in traffic driving through Vancouver."

Virginia stood ten feet away with her mouth open. Her eyes watered again. "How do I know you're real this time?"

Brad winked and pinched his arm. "I feel pretty real."

Virginia didn't recall crossing the distance as her arms threatened to break his ribs. She could smell the Irish Spring soap and found it pleasant for the first time. Virginia raised a hand to feel his beard before sobbing. The rollercoaster of emotions took its toll.

It was a few minutes before she regained enough control to ask, "How?"

"Five years ago, a time-loop was created, and we went on divergent paths. I couldn't interfere without changing too many things. It wasn't worth it, and I remained behind the scenes. Once the stone passed through the white hole, everything aligned, and the alternate timelines vanished."

Virginia tried to make sense of what had happened. "It all makes sense, I'm sure." An idea came to her. It was the only possible answer. "There's one thing that the meteor could be. Dark matter."

"What's dark matter?"

"Most of the universe is comprised of dark energy, upwards of sixty-seven percent. If we took all the matter in the universe and added it up, it would amount to less than six percent. The remainder is what scientists call dark matter. Dark matter contains its *own* energy, which may be why the universe keeps expanding."

"How does the stone figure into this?" Brad looked like this information was already over his head, but at least he tried to understand.

"The energy that created the stone was part of the universe itself. It was a basic building block and wouldn't be subject to the rules of space and time."

"If it makes sense to you, that's all that matters."

Virginia realized that she was still holding his hand. If he weren't going to object, she wouldn't either. It felt good. However, she had one more question. "What about the paradoxes that were created?"

"There isn't any such thing as a paradox. I returned fragments and the meteor where and *when* they came from."

Virginia noticed he wasn't wearing his gold band as they held hands. During a previous conversation, Brad tried to deny his ring had anything to do with time travel. She had noticed Clement also wore the same gold ring, and the stone chip matched the meteor. Eventually, Brad caved and gave her some information, but he didn't go into details. "What happened to your ring?"

"After the black hole had changed, I finished the events in the actual timeline so they would occur. I returned the fragments to where they should be, and the stone was returned. As to the ring, I returned it with the stone to the past. I no longer have any abilities. I'm normal now. The past Clement brought me back."

Virginia wiped the tears away, gestured to the Winnebago, and laughed. "How's that normal?"

The former FBI agent walked to the front of the motorhome and patted the hood. "Brad Holman, a special agent with the FBI, no longer exists. Multi-millionaire Brad Sheppard exists, and he loves his traveling home on wheels. He also owns several thousand acres in Wyoming that I have to go and get the keys in a few days."

Despite the mood, Virginia grew somber. "With all my years of schooling, research, and experiments in quantum mechanics, I can't return to work."

Brad held out a hand to stop her. "But without that knowledge, it would have been certain death, and everything on the planet would have been destroyed. It was *your* ideas that helped save the world."

Virginia took a deep breath and agreed, but it didn't make her feel better. "True, but I can't further experiment along those lines. I have seen behind the curtain, so to speak."

"I understand. Almost the same reasons why I can't go back to work for the FBI with what I know now. However, I like to help people, and now I have the resources to do so."

Virginia slumped her shoulders and mumbled. "What the hell am I going to do now?"

Brad took her hand once again and grinned. "I have a nice quaint twelve-room cabin in the country. Do you want to move in, and maybe we can go fishing?"

Instead of answering, Virginia threw her arms around Brad, and her lips finally found his.

Too bad I waited years for this. Wow!

Her tears dried as her toes curled. When the ring appeared in his breast pocket and pushed into her shoulder, Virginia ignored it.

The time to live was in the present.

The future could wait.

Epilog

"Sir?"

Clement stirred but fell back into a slumber. Someone reached down and gently shook his shoulder. "Sir? Mr. Wallace?"

As he slowly sat up, Clement realized he was in a chair. He had been there for a while by the stiffness in his back. He tried to recall what was going on but drew a blank.

He had a vague impression of Brad knocking on his door in Boston, coming over to update him, but it was like a faint memory of a dream. The details were quickly slipping away. He looked around at the pastel walls and tiled floor before the disinfectant smell hit him and rubbed his eyes.

He was in a hospital waiting room.

Clement had no recollection of what happened or how he got here, and he certainly didn't recognize the nurse standing beside his chair.

She was an older woman with her hair in a bun, wearing pastel green scrubs with white running shoes.

Clement had to clear his throat a few times before he could talk. "Yes?"

"You can go in now. Everything will be fine."

Clement struggled to his feet and tried to understand what was happening. What did Brad do?

"Go in where?"

She patted his shoulder. "To see your wife. Your brother brought her here in time."

Clement could barely talk. Centuries of emotions threatened to overwhelm him as he struggled to understand. The corner of his mind opened, and his repressed feelings threatened to drive him mad. "My wife?"

My brother?

"Yes, dear. We caught the double pneumonia in time. She's now on an IV with a hefty antibiotic dose. She's still fairly young and seems slightly confused, but she'll be fine."

Tears rolled down his cheeks and were wiped away with the back of his hand. Clement numbly followed the nurse down the hall as he silently thanked his friend.

"I'm coming, Jeanne."

"A secret of the centuries

born of lumination in the sky,

but the darkness swallows

answers

and can change the course of time.

Though with no meaning

there is no measure

of seconds or years that pass,

but he who holds the missing piece

holds this timing task."

J. Monroe

About the Author

David grew up in a small town east of Toronto, Canada. He has had many interests throughout the years, including the military, martial arts, playing guitar, and reading, and in his mind, he is quite an excellent fisherman. David is married and has one daughter, and he misses his chocolate lab beyond words.

Feel free to write to David Darling at:

author.david.darling@gmail.com or check out his website.

www.daviddarlingbooks.com

Afterword

Even as a young child, I was fascinated with time, and that feeling grew into adulthood. Countless novels have dealt with the subject, and I have read most of them.

However, I haven't read a novel that used the subject in the manner that I have proposed. A Temporal Paradox is usually approached in two ways, a Time Paradox or a Grandfather Loop. I believe I have come up with a third approach that leans toward a self-fulling prophecy caused by a time loop.

Time travel *does* exist, and it's a one-way ticket. We cannot get off the ride and journey to the final destination—forward or back. Within the novel, I also mentioned a second method of time travel. Time is not constant. But instead, it slows down the faster you move through space. True!

There are many theories for time travel from some of the most brilliant minds in our history. I spent many weeks and months reading their proposed concepts in preparation for this novel. Most of what I have talked about is real (in theory, at least). I also freely used a writer's artistic license and changed some ideas to suit the narrative.

As to what was real and historically/scientifically accurate versus imagination, I will leave that up to the future to discover.

From an author's point of view, I learned many things while writing this novel. Hand-written notes are invaluable, and the thirty-eight pages I spread over my living room floor, in an attempt to keep the timeline accurate, hopefully, made the difference. I also learned how to pace my efforts and pay attention to details. If I write about a cyclotron in Vancouver, I better thoroughly research that subject. When I read about the Quantum Bounce theory, the novel's ending fell into place. Am I now a subject matter expert on quantum physics? Not a chance! But I did enjoy the research and learning about the possibilities of the universe. While I intended to make this novel a standalone, I may have accidentally started a sequel. Not sure when that will be released, but most likely in 2024.

Edge of Time is a science *fiction* novel whose main goal is entertaining the reader. I hope that was achieved! If you have a moment, please leave a review from where you purchased the book/eBook. Something as simple as '4 Star – I enjoyed it' makes a huge difference and drives sales. The novel's original title was The Kronos Stone, but after months of changes, edits, revisions, and so on, Edge of Time stuck. However, it may tie into the sequel rather well.

Thank you,
David Darling

Serve in the Shadows: Recruitment

Available in paperback and eBook.

Serve in the Shadows: Recruitment

While on deployment in Afghanistan, Master Sergeant Derek Lawson of the 75th Ranger Regiment received a warning, barely in time to avoid a bullet from a hidden sniper. After a confused and thankful Derek looked for the person, there was no one to be found. Back at base camp, the master sergeant received news that his brother, Grant Lawson, was killed. Grant, a CIA officer, was murdered while he gathered pertinent information for a critically sensitive mission that involved a former Afghanistan bomb-maker coerced out of retirement.

After he arrived in Germany to collect his brother's remains, Derek was shocked when Grant suddenly appeared, and they were able to see and communicate with each other from beyond death's reach. Derek eventually accepted that he could see his dead brother's ghost and that he hadn't lost his mind. Grant did not have to work hard to convince Derek to help finish his last assignment and help bring his killer to justice.

With Derek's knowledge and abilities earned with the Rangers and Grant's skills, he learned from the CIA - they make a formidable team. Together, the brothers will attempt to stop a terrorist plot and expose corruption within the CIA's upper levels.

Grant's death was not the end. It was just the beginning

Prelude

28 July, 23:15 Hrs.

South Sudan

Surrounded by darkness, the thin figure dressed in a long brown robe resembled a specter of death. The fabric swirled about his feet and hung straight from his shoulders as he shuffled along the old jagged sidewalk. Each foot landed with care. A lifetime of aches and pains from old injuries caused him to walk with a shuffle and limp. The fabric swirled around the man's feet was coated in dust and dirt. However, the clothing kept him comfortable during the day and warm at night. With the daily temperature change in South Sudan, that was essential.

The night birds' usual sounds were absent, which usually signified the arrival of a storm.

The man walked home nightly after he finished the late evening *Isha* prayers at the mosque. He had left the temple with a small group, and after fifteen minutes, he was alone as he moved through the darkened town. The only illumination came from one old streetlamp that flickered dimly overhead and cast its light only fifty yards ahead. Most of the storefronts' neon signs were dark, and the metal gates spanned the doorways. He walked this same route countless times, and the darkness held no fear.

A slight vibration in his pocket gave him pause. The man fished out an older Android cell phone with a cracked screen that resembled a lightning strike.

The feeble light showed an old, weathered face, darkened and lined from a harsh life and outdoor living. He squinted with one eye while he scrolled through the screen commands. The left eye was covered in a mass of scar tissue, and the light showed the three outer fingers on his right hand were gone— only small stumps remained. Despite the two decades since he was disfigured in an explosion, he could still feel the aches and phantom pains.

He navigated through various screens and menus with his remaining index finger quite well. After a minute, the man paused and frowned, the deep lines on his brow furrowed. He raised the phone above his head and turned in various directions to acquire a signal. His attempts were futile.

The lone streetlight went dark, and the shops down the street plunged into darkness simultaneously. The man had turned to retrace his steps, but he stopped as the adrenaline kicked in.

The blackout wasn't an accident.

Only the immediate area had been cut off, yet two blocks over, the lights still shone.

A frail arm raised the phone above his head, and he tried to ignore the tremors in his hand. The phone's feeble illumination failed to pierce the darkness for more than two feet, not enough to drive back the shadows.

Old memories and fears surfaced, and frail fingers clenched the phone tight so it would not fall. Despite the cool evening air, Ymir gasped for breath and slowly spun in a circle. His heart pounded against his ribs, fast enough that it sounded like a drumbeat in his ears.

The darkness held to its secrets, and he had no success.

He sensed a movement out of the corner of his eye, but it was too late. A shadow emerged from the alley behind him, and a strong hand clamped a damp cloth over his face. It muffled any attempt to scream. Within seconds the man's knees buckled, and he collapsed into a boneless heap in his capture's arms. A gloved hand removed the cell phone from his grip, and it was slipped into a tactical vest with a practiced movement.

An old red minivan came around the corner and stopped beside the two men. The headlights and marker lights were dark, and the vehicle blended with the shadows. Despite the van's age and outward appearance, it ran smooth and quiet. The rear sliding door opened, and a tall figure reached down to help his partner. Together they lifted the unconscious man inside.

The side door closed as they drove away into the night.

Sixty seconds after the vehicle disappeared along a side street, the power was restored. A lone neon sign in a storefront flickered to life.

A scuff mark in the dust was the only trace left behind.

*****

3

The fabric on his nose itched, causing Ymir to rise from a deep sleep. When he tried to scratch, his arm wouldn't move. Confused, Ymir tried to see, moving his head back and forth. It took a moment before he could tell that a heavy cloth bag covered his head to block out the light and that his remaining eye wasn't blind.

His arms were firmly secured to a chair. Confusion warred with fear as Ymir fought against his bonds. He soon realized that it was futile; the harder he pulled, the deeper the bands of plastic dug into his flesh. An attempt to move his legs proved that they were bound in the same manner.

Beads of sweat rolled down Ymir's back and trickled between his bare skin and the metal. He was out of options. Naked and secured firmly to a chair gave his captors the upper hand. The fear of the unknown caused his imagination to escalate, and he twitched at every sound.

When the door opened and slammed into a wall, he couldn't help but flinch against his bonds. Through the cloth bag, he heard two men approach. He tried to think of his family, anything to take his mind off this moment. However, he knew that the nightmare was about to begin.

Without warning, the hood was yanked off his head, and a bright light temporarily blinded him. He felt the heat on his skin from the lamp. It was too close. The light burned bright enough that Ymir saw it through his closed eyelid. There wasn't a chance he could make out any details of the room or the men. He knew one would be at his back, and the other should be behind the lamp itself.

"Lays ladayna alwaqt lildhahab bibut'in. nahn bihajat 'iilana 'iijabat ealaa alfawr," the man behind the light said. *We do not have time to go slow. We need answers immediately.* As Ymir grew used to the intensity, small details emerged. The man in front of him seemed to be tall and broad at the shoulder. Ymir knew the man was an American, even though his Arabic was near flawless. A few words were off, but many wouldn't notice.

He continued in English. "I know you don't fear death, Ymir, but you have a family who needs you. How are your grandchildren? How is your daughter doing without her father nearby? I hope that nothing would ever happen to them."

Ymir knew what they would be after, and the fear began to swirl deep in his stomach. He tried his bonds again, but they were solid. He didn't have the strength. Maybe in his youth, but those days were long gone.

The light was redirected to the ceiling of the small room. Ymir stared straight into the eyes of his captor.

Neither man blinked at the sudden showdown. He appeared to be a forty-five-year-old American, with short brown hair and a gray touch at the temples. With one look, Ymir understood that he was dealing with a man used to getting results. There was a look of authority about him, a familiar appearance.

Ymir shifted his focus to a laptop that sat open on a small rolling table three feet away with the light out of his eyes. The screen had a live video feed of a small house with two little boys playing football out in front. Their mother watched while she talked on a cell phone on the step by the door—all taken from an aerial view.

It could only mean one thing.

Ymir moaned as his deepest fear began to play out before him and drove rational thought from his mind. He would gladly pay for his past and divulge no information, but he wanted his family left out of it. The man casually showed him his cell phone. Dozens of missed calls were displayed on the cracked screen. Password security was disabled, and they had full access.

The man behind him finally spoke. "Your daughter has been trying to call you all evening, as well as this morning, Ymir. She is deeply concerned as to where you are." Ymir could not see the man, but he sounded calm, and his deep voice lacked any emotion. It sent a chill of warning through him.

The man continued. "We have a drone in the air at this moment, and you can see the target. What happens next is up to you. You have less than a minute to tell me what I want to know before it is too late. Where is your son-in-law, and who is he working with?"

"No! Don't do this. My family is innocent, and they know nothing." Tears rolled down one side of his face and disappeared into his white beard. He was unable to blink or look away from the laptop. All his old resistance training melted away with each beat of his heart.

"Forty-five seconds, Ymir."

He tried to turn his head to avoid staring at the footage, but the man behind him wouldn't allow that luxury. Strong hands twisted his head forward, leaving him no choice but to stare at the screen.

The drone had zoomed out, and in the top corner of the screen, a countdown timer moved closer to zero. At twenty, his heart raced in his chest, and his pulse thundered in his ears. Their lives were more important than his own. They had him.

"Promise me you won't hurt them, and I'll tell you what you need to know. Call off the drone strike."

Ymir closed his eye and began to pray. He knew when to accept defeat. He was broken, all without a hand being laid on him.

The American closed the laptop and pulled out a satellite phone.

"Cancel Operation Orchid," he said.

Ymir exhaled in relief and rested his chin on his bare chest.

The man cleared his throat as he returned the satellite phone to his pocket and closed the lid to the computer.

He turned to Ymir. "At any time I feel you have left information out or have not told the truth, the drone strike is back on. Their lives are in your hands now. You understand?"

Ymir eagerly agreed and nodded. "My daughter's husband had just left South Sudan for Yemen. He should have arrived a week ago."

"And who is paying your son-in-law? Who hired him, Ymir?"

Ymir studied the man's face, realizing it could have been carved from stone. Those green eyes pierced his soul, and they would catch a lie. He would not be able to hold anything back. His daughter and grandchildren meant more to him than his own life. While he feared the man who had taken his son-in-law, he feared *these* men even more.

"A-a-an American found me, and he wanted to meet up with Mustafa. I was encouraged to comply with my continued health. I think he worked for the United States as the American accent was unmistakable. My old skills and knowledge I have taught and passed along to my son-in-law over the years. He is smart and has learned everything I knew without effort."

Ymir paused and tried to swallow. His mouth was dry. "I'm no longer able to work due to other issues. I enjoy the peace and stay with my family." Ymir watched the man in front of him. He seemed to take it in as his eyes narrowed and bored straight into his.

"Describe the man your son met up with."

"I had only met him a few times, but once Mustafa and myself left the mosque, the man met us nearby. He was a tall, white man with short white hair. He carried a briefcase." Ymir remembered a small detail that may help him. "Yes! He had a burn scar on his left cheek."

Instantly, Ymir saw that he'd said something wrong. The man in front of him paled, and his eyes widened as he looked at his partner.

"I'm sorry, Grant," the man behind him said. "You were never supposed to find out."

The sound of a slide being cocked and a round being chambered filled the small room.

The man in front of him, Grant, stepped back, his eyes narrowed in rage. He reached behind his back for his gun when two shots rang out. The first round entered the center of his chest and the second through his forehead. He went back as if punched and fell against the table, dead before he hit the ground.

Ymir's ears rang with the pistol fire as he struggled to breathe.

There was no escaping what would happen next. Ymir closed his eye and bowed his head as he began to pray for his family and forgiveness.

He never heard the shot as it entered the base of his skull.